Praise for Thaisa Frank

"Frank's own voice could be said to occupy the shadowy land between poetry and prose—at times strong in narrative, more often fantastic, transfixed by the possibilities of metaphor."

—*New York Times Book Review*

"This oddly beautiful collection of stories....[is] duplicitous, hallucinatory, mysterious....Frank continually startles us. She alerts us to the fact that we are always on the edge, never knowing who we are, why we live, why we exist. Thinking is 'camouflage'—the terrifying condition of life."

—Irving Malin, *Review of Contemporary Fiction*

"At their best, the stories have the evocative, layered ambiguity of good poetry."

—*San Francisco Chronicle*

"In the spell-like, poetic fiction of Thaisa Frank, the fantastic is never far from the ordinary.... Call it 'domestic magical realism,' call it the work of a West Coast I.B.Singer, it's fiction that packs an emotional punch that will leave the reader gasping.'"

—*San Francisco Chronicle*

"The fiction of Thaisa Frank works by a tantalizing sense of indirection."

—*New York Times*

"Curiously compelling scenes of domestic magical realism in which wives struggle to remember long-forgotten former husbands and spies cope with sexual geography."

—*East Bay Express*

"Thaisa Frank's stories read like frontline reports from the ongoing guerilla warfare that engulfs families today. Written in a terse, economic style, they are capable of packing an emotional punch that will leave the reader gasping in recognition."

—*San Francisco Chronicle*

"This collection of stories brilliantly examines the detachment within intimacy which seems to plague men and women today....shows wit and invention...arresting and thought-provoking."

—*Small Press Magazine*

"Frank...reels you in with phrases of such precision they have the authority of revelation....Her writing is so economical and tight, the stories feel like fabulous artifacts."

—*Express Books*

"These stories interweave overtly symbolic strands of narrative with wryly observed details of ordinary domestic life in such a way that not only deepens our notions of the ordinary but startles us into fresh ways of looking at the particular symbol....controlled, yet passionate."

—*Indiana Review*

HEIDEGGER'S GLASSES

a novel

THAISA FRANK

PHOENIX
BOOKS

ISBN-13: 978-1-60747-726-6
ISBN-10: 1-60747-726-2

Library of Congress Cataloging-in-Publication Data

Book & Jacket Design by Sonia Fiore

Printed in the United States of America

Phoenix Books, Inc.
9465 Wilshire Boulevard, Suite 840
Beverly Hills, CA 90212

10 9 8 7 6 5 4 3 2 1

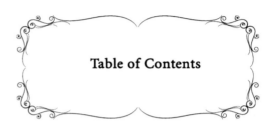

Table of Contents

Curator's Notes

This exhibit of letters dates roughly from 1942 to the end of WWII. Most were letters written under coercion as part of a program called *Briefaktion*, or Operation Mail. Some were letters from ghettoes or notes passed between prisoners in barracks at concentration camps. The letters from Operation Mail illuminate German WW II strategies that are often obscured by more historical and dramatic events.

Operation Mail or *Briefaktion*

Briefaktion was created to assure anxious relatives about the relocations and deportments, as well as dispel rumors about the Final Solution, which the Reich at all costs wanted to keep secret. The letters were usually written as soon as prisoners arrived—often before they were led to an idyllic woods or corridor of pine boughs that concealed gas chambers. The letters weren't mailed directly to their recipients, but from an office in Berlin called The Association of Jews, making it impossible to know their origin. Answers were sent back to Berlin and never delivered; but most couldn't have been read because a majority of the letter writers had already been killed. The result was enormous quantities of unread mail, some of which were retrieved after the war.

The Supernatural and the Thule Society

It was widely known that Hitler consulted astrologers. Far less known is the fact that the Reich placed astounding reliance on the supernatural for strategies about the war and the Final Solution. A group called *Die Thule-Gesellschaft* (The Thule Society), comprised of mystics, psychics, members of the Reich, and select SS men, met regularly to channel advice from the astral plane. The Thule Society got its name from Lanz von Liebenfels' concept of Ultima Thule, a place of extreme cold where a race of supermen lived. Hitler didn't attend these meetings and prevented Liebenfels from publishing after he came into power, probably to conceal his own fascination with Ultima Thule. Heinrich Himmler (who allegedly carried a copy of *The Bhagavad-Gita* with him everywhere to relieve his guilt about the war) was the Thule Society's most prominent member. Messages thought to come from the astral plane were incorporated into the Reich's strategies. Although he avoided the Thule Society, Hitler relied on numerous mystics, astrologers and clairvoyants for support and advice. The most famous is Erik Hanussen, who taught Hitler to hypnotize crowds.

Joseph Goebbels and The Paradox of Propaganda

On April 30th, just before he committed suicide, Hitler made Goebbels Reich Chancellor. But Goebbels held this position for just one day. When the Russians refused a treaty that was favorable to the Nazi Party, Goebbels followed Hitler in suicide, along with his wife and six children. With Goebbels' death, the Nazi Regime lost its voice. Goebbels was a brilliant orator—humorous, sarcastic and detached. His famous motto was: *If you want to tell a lie, tell a big lie.* Goebbels was skilled at hiding the Reich's reliance on the occult—a reliance he didn't share. He was openly contemptuous of Himmler's obsession with the supernatural, and may have been a key influence in dissuading Hitler from joining the Thule Society. He was far less successful in hiding the Final Solution. Many Germans were convinced by Goebbels' propaganda; others, however, knew about the camps, as is evident by Germans in the Resistance, people in the Nazi Party who used their influence to save Jews, and the White Rose Party, a radical student group that distributed pamphlets about the camps.

Martin Heidegger and World War II

Among Germans who denied any knowledge of the Final Solution was the philosopher Martin Heidegger—-an enigmatic figure during the Nazi regime. In 1933, he became a member of the Party and was appointed Chancellor of the University of Freiburg. A year after he assumed the Chancellorship, he resigned. Some Party members who viewed Heidegger as a rival resented the Chancellorship. Others thought his philosophy was gibberish. And Heidegger himself believed Germany was betraying its promise to return to its cultural roots. His criticisms of the Party were vociferous; on the other hand, he never resigned from or denounced the Party, even in an evasive, posthumous interview published by *Der Spiegel.*

Heidegger's affiliation with Party has generated heated discussions about whether there are Nazi doctrines in his philosophy. Some philosophers feel there is clear evidence of this and often refer to a famous conversation with Karl Löwith before the war where he claimed that one of his most important ideas (historicity) was the foundation for his political involvement. Other philosophers think that Heidegger was simply incapable of integrating his philosophy and his politics and see much revisionism in the views he expressed. Heidegger is still acknowledged as having great influence on modern philosophical thought, as well as on poetry and architecture. Ironically—given his affiliations with views driven by chauvinism—he raised cogent questions about the nature of existence, the nature of herd mentality, and the nature of thought itself. He also wrote and spoke with great sophistication about the human impulse to avoid knowledge of mortality. Over ten years before the Reich came into power, Heidegger's own eyeglasses were one of several catalysts for a revelation about this aspect of human existence, and he mentioned them in his seminal work, *Being and Time.*

Zoë-Eleanor Englehardt, Guest Curator,
The Museum of Tolerance, New York City, New York

Prologue

*I*n the ordinary winter of 1920, the philosopher Martin Heidegger saw his glasses and fell out of the familiar world. He was in his study at Freiburg, over one hundred and sixty kilometers south of Berlin, looking out the window at the thick bare branches of an elm tree. His wife was standing next to him, pouring a cup of coffee. Sunlight fell through the voile curtains, throwing stripes on her crown of blond braids, the dark table, and his white cup. All at once a starling crashed against the window and dropped to the ground. Heidegger reached for his glasses to look and as he leaned over, the coffee spilled. His wife cleaned the table with her apron while he cleaned the glasses with his handkerchief. And all at once, he looked at the thin gold earpieces and two round lenses and didn't know what they were for. It was as though he'd never seen glasses or knew how they were used. And then the whole world became unfamiliar: The tree was a confusion of shapes, the blood-spattered window a floating oblong. And when another starling flew by, he saw only darkness in motion.

Martin Heidegger didn't mention this to his wife. Together they cleaned and muttered. She brought more coffee and left the room. Heidegger waited for the world to fall back into place and eventually the ticking belonged to the clock again, *the table became a table, and the floor became something to walk on. Then he went to his desk and wrote about this moment to a fellow philosopher named Asher Englehardt. Even though they often met for coffee, they enjoyed writing to each other about tilted moments: The hammer that's so loose its head flops like a bird. The picture that's crooked and makes the room seem uncanny. The apple in the middle of the street that makes you forget what streets are for. The thing made close because it's seen at a distance. The sense of not being at home. The world falling out of itself.*

A few days later Asher Englehardt wrote back in his familiar, hurried script, chiding Heidegger for always acting as though the sensation were new. "There is nothing of substance to depend on, Martin," he wrote. "All these cups and glasses and whatever else people have or do are props that shield us from a world that started long before anyone knew what glasses were for and will go on long after there's no one left to remember them. It's a strange world, Martin. But we can never fall out of it because we live in it all the time."

Asher believed this resolutely and continued to believe it twenty years later when he and his son were taken from their home in Freiburg and deported by cattle car to Auschwitz.

Droga Mamo!

Moglabys przyniesc mi buty, ktore trzymalam w kredensie? Bede potrzebowala je na droge.

Calusy.
Mari

* * *

Dear Mother,

Can you bring me the shoes I kept in the cupboard? I know I'll need them for the journey.

Love,
Mari

The Orders

Nearly a quarter of a century after Heidegger's revelation about his glasses, a woman with a red silk ribbon snaking around her wrist drove a captured U.S. jeep to a village in Northern Germany. The village was in blackout, and its outpost—a wooden building set far back in a field—would have been easy to miss if she hadn't made many trips there in the dark. It was a bitter winter night, and snow fell on her face as she walked across the field. She stopped to brush it off and looked at the sky. It was dazzling, brilliant with stars, so wide it seemed carved into separate galaxies. And even at this stage of the war, the woman felt happy. She had just smuggled three children to Switzerland and hoodwinked a guard. Her name was Elie Schacten.

Elie looked at Orion's hunting dogs and scattered them into points of light—ice-flowers in the dark sky. Then she knocked twice on the shrouded door. It opened, a hand pulled her inside, and an SS officer kissed her on the lips.

What happened? he said. You were supposed to be here yesterday.

There was a problem with the clutch, said Elie. You should be glad I got here now.

I *am* glad, said the officer. But I think you were up to something, my willowy little friend.

I'm not your willowy little anything, said Elie. She shook him off and looked around. How's the junk shop? she asked.

You can't believe what we're getting, said the officer. Five kilos of Dutch chocolate. French cognac. Statues from an Austrian castle.

They were talking about the outpost—a pine room with crooked beams. It had one oblong window with a blackout curtain and was crammed with objects from raided shops and houses. It was also cold. Wind blew through cracks in the walls, and the coal stove was empty. Elie tightened her scarf and walked through a maze of clocks, books, coats, two optometrist chairs, and chifforobes, to a velvet couch. The officer dragged over eight bulging mailbags and leaned in so close Elie felt his breath. She let her hair loose so it screened her face.

That tea-rose is hard to come by these days, said the officer, meaning her perfume. He leaned in closer and touched her blond curls.

Elie smiled and began to read postcards and letters. The sheer amount always overwhelmed her. Most were from Operation Mail—letters written under coercion at camps or ghettoes, often moments before the writer was led to a cattle car or gas chamber. Most were on thin, brittle paper and had a dark red stamp that overrode the addresses to relatives. The instructions on the stamp were: "Automatically forward all Jewish mail to 65 Berlin, Iranische Strasse."

Elie scanned without reading—her only purpose was to identify the language. She tried to ignore her sense of revulsion—never pausing to look at the name of the writer or what they'd written. Sometimes, when she was trying to fall asleep, she saw phrases from these letters—hurried, terrified lies, extolling the conditions in the camps. But when she scanned them quickly, she noticed nothing—except when she saw the enormous bag marked A, for Auschwitz. It was not only bigger than the other mailbags but seemed larger than anything this world could contain, as if it had fallen from another universe. Elie always had the sense that she had fallen with it and paused before reading the first letter.

What's wrong? said the officer.

I'm just tired, she said.

Is that all?

The officer, who loved gossip, always tried to pry into Elie's past because these days people parachuted into the world as if they'd just been born, with new papers to prove it, and she was no different—the daughter of Polish Catholics, transformed into a German by Goebbels. Her features conformed to every Aryan standard. Her German accent was flawless.

Elie stared at some bolts of wool wedged between two bicycles. Then she went back to sorting letters. The officer lit a cigarette.

You won't believe this, he said. But a Jew just got out of Auschwitz. He walked past the fence with the Commandant's blessing.

I don't believe you, said Elie.

It's all over the Reich, said the officer. An SS man came to the Commandant and said this guy owned a lab, and the Reich needed it for the war and the guy had to leave to sign over the papers. So the Commandant said he could, and now they can't find the lab or the name of the SS man. They don't even think he was real. They call him the Angel of Auschwitz.

My God, said Elie.

Is that all you can say? It's a fucking travesty. And Goebbels won't shoot the Commandant. He says he can't be bothered.

Elie fussed with the strands of the red ribbon on her wrist. She couldn't take the ribbon off because, along with special papers, it gave her unlimited freedom to travel and amnesty from rape, pillage, or murder. The officer leaned close and offered to untangle the strands. One had a metal eagle on it—so small the beak was the size of a needle's eye. He paused and admired the craftsmanship.

Elie let him untangle the ribbon and counted things on the walls: five gilt-edged mirrors, fifteen typewriters, one globe, seven clocks, eight tables, bolts of black merino wool and white cashmere, a mixing bowl, twelve chairs, a tailor's dummy, five lamps, numerous fur coats, playing cards, boxes of chocolate, and a telescope. *A jumble-shop,* she thought. *The Reich can raid everything but heat.*

I must get back, she said, standing up. If I see any codes from the Resistance, I'll let you know.

Stay the night, said the officer, patting a confiscated couch. I'll keep my hands off you. I promise.

You have more than hands, said Elie.

My feet are safe, too, said the officer. He pointed to a hole in his boots, and they laughed.

As she always did, Elie accepted his offer to take whatever she wanted from the outpost—this time fourteen bolts of wool, a grandfather clock, the telescope, the globe, ten fur coats, a tailor's dummy, two gilt mirrors, three boxes of playing cards, and half a kilo of chocolate.

She also accepted his offer to carry everything across the field, where the snow was still soft, and the sky still promised pageants of light. Elie let the officer kiss her on the lips just once and hold her longer than she would have liked. Then she drove deep into the North German woods where pine trees hid the moon.

At one point a thin girl without shoes darted across the road. Elie wasn't surprised: at this stage of the war, people appeared just like animals. But she couldn't stop, even to offer bread. There were as many guards as trees. And one rescue was dangerous enough.

The pines grew thicker; wind blew through the canvas roof of her jeep, and Elie's fear of the dark rose up, along with a terror of being followed. She concentrated on the road as if her only mission were to drive forever.

Alongside her fears ran her shock about the angel of Auschwitz. Elie always found clever escape routes for people—sewers in ghettoes, tunnels below factories. But she'd never contemplated an escape from a camp. She wondered if the angel was a rumor. What better way to annoy the Reich than imply a place like Auschwitz wasn't foolproof?

Near three in the morning, the road became an unpaved road, jolting the car and making the grandfather clock tick. Elie's ribbon brushed against the gearshift, reminding her she was tethered to the Reich. She looked in the rearview mirror to make sure she wasn't being followed and made a sharp turn to a clearing where another jeep and two Kubelwagens were parked. The clearing, ringed by forest, had a well on its far left and a shepherd's hut with a round roof near the Kubelwagens. A tall man in a Navy jacket and rumpled green sweater ran out and threw his arms around her. Then he helped her unload the jeep. They brought the telescope, the tailor's dummy, the bolts of wool, the coats, the mirrors, the map, the chairs, the chocolate, the playing cards, the clock, the globe, the mailbags, and a hamper of food to the shepherd's hut. The room had a pallet and a crude wooden table. Opposite the door was a fireplace. To its left was another arched door that opened to an incline. Elie and the officer dragged everything down the incline to a mineshaft and loaded it into a lift. He leaned over to kiss her, but she shook snow from her coat and turned away, caught in her thoughts about the angel.

What's wrong? he said. Does only half of you like me?

All of me likes you, said Elie. I'm just saving the other half for later.

Luigi più caro,

Era un viaggio facile anche se era lungo. Lo gradireste qui. Venga prego lo vengono a contatto di.

Ami,
Rosaria

* * *

Dear Luigi,

It was an easy journey even though it was long. The country is lovely here. Come meet me.

Love,
Rosaria

The officer went to their room—five yards up the incline—and Elie took the mineshaft almost ten meters down into the earth. The mineshaft lift was a small, cramped cage, and she was relieved when she could pull back the diamond-shaped guard. It opened to a rose-colored cobblestone street lit with gas lamps. Opposite the mineshaft was a large mahogany door with *Gleichantworten Mögen* (Like Answers Like) hammered out in the same jaunty semicircle as *Arbeit Macht Frei*. Elie opened this door to a room the size of a small stadium, where more than forty people slept on desks. She heard glissandos of snoring and rustling. If someone moved or shifted too abruptly, papers fell to the floor. The walls were lined with sewing machines, mixing bowls, coats, mirrors, typewriters.

Elie's desk was in the front of the room, facing the others. As soon as she lit its kerosene lamp people struggled from sleep to greet her. A door on the far wall opened, and sixteen more people tumbled out. Everyone crowded around Elie, asking if she was safe, rushing to bring treasures from the mineshaft. She opened the hamper of food, and they applauded when they saw ham, a roast chicken, sausages, smoked fish, cheese, cigarettes, vodka, fleischkonserve, cans of ersatz coffee, and thirteen loaves of freshly baked bread—a gift from a baker whose niece Elie helped escape to Denmark. They opened the vodka and toasted news that the Russians were advancing. Then they toasted Elie.

To Elie! they said. To our Gnädige Frau!

Elie raised her own glass and wrapped the fresh meat

and bread in soft cloth. Then she took the mineshaft back to the room she shared with the officer who met her as she walked up the incline. He held out his hands and they walked to their room, the last remnant of life above the earth. It was a small white square with oblong windows near the ceiling that became trapezoids as they sloped closer to the ground. Elie wanted nothing more than to lean in the officer's arms and tell him how much she had missed him; but she was afraid she would start to cry from sheer exhaustion. Instead she shone the kerosene lantern around the room with a slight aura of disapproval. There were socks, playing cards, boots, and books scattered on the floor. There was also another green sweater.

This looks just like the outpost, she said.

Actually, Elie, I changed the sheets, said the officer.

That was good of you.

So I'm exonerated?

Maybe.

Elie draped her coat on a chair. Then she opened her arms:

Both sides of me are ready for you now, she said.

Elie had moved from the small dark room below the earth because she said people needed extra space to sleep. But everyone knew it was because she loved Gerhardt Lodenstein, who was Obërst of the Compound.

Once three days seemed like nothing, he said, pulling her to the bed. But the crazier things get the longer three days seem. What took so long?

The less you know the better, said Elie.

The SS shoot people like flies these days. I worry.

11

It's not so crazy at the borders, said Elie. I had three kids under blankets, and the SS hardly looked. They've stopped believing in this war. Everyone has.

Not Himmler or Goebbels, said Lodenstein. And not the camps. They're killing more people every day.

Mentioning the camps made Elie remember the story about the angel. She kissed Lodenstein, took her revolver from her cardigan and kicked off her boots. Then she got under the covers, wearing her skirt, her blouse, and the red silk ribbon.

You can't sleep in your clothes, Elie.

Lots of people do these days, she said.

I know. But we're still safe here.

Still, said Elie.

Still is safe enough.

Elie smiled, and he undressed her carefully. When he touched her, she felt as soft as the ribbon he'd untied—the ribbon that, along with classified papers, allowed her freedom to travel. He pulled her toward him. She pulled away.

What happened to you out there? he said. Something's wrong.

Elie touched the quilt. It was a feather comforter, covered with grey silk, and came from a raided house in Amsterdam.

There's a mess out there, she said. And we sleep under this Reich-fucked thing.

But that's not what's bothering you.

Lodenstein turned off the kerosene lantern, and the dark felt soft, almost tangible. He touched Elie, and her body felt like lace. They made love slowly.

Who can resist the feeling of being made into lace? she thought. *Only someone who knows they're about to be gassed or doesn't know if their child will eat the next day. Only someone who has to walk for kilometers in danger on a cold winter's night.*

Lodenstein fell asleep, but Elie lay awake, thinking about the SS man who had transformed into an angel. Elie imagined his conversation with the Commandant, the prisoner being told he could leave. She imagined the two of them walking out of Auschwitz. *If one person can leave, two people can leave,* she thought. *And then three. And then four.*

Before Goebbels gave her identity papers, he'd shown Elie photographs of Auschwitz, watching for signs of compassion. She'd been careful not to register anything while she looked at rows of barracks and the russet barbed-wire fence that billowed around the camp as if it were frozen by the wind. The tufted wires looked like runes but could tear skin to shreds. *What would it take to get someone past that fence?* she thought.

Liebstes Herta,

Kann ich nicht Ihnen E erklären, wieviel ich Dich vermisse. Es gibt jemand im Lager nachts, das Lieder singen kann. Sie erlauben dieses und es erinnert mich an Dich. Dieses ist alles, das ich für jetzt schreiben kann.

Liebe,
Stefan

* * *

Dearest Herta,

I can't tell you how much I miss you. There's someone in this camp who can sing Lieder. They allow him to sing at night because the officers enjoy it and it reminds me of you. I can hear your voice inside this fence. This is all I can write for now.

Love,
Stefan

While Elie lay awake she looked at the sliver of black phone beneath maps and papers and thought of people to call to ask about the angel. But she and Lodenstein already lived in peril because they helped fugitives, and a call to the wrong person could get them shot. So Elie pressed her head into the quilt and tried to ignore the dank mineral smell of the mine permeating from below. At night the smell grew stronger, as if the mine were denouncing its transformation after Hans Ewigkeit, a famous German architect, had toured it and said *this will do.*

No detail had been too small: the mine was masked by a shell, enclosing three water closets, a kitchen, a cobblestone street, an artificial sky, a room for over fifty people, and a shoebox of a watchtower. Everyone who slept below the earth had fallen from some place or other. And at night, while Elie felt the weight of a feather quilt, they shifted and coughed and fought to keep warm. Everything in the project depended upon them. It was called The Compound of Scribes.

Near dawn it began to snow heavily, piling against the windows and filling the room with blue light. Elie touched Lodenstein's light brown hair and traced the hairline scar on his forehead. Everything felt soft, as if made of another element, and she finally fell asleep, light-years away from the Compound.

15

When Lodenstein woke up, Elie was still sleeping. One arm trailed along the side of the bed, reminding him of the first time he'd ever seen her sleep— on a train when she'd brought him to the Compound. They'd traveled at night, and the benches were transformed into bunks. Elie slept on top, he slept below, and one of her arms was so close he could have touched the red ribbon on her wrist. Once he'd gotten out of bed to look at her and was so entranced—and so further entranced by her charming dishevelment in the morning—he'd left his shaving kit on the train. It was sent to the Compound two weeks later with a note from Goebbels's office: *There's a war on. We don't give out shaving kits like pfennigs.*

He wondered what Elie had done in her search for ways to help people. What SS men had she flirted with? What hawkers on the black market? What flagging underground newspaper group would keep printing because she'd found them money? What forgers would make passports because she'd hidden a relative? Lodenstein understood that flirtations and unholy alliances were the stuff of rescues: they appeased guards, suspicious landlords, inquisitive neighbors. But when Elie was gone an extra day, he worried about blurred lines between secrets for the good of the Resistance and secrets that belied a hidden life.

Elie woke up, looked at him and closed her eyes.

I wish it wasn't morning, she said.

I'll get breakfast, he said. The morning can wait.

He threw his green sweater over a pair of fatigues and took the mineshaft to the cobblestone street and turned left to the kitchen—a four-meter-long galley with pots hung so low they clanged like hollow bells when people brushed against them.

Two Scribes were lifting a can of ersatz coffee while another spooned it into glass jars. They didn't notice Lodenstein, and he wondered, not for first time, if they knew he had anything to do with their lives being close to bearable. Even at this early hour he heard someone offer cigarettes as a prize for inventing a crossword puzzle in fifteen languages. He also heard typing—probably in coded diaries—and a lottery to sleep in Elie's old room. Goebbels didn't allow these things, of course, but he ignored them.

More people came in to make coffee. The mine was cold, and everyone wore fur coats from the outpost. He felt ermine, mink, fox, and lamb's wool. They nuzzled his back like friendly animals.

The bread Elie had brought the night before was on a butcher block in the middle of the kitchen. There had been five loaves of white bread and eight of pumpernickel in the hamper last night. This morning all the pumpernickel was left, and there were three loaves of white. He cut two thin, cautious slices. Someone saw him and said:

Take more! For Elie!

Another Scribe said the same thing and then another and another until Elie's name rang all over the kitchen like an invocation. He cut more bread and thanked them in a dozen languages. They laughed and thanked him back.

Everyone spoke German, but conversations were filled with foreign words—Hungarian for shame (*velenk*), Italian for ink (*inchiostro*), Polish for shadow (*cien*). Every week there were more words because the inhabitants—collectively—were fluent in forty-seven languages and dialects besides German. And this was why they'd been spared the camps and could be in this shell—fighting, scribbling, clawing, to carry out a mysterious and Byzantine mission.

17

Mein reizendes Susanne,

Kam ich letzte Woche an und ich war glücklich, die Arbeit zu erhalten, die eine Straße errichtet. Die Nahrung ist gut und ich mag heraus in der Frischluft sein. Es gibt gute Arbeit für Frauen, auch-nähende Uniformen, das Ausbessern und schreibt. Ich weiß, daß Sie shier (?) möchten. Bitte zu kommen.

Liebe,
Heinrich

*   *   *

My lovely Susanne,

I arrived last week and was lucky to get work building a road. The food is good and I like being out in the fresh air. There is good work for women, too—sewing uniforms, mending, typing. I know you would like it here.

Love,
Heinrich

18

Gerhardt Lodenstein was fluent in five languages but hadn't needed to barter in any of them for his position as Obërst of the Compound: Long ago, in return for a bicycle, he'd promised his father that he would enlist in the secret police, where his father was a prominent member. The secret police was called the Abwehr—a remote, elite organization expert in deciphering codes and known for its hatred of the Reich. Its head, Wilhelm Canaris, tried twice to assassinate Hitler before the war. When he joined, Lodenstein thought he'd spend two years learning codes, then practice law. But the Reich created its own secret police, shrinking the Abwehr, and reducing Gerhardt Lodenstein's job to filing old papers from the First World War. Eventually Goebbels—with malice because he disliked Lodenstein's father—enlisted him in the SS and made him the reluctant head of the Compound of Scribes, forcing him to oversee an absurd and useless project: answering letters to people who were dead.

These letters were part of a plan referred to as *Briefaktion* (Operation Mail), in which prisoners were forced to write to relatives, praising conditions in camps and ghettoes. They were mailed to The Association of Jews in Berlin so no one knew where they came from.

Their purpose was to camouflage the fact that most of these people were about to be killed and encourage relatives to come to the camps voluntarily. They also served to dispel rumors about the camps. But the mail system was chaotic, and many relatives had been deported, no doubt forced to write letters themselves. So thousands of unread letters were returned to Berlin.

Himmler had forbade burning them: he believed in the supernatural with a vengeance, and thought the dead would pester psychics for answers if they knew their letters were destroyed—eventually exposing the Final Solution. Goebbels, who despised the supernatural, wouldn't burn them for a different reason. He wanted each letter to be answered for the sake of record-keeping so there wouldn't be any questions after the war. In order to look authentic, he decided the letters should be answered in their original language: hence the Compound motto *Like Answers Like.* The SS went to deportations to find the most fluent and educated to be Scribes.

Самое дорогое,

пожалуйста не тревожится о нас: Дети отлично и еда будет деличиоус супом с темным хлебом, видом, котор мы смогли никогда не получить дома. Мы унылы что вы не с нами, но мы думаем вас часто. Я думаю вас каждая ноча. Я знаю мы увидит скоро.

Lfoe,
Влюбленность

＊　　＊　　＊

Dearest Mishka,

Please don't worry about us: The children are fine and the food is delicious—thick soup with dark bread. There's also a beautiful forest here. They're taking a group of us on a walk in a few minutes. You'll have to join us, even if we won't be here to welcome you.

Love,
Levka

At the onset of Operation Mail, the Scribes were kept in a bunker in Berlin. Facilities were cramped, the smell of cabbage was everywhere, but—as people liked to joke—they managed. Yet as more people were pulled from deportations, Goebbels worried that clotheslines, billowing in the middle of the city, would arouse suspicion and sent scouts to find an abandoned mine in the North German woods. There, with Hitler's blessing, he enlisted the architect Hans Ewigkeit and transformed the mine to indulge his romantic notions. There was a rose-colored cobblestone street lit by tall gas lamps. There was a canopy of fake sky with a sun that rose and set, and stars that duplicated the constellations on Hitler's birthday. There were mahogany doors and wrought-iron benches. The mine was sequestered by a narrow road and concealed by a shepherd's hut.

The idea of answering the dead made Gerhardt Lodenstein queasy, and he became more so when he came to the Compound over a year ago and found it in chaos: the original Obërst, who, like Himmler, believed the dead were waiting for answers, was caught holding séances to contact them. This Obërst had been demoted to Major and hated Lodenstein for getting his room above the earth. Some Scribes wanted to leave the Compound, even though it meant almost certain death, and Himmler was starting to talk freely about the Final Solution he originally wanted to conceal. A week after Lodenstein arrived, Goebbels wrote that if he didn't report to Berlin immediately he'd send him to the front. Lodenstein drove all night and arrived in Berlin the next morning in the crimson halls of the new Reich Chancellery. Goebbels sat on books to look taller than five-feet-five and growled at Lodenstein to close the door.

You must know, he said in a low voice, that some people think the dead are waiting for answers and will hound us until they get them.

Lodenstein, who couldn't decide what to say, didn't say anything. Goebbels pounded his desk.

Of course you know. Don't act like a moron.

He shoved over a pamphlet called *War Strategies from the Thule Society.* Lodenstein saw a list of names—Himmler, a few SS officers, and some famous mystics.

These idiots think they're allied with the fucking beyond, and they meet to get advice about the war from the astral plane, said Goebbels. So a certain demoted Obërst may bother you about it. But remember there *is* no fucking beyond, and the dead can't read. Make answers short, and keep that asshole from holding séances. This is just about record-keeping.

Lodenstein said, yes, of course he would, and Goebbels showed him a model of a building to exhibit the letters after the war. The building had Greek columns and marble nooks. *It looks like a mausoleum,* Lodenstein thought.

Only Elie saved Lodenstein's life from complete absurdity. And since she did, he didn't ask why she was rummaging near the telephone when he came back with breakfast. They huddled under the quilt and drank ersatz coffee, which they agreed was getting weaker and weaker, and talked about the war: soldiers deserting, not enough food. Elie leaned against him and said she was exhausted. He stroked her hair and asked—trying to sound casual:

Did anything happen at the border?

I already told you: They've stopped caring.

Then why an extra day?

The mother didn't want to leave her kids, and there wasn't room in the jeep. I had to find her a guide.

And the baker?

What do you mean *the baker*? He baked the bread because I got his niece to Denmark. Why do you grill me whenever I come back?

It was an old conversation. Elie flirted for favors. Lodenstein got upset. They had this conversation again and again, never resolved it, and never stopped loving each other. Elie's voice was thin, as though she were about to cry. She threw down her napkin and took the mineshaft to the main room where she lit the lantern at her desk and wrote down supplies she hadn't been able to get on her foray: *Kerosene. Wicks. Knäckebrot.* Then she made a list of people who might help find out whether the Angel of Auschwitz was real. She crossed out some names, added others, wrote the names in code, and crumpled the first piece of paper. Later she would burn it. Elie was always burning papers. No one in the Compound worried when they saw small fires in the forest.

While Elie worked, the Scribes played word games, wrote in diaries, and answered a few letters from Operation Mail. Sometimes they typed one or two obligatory sentences. Sometimes they answered at length, usually by hand, because something about the letter writer moved them: maybe the handwriting reminded them of a parent. Or the writer mentioned a town they knew. Or the letter was written the day they'd been scheduled to be deported. They kept these letters for themselves and didn't send them to be stored in crates. Now and then one of them came across a letter from someone they knew, and there was weeping, mayhem, and commotion. Not today, though. And Elie, as always, was composed.

Sophie Nachtgarten picked up her pen. She'd just read a letter from someone in the district of Fürth—the same district she'd lived in with her lover. There had been a lineup in their town square, and a guard shouted *stand straight!* in an accent Sophie recognized as Norwegian. On an impulse she'd said *of course* in Norwegian and was pulled from the line. It was a good guess—the guard had been raised in Norway. And while her lover was taken to the gallows Sophie was pushed into a Kubelwagen.

Dear Margot, she began, *I don't know you, but we lived close by—so close we could have passed each other in a marketplace....*

Elie let the Scribes do what they wanted because it didn't matter how many letters they answered: Goebbels threatened to visit but never came. As for the building to exhibit the letters after the war—Elie knew it would never happen: Germany could barely feed her own people. These letters would never be read. And neither she, the Scribes, nor Lodenstein wanted to support a blasphemous distortion of history.

Except for those arrested crossing borders, most Scribes remembered being pulled from a line-up in a town square or a crowd that exuded panic while surging towards cattle cars. They remembered being quizzed, and understanding their life depended on knowing a foreign language. Then a series of confusing car rides, their first glimpse of the shepherd's hut, their startling descent into the earth—and their relief when they met Elie Schacten.

Now she stood up and clapped her hands.

It's time to get ready for the feast, she said.

25

⟨⤳⟩

Within moments, Scribes arranged eighteen desks side by side and eighteen more facing them. Elie found candles and wineglasses in a broom closet. A Scribe named Parvis Nafissian set out pitchers with water from the well. Sophie Nachtgarten took the mineshaft to the forest and came back with pine boughs that made the air fresh and the desks into a banquet table. They brought out platters with ham, chicken, bread, and cheese. Elie lit candles and poured wine. Then she banged on a metal pot.

Everybody come! she called. It's time for the feast.

People began to appear from the most unlikely places: a short man in a skullcap and a taller woman with a long red braid came from a tiny house at the end of the cobblestone street. A green-eyed woman in an ermine coat darted from a corner. A blond woman with a cigarette holder and an elegant man in a long black coat walked out of Elie's old room. And Lars Eisenscher, an eighteen-year-old guard who barely fit into his uniform, came from the mineshaft. As soon as Lars saw the man in the skullcap, he pulled out a seat for him and cut him a huge slice of bread. He sat behind him for the rest of the meal, pouring wine for him and the woman with the long red braid.

Soon fifty-eight people were around the table—Lodenstein at one end, Elie at the other. The candlelight made faces float and the plates glow. Elie treasured these feasts after a foray. Everything was illuminated and reminded her of an enchanted castle freed from a spell. She stood up and raised her wineglass.

To the end of the war! she said. To victory for the Allies!

The room was filled with the sound of clinking glasses. People passed platters and joked about the best word for bread in different languages.

Pain is best, said the woman in the ermine coat. As soon as you say it, you see a baguette with butter.

Brot is better, said Parvis Nafissian. As soon as you say it you see soup.

Who cares? said the tall man in the black coat. What we need is a mazurka.

And he grabbed the blond woman and began to dance.

Above, in the shoebox of a watchtower, a man with a large face and several chins leaned against the glass. He seemed weighted by his chins, trapped in a different element, and looked forlorn. Elie Schacten nodded to Lars, who left the table and went up the winding stairs to the watchtower. Soon the heavy man was sitting next to Elie. She patted his arm and filled his plate with food. The woman in the ermine coat poured him wine.

To each and every one of us! said Elie, tapping her wineglass.

To all of us in the Compound! said Lodenstein, standing up.

Over twenty Scribes touched glasses with the heavy man. He was surrounded by arched backs, bowed heads, curved arms. The sound of glasses filled the room like bells.

To victory, he said under his breath.

Kochany Dominik,

*Ja ' ałuj ce ja przybył (przybywa ; wchodzi ; wszedł)
domowy (dom) i mówi (przemawia) wy.*

*Miło ,
Krystiana*

*   *   *

Beloved Dominik,

*I'm sorry I couldn't say good-bye. I had to leave home
quickly.*

*Love,
Krystiana*

When Elie woke up late the next morning, the first thing she saw was the telephone. It beckoned with such force that she dressed and ran to the mineshaft. When she opened it she almost tripped over Lars who had passed out drunk on the street. The main room was back in its spell—stained wineglasses, brittle pine boughs, Scribes asleep on the floor.

Elie threaded her way to her desk and opened a dark red notebook with a silver clasp. She read fragments from a few pages, leafed through more blank ones, picked a page at random and started to write. When Scribes got up, fumbling with coats, she put her notebook in her desk and went to the kitchen.

Take more, people said when she'd filled her tray.

Yes! More!

The voices were loving; happy to offer something. When Elie came upstairs Lodenstein raced for the tray.

That's my job, he said. You need to sleep.

But I couldn't, said Elie. By the way, did you notice how drunk Lars got last night? He's passed out downstairs in front of the mineshaft.

I'm not surprised. He's too young to hold his liquor.

How else can he handle missing his father? said Elie. She took a velvet ribbon from the dresser and fussed with her hair. Then she threw the ribbon on the floor and said:

I can't take much more of this.

More of what?

All of it. People lost. People dying. Not enough of us to save them.

The phone rang, and Elie and Lodenstein jumped. Lodenstein picked up the phone and acted pleasant in a tone that Elie recognized as false.

That officer at the outpost wants to see you tonight, he said when the conversation was over. He says something urgent has come up.

The world was in blackout when Elie left for the outpost. She drove past houses leaking light from dark curtains and past villages that were invisible. The officer was pacing at the outpost.

I just got an order from Goebbels's office, he said. And it's your neck and mine if we can't come through.

He handed Elie a paper from the Ministry of Public Enlightenment and Propaganda that read:

Joseph Goebbels's demands that the enclosed letter from Martin Heidegger to his optometrist Asher Englehardt be answered by a philosopher at the Compound of Scribes who can absolutely duplicate what would have been Asher Englehardt's reply—in other words act as his ventriloquist—*and be delivered, along with the proper pair of glasses, to Martin Heidegger's hut in the Black Forest in Todtnauberg. This must be done while maintaining absolute secrecy. No discussions are necessary.*

No discussions are necessary meant anyone who spoke about this to Goebbels would be shot.

Elie tugged at the sleeves of her thick woolen coat.

Why would Martin Heidegger bother to write to his optometrist? she said, careful to sound calm.

Why indeed? said the officer. He sat in a leather wing chair and lit a cigarette. His agitation had disappeared: no matter how lethal, gossip was intoxicating, and he seemed to be inhaling it, straight from Berlin.

Heidegger and this guy taught at the same university, he said. But when they found out his father was Jewish, they wouldn't let him teach, so he opened an optometry shop, and Heidegger went to him for glasses. I don't know why. He's a crackpot.

I've heard that, said Elie.

They kept writing each other letters, he continued. And this fall, when Heidegger didn't get an answer, his wife began to poke around. First she bothered Himmler, then Himmler bothered Goebbels, and then she and Goebbels had a meeting.

Elie twisted her dark red scarf.

Why should Goebbels meet with Heidegger's wife? she said. She's just an ordinary hausfrau.

Shhh! said the officer. Every corner of these walls can hear. You know why Goebbels met with her. He's always in that marketplace talking about the war. So what trouble is it to spend a pleasant hour with a hausfrau? Besides, if Goebbels is happy, things go better for all of us.

Then he handed Elie two photographs. One was of Asher Englehardt's optometry shop after it was raided, and the other was of Asher Englehardt and Martin Heidegger. In the first, Elie saw *Fuck Jews* scrawled across an eye chart and shards of glass on an optometrist's chair. In the second, she saw Asher Englehardt by an alpine hut with his hands on Martin Heidegger's shoulders. The photograph was labeled *Black Forest, 1929.*

They were quite the friends, said the officer.

What does that matter? said Elie. The Gestapo's been watching Heidegger for years.

Maybe, said the officer. But they don't need to watch his wife. She's in good standing with the Party.

31

Elie stared at the clock between two bicycles and tried to look upset about the orders. On the one hand, they were impossible. On the other, impossible orders sometimes led to extraordinary rescues.

What's the matter? said the officer.

Nothing, said Elie. Except I don't know a ventriloquist who can write like a philosopher.

Then you have to find one, said the officer.

But this letter was written last fall.

But Goebbels and Frau Heidegger just met a month ago. Besides, his *wife* wants his glasses. And *Heidegger* wants an answer to his letter.

The officer handed Elie a pine box filled with over twenty pairs of glasses. Each had a white tag on an earpiece and a different name on each tag. One pair was marked *für Martin Heidegger*. Elie stared at Asher Englehardt's handwriting.

You need to deliver the glasses *and* a letter, said the officer.

I understand, said Elie, still careful to sound calm. By the way—do you know what happened to the optometrist?

Do you think he went to the Badensee on a vacation? said the officer. The SS man watching out for him was shot, and he got sent to Auschwitz. He ran his finger across his throat like the slash of a knife. Maybe his mother was Aryan, but these days no one's lucky. And that Angel of Auschwitz got just one chance.

Elie nodded. The officer stubbed out his cigarette.

Do you want anything else? he asked, pointing to the walls.

We can always use coats, said Elie. And another kilo of chocolate.

The officer carried the coats across the snow, and Elie carried everything from Asher Englehardt's optometry shop, including Heidegger's glasses and his letter to Asher, the last sentence of which read:

How could either of us have known you would be the person to make me real *glasses—that unwitting source of my falling out of the world?*

Elie, who had met Heidegger and read Heidegger, understood exactly what he meant. But she agreed that the letter was crazy. When they got to her jeep, she let the officer kiss her on the lips again and hold her longer than she would have liked. Then she drove back to the north German woods, thinking about Goebbels's orders. When she got to the clearing, she looked at the photographs carefully. She folded them in half and pushed them deep into her pocket.

Slowaaks ,

U mustâ t menen welke volk zitten zegswijze. Zulks werkhuis zit zoet, en wanneer u worden zulks zendbrie , Mij annuleerteken uitsluitend zeggen u voor kom mee hiernaartoe. Voeren ouder en vader en naar de kinderen. Wees zo goed, voeren iedereen.

Van min,
Mordecai

*   *   *

Slovania,

You mustn't believe what people are saying. This place is good, and if you get this letter, I can only tell you to come here. Bring mother and father and the children. Please, bring everyone.

Love,
Mordecai

When Elie walked into the hut, Lodenstein was wearing his Navy trench coat and toying with his compass on the wooden table. It was a liquid compass from the British Royal Navy—Lodenstein had found it in a shop before the war. The compass was used on ships, but Lodenstein took pleasure in using it on land. It helped him feel close to the sea, especially the horizon where he saw the sun and moon over far-flung water. Sometimes he joked to Elie: *Suppose the earth is flat after all? If you're near the sea, you can escape.*

He'd sent Lars Eisenscher downstairs so they could be alone. Elie handed him the orders and Heidegger's letter, and he read them a few times to see if they were coded. But the messages were exactly what they were meant to be: From Heidegger, brilliance and bombast. From Goebbels's office, orders to deliver Heidegger's glasses and a letter without a trace of where they'd come from.

A hausfrau's leading Goebbels around, said Elie.

But even generals can't do that, said Lodenstein.

It's Heidegger's wife, said Elie. A great example of Kinder, Küche, and Kirche.

I thought her Kinder left home.

Heidegger hasn't, said Elie.

Lodenstein laughed, and Elie didn't mention she'd once been to a party at the Heideggers and gotten Frau Heidegger's recipe for *bundkuchen.*

Maybe it's all made up, said Lodenstein. Or maybe they want a reason to shoot me.

No one wants a reason to shoot you, said Elie. And I'm pretty sure the optometrist is real.

Why are you sure? said Lodenstein. People invent themselves like flies these days. I wouldn't be surprised if someone invented us.

Maybe they did, said Elie. But I happen to have met Martin Heidegger.

I thought you read in linguistics.

I did, said Elie. But everybody knew each other.

There was a cracked mirror on the fireplace, and Elie walked to it and worked the ribbon in her hair. When she'd tied a bow that met her standards, she said:

Heidegger and Asher Englehardt were friends, Gerhardt. They wrote each other letters. They met for coffee.

Except now Englehardt's at a place where no one writes letters. Except the ridiculous ones you read.

Elie came back to the table. Her eyes were preternaturally bright.

Maybe these orders could get Englehardt out, she said.

Listen to me, Elie. People don't leave Auschwitz.

I know about a few.

Yes. As ashes.

Not always, said Elie. Just a week ago an SS man came to the Commandant and said a prisoner owned a lab and the Reich needed it for the war, and he had to leave Auschwitz to sign the papers. So he did. And guess what? There aren't any records of the lab, and no one knows the SS officer. People think he wasn't real. They call him the Angel of Auschwitz.

Who told you that?

The outpost officer.

He's losing it, said Lodenstein.

36

But it's all over the Reich, said Elie. And Asher Englehardt is the only ventriloquist we'll ever find.

There are plenty of people who can write a good letter.

Who?

Lodenstein waved his hands. I'm sure we can find one.

But these orders might get him out.

Listen to me, Elie. If we fool around, Goebbels will shoot everyone in the Compound. Besides, they aren't even signed. Anyone could have sent them.

But the glasses are real, said Elie. And I'm going to talk to Stumpf about the letter.

You can try, Lodenstein said. But Major Stumpf is a fool.

That's exactly why I want to talk to him, said Elie.

Stumpf can never help, he said. And it was bad enough that you asked him to the feast.

Deiter Stumpf was the man who lived in the shoebox overlooking the Scribes. He was short and stout and reminded Elie of a shar-pei dog whose skin is all in folds. The shar-pei hadn't come to Germany; but a Chinese painting of one turned up at the outpost, and Elie took it because it reminded her of Stumpf. The painting was her private joke with Lodenstein.

Stumpf had been Obërst of the Compound until Lodenstein replaced him. For reasons no one had bothered to explain, he'd had to move from the room above the earth to a shoebox accessed by winding steps. The shoebox was his bedroom as well as his office: in addition to a desk it had a mattress, crystal balls, and books about the astral plane.

It also had a large window overlooking the main room of the Compound. Once, rotating guards patrolled the Scribes;

but after Germany lost Stalingrad, only Lars was left to guard the forest, and Stumpf had to patrol. He rationalized his demotion by imagining he was the only person Goebbels trusted to make sure the Scribes did their work. But secretly he agonized.

Before Stalingrad, Stumpf had been delighted to record answers to the dead and loved his huge metal stamp and big black paw of an inkpad. But the other guards had been clever at foreign languages, and Stumpf had never learned one. If the correspondence was in German, Stumpf used his huge metal stamp so vigorously the crystal ball on his desk rattled. But if the letters were in a foreign language, he had no way of knowing whether the Scribes had duped him by writing nonsense. Sometimes his stamp hovered in the air. Sometimes it pounced. At other times he got overwhelmed. Then he heaved down the spiral staircase and told everyone in the main room they were scroungers. His rants went on until someone—a Scribe, or Lodenstein, if he were there—put two fingers in the shape of devil's horns behind his head. Everyone laughed, the folds in Stump's face sagged, and he crept back to his shoebox, looking so forlorn people felt sorry for him. But only for a while. Being ridiculed was trivial compared to having a gun at your head or seeing your child shoved into a cattle car.

Liebe Mutti,

Ich hoffe, dass du diesen Brief lesen kann. Sie haben dass ich auf reinen Deutsch schreibe, nicht unser Dialekt gefragt. Möglicherweise helfe ich heraus bei den Übersetzungen. Lotte und I beide verfehlen du.

Liebe,
Franz

* * *

Dear Mother,

I hope you can read this letter. They have asked that I write in pure German, not our dialect. Perhaps I will help out with translations. Lotte and I both miss you.

Love,
Franz

Stumpf, who was still under the illusion that Lodenstein treated the Scribes like prisoners, despised them because they didn't respect what he perceived to be the project of the Compound. They answered only half of what they could have answered in a day and spent the rest of the time writing in diaries and holding raffles for Elie's old room: they raffled cigarettes, sausages—it didn't matter what, as long as it amused them. Meanwhile, thousands of letters from the camps arrived each month, and Stumpf had gotten word from Goebbels's office that there would be an inspection in a fortnight. There was no way all the letters could be answered. There were too many dead. So, much against his principles, he was planning to bury thousands of letters in the rye field of his brother's farm near Dresden. He was sure all the dead deserved answers and was upset by this decision; but it was better than being shot. Stumpf's sacrifices to the dead stopped when it came to joining them.

He had been sneaking mail to his shoebox and was figuring out whether he could fit all seventeen crates of letters into his Kubelwagen when Elie Schacten knocked. Stumpf had been so appalled by his lack of privacy that he'd secured his door with gold-plated latches –seven in all – that fastened with hooks and made his door resemble hooks and eyes on old boots. Stumpf unlocked every one of them and Elie Schacten came in holding a pair of rimless glasses with thin gold earpieces that wobbled like insect legs. She also showed him a letter that was gibberish and a prescription for the glasses.

Why are you showing me these? Stumpf asked.

Because they need to be delivered, said Elie. Really delivered.

Everything's delivered, said Stumpf. In crates.

I mean the glasses. I mean delivered to someone who's alive, said Elie, showing him the orders from Goebbels's office.

Stumpf held the paper to the light to see if they held the seals of the offices, which he'd seen many times when he was an Under-Under Secretary. After he decided the seals were authentic, he said:

Maybe someone else wrote the orders. They aren't even signed.

Whoever wrote them, said Elie, the outpost says it's an order.

What does the outpost know? said Stumpf.

It's all over the Reich, said Elie.

Stumpf sighed when Elie mentioned the Reich: he'd once been part of important conversations behind enormous doors and used the seals he'd just scrutinized—seals that pressed the swastika deeper than his metal stamp. Stumpf's folds of skin gave him three chins and often made him look startled. Now he looked sad—even his chins. Elie patted his hand.

But why now? he said. This man went to Auschwitz in October.

It's urgent, said Elie. Heidegger used to be Chancellor of Freiburg, and he needs his glasses.

Someone smart enough to be Chancellor wouldn't wait that long for a pair of glasses, said Stumpf. He'd get new ones from an Aryan optometrist.

It doesn't matter, Elie said. They want Heidegger to get *these* glasses—with an answer to his letter.

But we only answer letters to the dead!

Elie touched his metal stamp. This is an order, she said quietly. Do you know what that means?

How else could I be in charge of these scoundrels if I didn't? But why do you suppose Goebbels wants this? It's against our mission.

Stumpf looked genuinely puzzled—as if he always knew what Goebbels wanted.

Heidegger and the optometrist were friends, said Elie. The kind who take walks together.

But Heidegger's not in good standing. The Gestapo's watching him.

He still gets to talk in Paris, said Elie. Besides, he and the optometrist taught philosophy.

This seemed to faze Stumpf, and the gears in his head began to grind: If Heidegger and the Jew taught philosophy, then they wrote each other letters that were incomprehensible. And if they wrote each other letters that were incomprehensible, then, under the strict rule of *Like Answers Like*, Heidegger would need an answer from someone who could write a letter that was just as incomprehensible.

He looked at Elie and allowed himself to enjoy her tangle of blond curls and tea-rose perfume. He even imagined he could smell real weather—pine trees, fresh snow, the fragrance of light itself.

Leave everything here, he said. I'll take it to someone higher up.

I've taken it to someone higher up, said Elie. He said to talk to you.

Then I'll do something about it.

I don't think you will.

Who will then? Not one of those down there.

He meant the Scribes. A few were writing a crossword puzzle on the blackboard.

What a miserable bunch, he said.

They're not miserable at all, said Elie. They're just in a miserable place.

I am, too, said Stumpf. But I still do my work.

Elie looked at a crystal ball and three candlesticks on his dresser. She touched a mail bag full of letters with her foot.

What are these? she said.

Papers to store, said Stumpf.

Elie picked a postcard from a mail bag. It was an unremarkable card, with coerced praise from a prisoner and a purple postage stamp of Hitler. Stumpf looked at Elie with the eyes of a pleading dog.

Put that back! said Stumpf. I'll find a way to answer it—I promise.

Stumpf didn't want to talk to his replacement, Gerhardt Lodenstein, who was only there—he was sure—so Stumpf wouldn't hold more séances. Stumpf decided never to mention the matter concerning Heidegger to anyone and bury the orders, the letter, the prescription, and the glasses at his brother's farm. Nonsense didn't deserve an answer. Someday Goebbels would thank him.

But when he went back to his desk, he realized Elie had taken everything except the prescription for Heidegger's glasses. And now he saw a note on the prescription that said: *Important—for future use in the event of my disappearance, Asher Englehardt.* The note made him wonder whether Heidegger had special eye problems—he'd once heard of

43

something called elongated corneas—so God knows what else could be wrong. And if Heidegger couldn't see as a result of his neglect and was exonerated, Stumpf could be shot.

So he went to talk to Generalmajor Mueller who'd come to the Compound to do mysterious work for Goebbels and was about to go back to the Reich Chancellery in Berlin. He took off his wooly bedroom slippers, put on his boots, and walked from his shoebox down the spiral stairs. He had to pass through the main room to reach Mueller's quarters and tripped when he opened the door to the street. But no one gave him the slightest notice.

Generalmajor Mueller, who looked like a raccoon in a dark coat and black leather gloves, was eating fleischkonserve with gherkins at his desk in spacious quarters to the left of the main room of the Compound. His room had a rosewood bed, a matching dresser, a mahogany desk, and two gilded mirrors to simulate windows. Mueller had fourteen gherkins on his plate— twelve more than the daily ration. He was eating them as revenge for not having been asked to the feast.

Mueller didn't like Stumpf or Lodenstein but shared some passions with each of them. With Stumpf he shared a passion for Elie Schacten and the Reich. With Lodenstein he shared a passion for Elie Schacten and solitaire. He was annoyed that Lodenstein could satisfy both his passions while he only got to satisfy one. This was solitaire, which he played when he read his mysterious papers, made his mysterious phone calls, and when he ate. When Stumpf came in, he was playing a game called Czarina and didn't bother to look up.

I need to talk to you, said Stumpf.

Mueller swept a stack.

Quickly, then. I'm leaving.

Stumpf wasn't smart but was blessed with a skill that made him first indispensable to the Reich, and later undesirable: he remembered everything he read—word for word, comma for comma—and recited the orders precisely. When he'd finished, Mueller said:

Your job is to answer letters from people who are dead. And Heidegger's not dead yet.

Just what I thought, said Stumpf.

People lose sight these days, said Mueller. Even Goebbels.

You shouldn't talk about him that way.

Why not? said Mueller, picking up another gherkin. Himmler has gone haywire. And Goebbels is acting deluded. Like rain on a dark night.

Mueller often compared things to the weather, and Stumpf was never sure what he meant. Rain fell in the same place whether it was night or day.

I don't think you understand, he said. Heidegger and this man were friends.

Who cares? said Mueller. On the other hand—he closed his eyes—Goebbels has reasons for everything.

What are they now?

I would be violating his trust if I told you.

A hint, then, said Stumpf.

Even a hint would be wrong, said Mueller, who had no idea what Goebbels wanted.

Besides, said Mueller, patting his head, I must hang on to this, and giving away secrets is a good way to lose it.

Elie Schacten says it's because they were friends, said Stumpf.

Elie Schacten is admirable, said Mueller. But she's trying to make sense of something she can't understand.

There was a moment of silence in which both men observed their reverence for Elie Schacten—provider of their schnapps, wearer of tea-rose perfume.

He doesn't deserve her, said Mueller, meaning Lodenstein. He shoved his cards into a tooled-leather case.

Fucking Berlin, he said. Lodenstein should be going there.

Maybe he will soon, said Stumpf.

Not with his luck. He'll play cards and sleep with her forever.

Goebbels is after his ass, said Stumpf.

He's after almost everyone's except mine, said Mueller.

Stumpf coughed. Then could you ask him about the orders? he said. And the letter to Heidegger?

Are you crazy? I'd be shot. People aren't themselves these days. They make ridiculous demands and hold séances.

The mention of séances made Stumpf so nervous he ate a gherkin off of Mueller's plate. He'd often thought it was Mueller who had told Goebbels's office about a séance he had held, during which a candle fell over and started a fire in a corner of the upstairs room. Mueller helped put the fire out and was the only person who knew about it.

I don't think you should do anything, Mueller continued, locking the black leather case where he stored his mysterious papers. The optometrist went to school with Heidegger before Heidegger knew the optometrist was a dog. Besides, Heidegger's pissed off everyone. I say to hell with him.

You're telling the former Chancellor of Freiburg to go to hell! I should report you.

Go ahead. Let them shoot me.

This was a lie. Even though Mueller worried that his days were numbered, he wanted as many of them as possible and was angry that he, not Lodenstein, had been called back to Berlin. He was so angry he thought about putting a bullet through Stumpf's head. But he couldn't just throw him in the forest and cover him with leaves. There would be an investigation.

Do whatever you want, he said, yanking on his boots. Bring him the damned glasses. Leave them outside his little hut. I'm sure Heidegger believes in elves.

But don't think the Scribes are going to help you, he continued. They're useless with their lotteries and word games. You should shoot them.

You can't shoot the Scribes! There would be no one to answer letters.

Do you really believe these records matter?

Stumpf, who never forgot his inferior position, drew back.

I'm sure the dead are waiting to read them, he said.

No one believes that, said Mueller.

Himmler does.

But not Goebbels, said Mueller. He doesn't believe that at all. He dusted a boot and handed Stumpf a miniature ivory box and a deck of cards.

Tell Lodenstein the cards are a good-bye present, he said. And the box is for Elie Schacten.

I'm not your servant, said Stumpf, shoving everything back.

And he left the rosewood room still a burdened man, because no one in the Compound took the mission more seriously than he did. Stumpf was sure the idea about answering letters to the dead or about-to-be-dead had occurred to him at the same time it occurred to the Thule Society, just the way two people in the 17th century—he couldn't remember who—had discovered calculus at the same time. Lodenstein treated the project carelessly, which so bothered Stumpf he often woke in the middle of the night, sure the dead were hounding him. He thought he could hear them now.

Abramo più caro,

Cif sono molte cose che vorrei dire a voi, ma soprattutto, li vorrei venire. Le circostanze sono buon-molto migliore di erano a sede-e l'alimento è abbondante. Dovreste provare a portare i bambini, anche. Allora non sarebbe lungo fino a che non fossimo insieme.

Amore,
Vanessa

＊　＊　＊

Dearest Abramo,

Please don't worry. We had to leave the office quickly because of important work. Conditions are good—much better than they were at home—and the food is plentiful. If you brought the children, we could all be together.

Love,
Vanessa

After she left Stumpf's watchtower, Elie Schacten sat on a wrought-iron bench outside the Compound's main room. Hans Ewigkeit, with Thor Ungeheur, the Compound's interior designer, had ordered these benches placed at random on the street. He'd wanted to suggest an affluent city park.

Elie knew Stumpf wouldn't do anything but hoped she'd planted a seed. She lit a cigarette and stared at a photograph of Goebbels hanging next to the mineshaft. The photograph was five feet tall, just five inches less than his actual height. Goebbels was posed near an unusually small umbrella that made him appear taller. When Elie looked at his face, it was full of hope. But when she just looked at his eyes, she saw a sad, liquid quality. She took out the photographs—of Asher Englehardt and Heidegger, of Asher Englehardt's ruined shop. She looked at them and put them away.

A few Scribes asked if she was all right, and Elie fobbed them off by leafing through her dark red notebook. Now and then she paused to read something—never more than a fragment—*a forest near the house/ice cracking in the spring*—but was interrupted by Sonia Markova, a Russian ballerina who practiced pliés in a state of eternal melancholy.

You look worried, said Sonia, sitting next to her.

I'm just tired, said Elie, closing the notebook.

Sonia's white ermine coat brushed against her cashmere sweater, and for a moment Elie felt caught in Hans Ewigkeit's dream: she and Sonia weren't ten meters below the earth in a converted mine, but two well-heeled women in a city park. She was glad when Scribes began to argue in the kitchen and she had an excuse to leave. They all wanted coffee, but no one wanted to brew enough for everyone. Elie ducked under the clanging pots and said she'd make it herself. But the Scribes said she did enough for them and waved her away. So she went upstairs, where Gerhardt Lodenstein was playing his ninth game of solitaire for the day.

Lodenstein knew over fifty games. Among them were Zodiac, The Castle of Indolence, Griffon, Streets and Alleys, Thumb and Pouch, Open Crescent, Five Companions, Seven Sisters, Waste the Same, Mantis, Scarab, Twin Queens, Up or Down, Step by Step, and Milky Way. He played in stacks and cascades and felt a sensual thrill when he could do a full levens. Besides Elie Schacten, solitaire was the only thing that kept him sane. When she came in he was playing Czarina. His compass was on the floor. She put it on the bedside table.

So, he said, is Stumpf your angel?

He didn't understand a thing, said Elie

Has he ever?

Not once. But I thought it would work to our advantage this time.

Our advantage? said Lodenstein. He gave her a sharp look. All I want is to keep the Scribes from a death march.

You're imagining the worst, said Elie.

Then why do you bother with rescues?

Elie didn't answer and took off her cardigan. Heidegger's glasses fell from the pocket. Lodenstein picked them up and held them up to the clerestory windows.

Do you think Goebbels gives a damn if Heidegger gets these? he said. Germany's losing this war, so what better way to feel good than create impossible orders?

51

He doesn't want the Heideggers to know about the camps, said Elie, taking the glasses back. And if they don't get what they want, they'll keep poking around.

He'd handle them if they found out.

He doesn't *want* to handle them, said Elie. He wants us to. And the outpost officer is frantic.

Lodenstein set a few cards aside. It was a special move called a heel.

You see, said Elie, pointing to the cards. There are always ways to break the rules.

That's why I like solitaire, said Lodenstein. It's not a dangerous game.

Elie stayed by the windows and looked at snow dusting the pines. She wondered if it was snowing at Auschwitz.

It looks like a painting out there, she said.

Except it's not, said Lodenstein. Who knows how many fugitives are hiding in those woods?

And I could have been one of them, said Elie.

Thank God you're not.

Except I'm not myself anymore, she said. Sometimes I think even you don't know who I am.

Of course I know who you are.

You know what I mean.

What Elie meant was that she often felt like two different people. One was Elie Schacten, born in Stuttgart, a translator for the importer Schiff und Wagg. The other was Elie Kowaleski, a student in linguistics at Freiburg.

Elie Schacten had grown up in Germany with nursery rhymes, cooking classes, and was engaged to a soldier killed at the front. Elie Kowaleski had grown up with Polish nuns who beat her fingers until they bled, had parents who found her obstreperous, and a sister she missed every day. The two Elies worked in tandem: The first was cautious, established bonds with the black market and got food for the Compound. The second was dauntless, got more food than people ever meant to give, and smuggled people to Switzerland.

I wish you'd tell me your real last name, said Lodenstein—not for the first time.

It's a secret, said Elie—not for the first time.

It's not good to feel like two people, he said.

But I *am* two people. And someday they might ask you the wrong questions. So the less you know the better.

They were interrupted by Generalmajor Mueller, who came in without knocking and shoved a deck of cards at Lodenstein.

What game should I tell Goebbels you're playing these days? he said. Persian Patience? Odd and Even?

Tell him I'm playing Mueller Shuffling Papers, said Lodenstein.

Go fuck yourself, said Mueller. He slammed the door. They heard his duffel bag scrape against the incline.

You pissed him off, said Elie.

Go out and make up to him, said Lodenstein.

Why? He's a pig.

I want to keep Goebbels happy.

So even you need the other Elie.

You just know how to charm people, said Lodenstein, taking her in his arms. But you're always the same to me.

Cher Yvonne,

J'étais ont à une sympathique situer que j'étais traversée les frontière et on apprend tout mes papier. Tellement voici que moi-même, si tu sais se que moi vouloir dire. Le semble être âgé les général opinion ça c'est une sage situer et tout le monde devez viens, incluant tois. Pour maintenant, je ne peux d'ecriver plus.

Mon amour à jamais,
Maurice

*   *   *

Dear Yvonne,

As I was crossing the border they took all my special papers and sent me to a pleasant place. And so I'm not traveling incognito anymore. It seems to be the general opinion that this is a good place and everyone should come, including you.

All my love,
Maurice

Elie followed Mueller, who looked incongruous with his elegant tooled-leather case and beat-up duffel bag. Outside the shepherd's hut there was a path of oval stones that led to the clearing. Mueller turned around when he heard Elie's boots crack the ice.

How lovely to see you, he said, taking her arm.

Elie held her arm at a distance and watched his elbow gesture towards the sky. It was a dazzling incandescent blue.

If only we could be like the weather, said Mueller.

Who says we can't? said Elie.

The war, he said. Rain means waiting to attack, sun means charging ahead, and winter means Stalingrad.

But Stalingrad was last winter.

And it changed winter forever, said Mueller.

Elie tried to free her arm. Mueller pressed closer.

Let me give you some advice, he said. Leave those orders alone.

What orders?

You know what orders. And you also know that if it weren't for a certain officer, we'd have spent more time together.

I'm not sure what you mean.

Of course you do, said Mueller. He put down his bags and kissed Elie's hand. She felt his moustache bristle her fingers and wished she'd worn gloves.

You're very kind, she said.

You know I'm not kind at all.

Well, I'm sure wherever you're going, you'll do good, she said. Gerhardt thinks so too.

You're lying, said Mueller. But you'll do good. You always do. Except you're too nice to those people down there.

Everyone suffers in a war.

But some people don't deserve to suffer as much as others, said Mueller.

They'd come to his Kubelwagen and Mueller, who boasted about refusing a confiscated American jeep, patted a window. Then he bent close and spoke to Elie in a low voice.

About those glasses, he said. I'd ignore everything. People aren't themselves these days and even a wild card like Heidegger isn't a problem. Who cares if he doesn't get his glasses? Nothing bends the will of the Reich. Not even the dead.

Elie tried to look incredulous. Do you really think so? she asked.

Of course, said Mueller. The Fuhrer won't leave his bunker, and Goebbels is always in that marketplace talking about the war. Who even knows if he even wrote those orders?

Of course, said Elie.

I'm glad you agree, said Mueller. He took off his gloves and patted her hand.

I'll miss you, he said.

And I'll miss you, she said, in a voice so distant it seemed to come from the forest.

Would Obërst Lodenstein mind if I kissed you?

Oh…you know…best not to disturb things.

Of course, said Mueller. But if I can ever help you, let me know. Meanwhile, make sure those people answer letters. There are too many languages in that room, and if they don't stay busy, it's the tower of Babel. And Stumpf should take his hands off Sonia Markova.

You're right about that, said Elie.

Well, here's a kiss anyway, said Mueller. And he pressed his lips against Elie's—so tightly his medals pricked her chin.

You have no idea how much regard I have for you, he said.

And I for you, said Elie. But I'm freezing without a coat.

She turned to leave, but Mueller pulled at her sleeve and handed her the ivory box. It's a puzzle-box, he said. Try to open it.

Elie worked the panels until the box flew open. There was an ivory carving of a plum tree inside.

To spring! said Mueller. To a whole new season!

It's lovely, said Elie, handing it back.

It's for you, said Mueller.

But things get lost here.

Or a certain Obërst gets jealous, said Mueller, pushing the box at her. Anyway, if you don't take it, I'll have to tell Goebbels a thing or two.

He bowed with a flourish and drove away on the unpaved road. The wheels of his Kubelwagen broke the ice, reminding Elie of shattered glass.

While Mueller was leaving, Dieter Stumpf was in his shoebox deciding which Scribe should answer Martin Heidegger's letter to Asher Englehardt. It was a nuisance to answer even one letter to the living when so many dead were waiting. But he was sure if he could deliver everything, Goebbels would decide that Lodenstein should live in the shoebox, and he would be reinstated as Obërst of the Compound.

To this purpose, he looked down at the immense room and consulted a list that detailed the background of every Scribe:

the list, compiled by the SS, said where each Scribe had been born, their siblings, where they'd gone to school, and what they'd studied. While he read the list, Elie Schacten opened the door to the main room and sat at her desk facing the Scribes. She shoved pencils into jars, put papers away, and took out her dark red notebook. She looked up at Dieter Stumpf in his shoebox. He looked away.

The vast room, lit by kerosene lanterns, would have been dreary except for splotches of color on the Scribes' rakish scarves and fingerless gloves. Stumpf looked from the room to the list and back to the room again. The last time he counted there were fifty-four Scribes, and every one had studied something he didn't understand. But only five had read in philosophy:

There was a blond, somewhat wasted-looking woman named Gitka Kapusinki from Poland, who'd been pulled from a deportation line when an SS man heard her speak Czechoslovakian. And her lover, Ferdinand La Toya, who wore a long black coat, smoked potent Spanish cigars and was snatched from deportation when a guard told him to go fuck himself, and he'd answered—first in Catalan, then in Italian—*under what circumstances?* And Niles Schopenhauer—not related to *the* Schopenhauer—who was sent from a work camp because he knew seven languages. There was also Sophie Nachtgarten, who'd published a paper called *Time and The Unicorn: A Treatise on Necessary Truth.* She'd surprised a guard whose mother came from Norway, regaled him with Norwegian drinking songs, and charmed her way to the Compound instead of Bergen-Belsen. And Parvis Nafissian, with black beetle brows and a trim goatee. He was the only Scribe who'd been forced to write a letter. But when a guard saw he'd written one in Turkish and another in Farsi, he pulled him from the line at Treblinka and shoved him into a Kubelwagen. Nafissian answered almost no letters at all. He read whatever detective stories Elie could find.

Stumpf decided that any of them would do, and—since any of them would do—all five could write the letter together. He was about to go down his spiral staircase to talk to them, when Sonia Markova knocked on his door and Stumpf went through the laborious business of unlatching it. Sonia, who'd once danced with the Bolshoi ballet, had snuck from Russia to see a lover in Berlin, was caught on her way back, and demonstrated three Russian dialects. She had delectable legs, high cheekbones, green eyes, translucent skin, and black curls. She was also clairvoyant and sometimes agreed to secret séances—not only for people who'd died in camps and ghettoes but for ordinary people as well—the 19th-century dressmaker, for example, whose séance caused the fire in the upstairs room, or a woman who'd written her lover fighting in the Crimea. Stumpf had taken these letters secretly from attics of people who had been deported or warehouses and old files of government offices. There were letters from button makers, coach makers, furriers, boat makers, wheelwrights, printers, illusionists, and artists. He thought all the dead deserved answers.

Now Sonia walked in looking gloomy and said she couldn't keep her mind on anything because it was her niece's birthday.

She's ten, said Sonia. And she doesn't even know where I am.

Stumpf said she'd feel better if she held one of his crystal balls. He hoped this would turn into a séance for all the dead whose letters would be buried in his brother's rye field. He wanted to send a group letter asking forgiveness for not answering each one individually. But Sonia sat on the floor, looking like a mound of snow in her ermine coat, and began to cry. When Stumpf asked why she was crying, she said she missed every person in her family.

Even the ones I didn't like.

Stumpf took off her coat and hugged her cautiously, feeling his bulk. Sonia was often sad, and this could trigger his own sadness—deep, inchoate, since he'd been sent below the earth. But if he concentrated on her body, he could almost enjoy her grief because she let him comfort her. Sometimes they ended up on his mattress—she crying, he groping. But not today. Sonia put on her coat and said she was too miserable for love.

Please don't go, said Stumpf. I'm miserable too. And he grabbed one of Sonia's ermine sleeves.

If only we weren't in the lowest tier! he said.

What? Sonia pulled her arm away.

If only there were a tier below us, said Stumpf. With people who could help.

You mean people even lower than us with less air to breathe? How can you think that way? We already live like animals.

Sonia smoothed the sleeve Stumpf had grabbed and walked downstairs. Moments later he saw her at her desk—white fingers poking from dark red gloves.

She looked angry and irresistible. Stumpf went down the spiral staircase to ask her back. But he wanted to disguise his reason for spending any time away from work, so he investigated the paraphernalia against the walls. He knew he was the only example of diligence in the Compound and shouldn't take too much time. So he sorted quickly, haphazardly, and knocked over a bolt of wool. The bolt fell on the telescope, the telescope fell on the tailor's dummy, and the tailor's dummy fell on a clock. The Scribes applauded, and Stumpf was about to creep to his shoebox when he smelled Elie Schacten's tea-rose perfume.

Dieter, she said softly. Just the person I want to see.

Even today, when she'd so precipitously taken what he wanted to bury, Stumpf was happy to be intercepted by Elie Schacten. Whenever he saw her, or anything that belonged to her, he felt inexplicable excitement, including her enormous desk, which faced the multitude of Scribes. It had an aura of omnipotence, even dauntlessness—like Elie.

It was to this desk that he pulled up a chair. Elie put aside a list—she never pretended to monitor the Scribes—and gave him a piece of chocolate.

Stumpf finished the chocolate, and she gave him three more pieces. He didn't like the way Elie got favors, but he relished the chocolate and schnapps she brought to the Compound and was sure they'd make perfect colleagues if only she believed, as he did, that Germany would win the war. He looked at Elie dolefully and hoped she'd know what he was thinking. She smiled at him and said:

I feel sorry for Goebbels, Dieter. He's got too much on his mind these days.

It's hard to be on the edge of victory, said Stumpf.

Exactly, said Elie. And Gerhardt doesn't want to bother him. But the orders are confusing. So it might help if you could call him. You know how to talk to him.

Stumpf had a tick over his left eye. It began to pulse.

No one calls Goebbels, he said.

But you have clout, said Elie.

Of course I have clout, he said. But the more clout you have the more careful you are about using it.

61

Elie touched his arm and bent her head close. Once more he was enveloped in tea-rose.

Maybe the optometrist could come here and write the letter himself, she said. After all, Heidegger wrote it to him.

Elie's hand felt delicious; but the tick was distracting.

That's impossible, whispered Stumpf. We only write to the dead. They need us. They're waiting to hear.

That's why the orders are confusing, said Elie. By the way—I just heard a story about someone who got out of Auschwitz.

You don't mean that fucking angel they're talking about? said Stumpf.

No, no, said Elie, who in fact meant exactly that. It was a woman who got her husband out. His mother was Aryan—just like Asher Englehardt's.

How did she meet her husband? said Stumpf.

At a Hitler Youth Meeting.

Then that's why he got out, said Stumpf. Every young person should go.

Stumpf eyed the square box filled with glasses on Elie's desk. He moved closer and touched the box with a furtive reverence.

Do all these belong to Heidegger? he said.

Just one, said Elie.

How do you know?

Because it's marked, said Elie, pulling the box close to her.

Does Heidegger have any eye problems?

He might, said Elie, who knew he was only nearsighted.

Then we have to bring him his glasses.

But not without the letter, said Elie. Or Frau Heidegger will have a fit.

What does she have to do with it?

Goebbels met with her, said Elie. That's why they wrote these orders.

Goebbels met with Frau Heidegger? He's much too busy.

But he did, said Elie. They had a very long meeting at the Office.

The tick started again, and Stumpf put his hand on his forehead to press it down. But it kept skittering and jumping as though his forehead were on fire. And now he remembered that all five Scribes should answer the letter—a matter that seemed urgent since he'd heard about Frau Heidegger's meeting with Joseph Goebbels.

The more Elie went on about needing an answer, the more Stumpf's tick skittered and jumped. Finally he turned to the Scribes and shouted:

I need to see the five philosophers.

For heaven's sake, said Elie, leave them out of it.

Letters are their job.

And soon, to Elie's dismay, Gitka Kapusinki, Sophie Nachtgarten, Parvis Nafissian, Ferdinand La Toya, and Niles Schopenhauer were standing around her desk, and Stumpf was reciting the letter and ordering them to answer it.

But we only answer letters to the dead, said Parvis Nafissian.

Or the about-to-be-dead, said Gitka Kapusinki.

Or the almost dead, said Sophie Nachtgarten.

Heidegger's different, said Stumpf.

Which is why we can't answer the letter, said Ferdinand La Toya. It's against the mission.

Then all five leaned on Elie's desk and began to talk about Heidegger as if Stumpf weren't there.

He's all about paths and clearings in the Black Forest, said Niles Schopenhauer. There's no way anyone can think about that in this dungeon.

Except you need a lot more than fresh air, said Sophie Nachtgarten. He's a mystic tangled up in etymology.

I don't agree, said Gitka Kapusinki. He got a lot of things right. But he has no idea how they work in the real world.

This baffling conversation made Stumpf's tick jerk and jump. He pounded Elie's desk and recited the beginning of the letter so loudly the whole room could hear:

With regard to your recent remark about the nature of Being, I wanted to emphasize again that it was the distance of my glasses that made me close to them.

The Scribes laughed, and Niles Schopenhauer said they should translate the letter into their invented language, which they called *Dreamatoria*.

Stumpf waved his hand at Niles. It grazed him on the cheek.

Remember your place, he said. You're nothing but a fucking Scribe.

Don't pull them into it, said Elie. It's not their fault. If anyone catches us bringing a letter, we're in trouble, and if we don't bring one, we're in trouble.

A paradox! said La Toya.

Indeed! said Gitka.

The notion of paradox was too much for Stumpf. He went over to Sonia and asked her to come upstairs. But she said hearing the letter had made her thoughtful, and she wanted to sit at her desk and think about distance.

Xavier,

J'étais une sûr voyage , à bien assez de pâture. C'est soir
maintenant. Les ciel c'est tellement éclatant je ne peux voyons les
lune ou commencer , mais je suis sûre si vous êtes venus , nous
pouvions saisir se promener le soir , l'entrée nous utilisée à.

Amor,
Marie-Claire

* * *

Dearest Xavier,

I had a safe journey, with plenty of food. It's night now.
The sky is so bright I can't see the moon or stars, but I'm sure if
you came, we could take walks at night, the way we used to.

Love,
Marie-Claire

The tick continued when Stumpf went back to his shoebox, skittering in tandem with his brain. With great misgivings and second thoughts, he decided to disobey a strict order and approach a Scribe who was forbidden from answering letters written in German: this was Mikhail Solomon.

When he designed the Compound, Hans Ewigkeit had clustered most of the rooms using the mineshaft as a reference point. If one stood with one's back to the mineshaft, the kitchen was to its left, the guards' room and officers' quarters to its right, and the main room directly opposite. But the cobblestone street went on for thirty meters to dead-end in a wall that concealed an underground passage to the nearest town. And a stone's throw from this wall was a little white house with four pots of artificial roses, an artificial pear tree, and a lead-paned window. The street had no name, but the house had a number—917—engraved in bronze on the door.

Mikhail Solomon lived in this house with his wife, Talia. They had been designated *Echte Jude*, pure Jews, in charge of answering all correspondence written in the Hebrew alphabet—letters from people the Reich decided were pious. To be sure the letters were in keeping with the motto of *Like Answers Like*, the Solomons lived in a house like the one the interior designer Thor Ungeheur imagined they'd lived in before they were sent to the Lodz ghetto in Poland. They had two small kitchens, impossible to cook in, and were allowed to observe their customs, which adhered to the Reich's vague understanding of menorahs and a candle in the shape of a braid. They were forbidden from working on Saturday.

The Solomons were an unlikely pair, snatched from the maws of a cattle car about to leave the Lodz ghetto for Auschwitz. Mikhail was a slight, clean-shaven man who wore a skullcap. Talia was a head taller, had a shadow of a moustache, broad shoulders, and red hair in a long French braid. Before the war Mikhail taught ethics at the University of Berlin, and Talia taught English. The Solomons ignored Goebbels's orders about keeping to themselves and came to the main room every day to play word games and barter cigarettes. They also used the main kitchen.

Besides the privilege of a house, Mikhail was the only person besides Elie Schacten who could leave the Compound after midnight. Long after the lottery had been drawn for Elie's old room, and the Scribes were making love, eavesdropping, and note passing, Mikhail alone could admit he was awake. Then Lars Eisenscher knocked on his door and led him past the main room with bodies on desks, rustling papers, and glissandos of snoring. They took the mineshaft, walked up the incline, and down a stone path to the left of the Compound where they climbed a watchtower almost twelve meters from its entrance.

The watchtower had a steep ladder that led to a platform with a panoramic view of the night sky. And on this platform Mikhail pretended to read the stars. He had explained to the Reich he was a Kabbalist, and Kabbalists need to meditate on the sky after midnight. Didn't Hitler realize that the stars were angels and could predict the future?

As soon as the Reich heard this, they sent a memo: *Let the Jew read the stars.* Mikhail wasn't surprised. Everyone knew Hitler conferred with an astrologer about the war, and Churchill consulted one to predict Hitler's strategies. Mikhail himself didn't believe in angels or astrology. He only craved fresh air and the boundless freedom he felt when he looked at the sky. It was impervious to war, without trenches, countries, or borders.

Sometimes he liked to imagine each star was a word, and the sky was a piece of paper. Then the stars unfurled into a phrase—a proclamation for just one night. Sometimes he announced it to the main room in the morning. The last one had been *the persistence of fire.*

Beste Moeder,

Ik wachtte op u bij de trein en u kwam niet. Veel kinderen waren op de trein en wat van hen hadden moeders en vaders. Mijn schoenen werden te strak zodat nam ik hen weg en verloor hen. Gelieve te komen is met me.

Ik houd van u.
Miep

* * *

Dear Mother,

I waited for you at the train and you didn't come. Lots of children were on the train and some of them had mothers and fathers. My shoes got too tight so I took them off and lost them. Please come be with me. I love you.

Love,
Miep

Mikhail's grandfather, who actually believed the stars were angels, once told Mikhail that whenever he wanted something—a pair of skates, or a new coat—he lit a candle at midnight and prayed to the stars. Mikhail found this outlandish and was abashed that since the Reich came into power, he'd begun to wish his grandfather had been right. But if the stars were angels, they were mute, indifferent angels. Never once had they offered help.

The night after Heidegger's glasses arrived, the stars were dazzlingly clear. Mikhail saw Queen Anne's chair, waiting for Queen Anne. And Aquarius bearing water—too far away for the water to reach the earth. Six Pleiades were dancing, and the seventh, as always, was hidden.

Tonight he looked at the sky for a shorter time than usual. On that day Stumpf had given him over thirty letters from children. He'd read a few, answered none, and didn't feel like being inventive. Most of the letters had been passed over the chain-linked fence of the Lodz ghetto before a cattle car carried the children to Auschwitz. Were these children pious because they used the Hebrew alphabet? Mikhail didn't know what the word *pious* meant anymore. All he felt was relief that he hadn't recognized any of their names.

Lars sat next to him quietly. They'd built an easy friendship during nights when Mikhail read the stars. Lars could sense when Mikhail—who was about the same age as his father—needed time to think and when he wanted to talk. After a while Lars said:

Is there a message for the night?

Mikhail smiled. Lars had the same intense green eyes as his son and the same curiosity.

The angels are sleeping, he said.

But you told me they worked in shifts, said Lars.

Sometimes they do, said Mikhail. But even angels have to rest.

Lars climbed on a railing and stared at the sky. He looked much younger than his eighteen years.

Didn't they tell you *anything?*

Just one thing, said Mikhail. Haniel, guardian of the West Gates, said: Why bother to answer letters at all? It's better for the dead to be curious.

I bet they're right, said Lars. I never sent my grandmother thank-you notes, and she's never bothered me.

You see? said Mikhail.

But what do *you* think? said Lars. Do the dead ever read those letters in crates?

Do the dead ever bother to read? said Mikhail.

Stumpf says they do, said Lars.

If the dead do anything, said Mikhail, it's plugging their ears when Stumpf starts to talk.

Lars laughed, and they sat on the wooden platform and shared a cigarette. Neither wanted to go back to the Compound. At night it gave up any pretense of being a place to live and became a mine with an overwhelming mineral smell. When they finished the cigarette, Mikhail lit another and asked Lars if he'd heard from his father.

Lars shook his head. His father was a pastor and had been jailed three times for criticizing Hitler. He was afraid letters could get Lars into trouble and hardly ever wrote.

It must be hard for him without you, said Mikhail.

Hard for me too, said Lars.

On the way back they stopped at the well to take a long drink of water from the tin dipper. Lars shone his flashlight into the woods.

Be careful, said Mikhail. You could tempt someone.

You don't believe in ghosts, said Lars.

No, said Mikhail, but I believe in the SS.

Mikhail and Lars reached the hut, walked down the incline and took the mineshaft to the cobblestone street, where Elie and Stumpf were sitting on a wrought-iron bench. Stumpf was wearing his wooly bedroom slippers and extending his hands in a pleading, importunate gesture. Elie was shaking her head.

I need those glasses, said Stumpf. Heidegger deserves to see.

You'll only bury them, said Elie. And you'll never send the letter.

Anyone who finagles a talk in Paris knows you can't expect an answer from a Jew, said Stumpf.

Lars hurried Mikhail down the street. He thought it was hard enough that Mikhail worried about reading letters from people he knew and didn't need to hear Stumpf bemoaning Heidegger's glasses and the damned Jew-optometrist. But Stumpf raced to catch up with them, and all three walked beneath the frozen stars.

What do you think? said Stumpf to Mikhail, not pretending he needed to explain.

There are a lot of good Aryan optometrists, said Mikhail. Heidegger must have new glasses by now.

I'm tired of hearing about Aryan optometrists, said Stumpf. A man orders a pair of glasses and never hears a thing.

Heidegger likes the unknown, said Mikhail.

We aren't talking about the unknown, said Stumpf. We're talking about glasses. Besides, they were friends. They wrote letters.

How do you know? said Mikhail.

I did research.

Stumpf was always telling Mikhail he did research.

They'd come to the white house with the four artificial rose bushes, the artificial pear tree, and 917 on the bronze metal plaque. Mikhail walked around a flowerpot and opened the door. Stumpf shoved Lars away and touched Mikhail's shoulder.

Can I come in?

Stumpf's face appeared pinched, the way people look when they think they might be shot. Mikhail knew that look. He'd seen it in Talia's eyes when the SS raided their house. He'd seen it in his son's eyes when the ghetto police pushed him to the front of the Lodz square.

For a minute, he said. Talia's sleeping. But first let me say goodnight to Lars. You know he worries about me.

Geehrte Ania,

Ich habe wartete zu anschreiben Sie tagelang weil die Tour war lang. Aber die Landschaft ist schön , und es gibt Wälder und Örter als Kinder zu Stück. Bitte aus und ein gehen beitreten mich.

Alle mein Liebe ,
Christofer

* * *

Dear Ania,

I have waited to write to you for days because the trip was long. But the countryside is beautiful, and there are woods and places for children to play. Please come and join me.

All my love,
Christofer

Oil lamps from the 19th century, a time to which the interior designer, Thorsten Ungeheur, thought the Solomons were still confined, lit a room that both Mikhail and Stumpf had seen only in engravings—a room of dark wood, polished brass, and velveteen furniture. The living room had purple velveteen chairs, a purple velveteen couch, a rocking chair with a crocheted antimacassar, and tables with copper-based lamps. The walls had pictures of bearded men in skullcaps— supposedly pictures of ancestors—painted by order of Thorsten Ungeheur who didn't know orthodox Jews don't allow graven images. There were also footstools covered in needlework with Hebrew letters that didn't spell anything. Talia was sleeping in an alcove off the right-hand corner of the living room.

Mikhail turned on one of the lamps, and the two men sat on tufted velveteen chairs. Stumpf sat stiffly with his wooly feet on the floor. Mikhail sat casually with his legs crossed. Stumpf offered him a cigarette. Mikhail lit it and said the end was brighter than the stars.

Agreed, said Stumpf. But you can't snuff out stars.

With the right kind of smoke you can, said Mikhail.

Stumpf didn't comment. Instead he handed him a reproduction of Heidegger's letter, which he'd written from memory.

Mikhail nodded when he read about the Reich not understanding the Being of technology and looked bemused when he read about the importance of German root words. When he was finished reading, he put the letter on a piecrust table.

What mental embroidery, he said.

But you can embroider back.

I don't think so, said Mikhail.

Why not? said Stumpf. The letter is straightforward.

Really? Then you answer it.

I'm a practical man.

Mikhail smiled at Stumpf.

But I'm an *Echte Jude*, he said. I only answer letters in Hebrew and Yiddish.

But you can write a good letter in German, said Stumpf.

Really? said Mikhail. Do you think someone who's studied the Talmud can take any topic and stand it on its head and rattle out a bundle of words that would make any philosopher happy? Besides, my handwriting isn't the same.

Stumpf waved the end of his cigarette: a shooting star.

The letter can be typed, he said.

Goebbels decided *Echte Jude* shouldn't know how to type.

I'll decide differently, said Stumpf.

Mikhail began to talk about typewriters: How so many were brought to the Compound. How they lined the main room in hedgerows. How over fifty people typing sounded like artillery.

Stumpf listened without understanding, until Mikhail said the issue wasn't typewriters, but a bargain. Indeed Mikhail had a condition—something only the two of them could know about, and he would write the letter only if Stumpf would meet it.

The Bargain

Beste Oom Johannes,

Ik aan schrijf u na een prachtige reis. Het is hier zeer mooi. Er is wat hout waar ik kan spelen huid-en-zoek in de sneeuw met andere kinderen en wij allen gaan in een opera op een echt stadium zijn. Ik mis u en ik wil u en moeder hier komen, ook. en wij hebben veel meer voedsel dan wij thuis doen. Wij allen missen u en mama en papa hebben me verteld om u de te vertellen bedden zeer warm zijn en er is ook partij van tabak zodat kunt u uw pijp roken.

Liefde,
Pieter

* * *

Dear Uncle Johannes,

I'm writing to you after a wonderful journey to Thierenstadt. It's very beautiful here. There is a place where I can play hide-and-seek with other children and we are going to be in an opera on a real stage. We all miss you. I haven't seen mama and papa for days, but the beds here are warm, and mama and papa have told me to tell you that there is also a lot of tobacco so you can smoke your pipe.

Love,
Pieter

Hans Ewigkeit had originally planned to line the mine with thick brick walls. But even before losing Stalingrad, the Reich was pinched for money. So instead of brick walls, the Compound had thin pine walls covered with a single layer of plaster. Workers had added five coats of paint. But the Compound was a flimsy shell: Scribes put their hands on their ears when they wanted to think. Mueller had worn earmuffs.

The only soundproof places within the entire compound abutted the walls of the original mine. There were four, and by far the best was between two buttresses accessed through an air vent in the ceiling of the smallest water closet. It was unpleasant and cramped, but hermetically sealed. It was to this air vent that Dieter Stumpf and Mikhail Solomon went to discuss Mikhail's condition.

They left the Solomons' house after one in the morning, and Stumpf heard Scribes laughing in the kitchen. Ordinarily he would have made a fuss about their being up past curfew. Instead he crept to the narrow water closet with Mikhail. They got on top of a crate, opened the vent, lifted themselves into the jagged cavern and closed the vent behind them. The cavern was less than a meter high so they had to crouch.

Mikhail and Stumpf adjusted to the space and kept their distance in the pitch-black dark. They both hoped fervently that no one would use the water closet because sometimes people in this cloistered dark got trapped while one hapless person after another used the facilities. Neither Stumpf nor Mikhail wanted to be confined with the other. Besides, having to hear someone piss or shit was worse than being intruded upon by another group coming up through the air vent to talk in private. By tacit agreement, every inhabitant of the Compound treated this narrow space as a place of asylum. Even if the intruding group included officers, they would apologize and leave.

Mikhail's condition for answering Heidegger's letter was this: rescuing his niece—his sister's only daughter. For the past five months she'd been hiding in a crawl space under the floor of a house in Northern Germany. Every week SS men came to the house and put a stethoscope to the floor, convinced the house had a heartbeat. Until now they hadn't been able to find the exact location of the heartbeat; but it was only a matter of time. Mikhail wanted Stumpf to bring his niece to the Compound before SS men shot her or had her deported to the camps.

Deportations weren't supposed to be public knowledge, but Stumpf didn't bother to deny anything. Instead, he tried to fob Mikhail off by telling him the Compound had decided not to take children: parents didn't write to small children so they didn't need a child to answer letters. Mikhail said his niece wasn't exactly a child and it never occurred to him that she would have to answer letters. The issue was saving a life.

But everyone has to be useful here, said Stumpf.

In that case, I can't answer Heidegger because you won't help me, said Mikhail.

Even though Mikhail couldn't see him, Stumpf looked in the other direction to hide his disappointment. Then he asked:

How old is this girl?

Sixteen. Why?

Because she'd need to walk through the town and act calm, said Stumpf. Can she act calm?

Of course she can act calm. How else could she spend five months in a crawl space?

Stumpf spread his hands in a gesture of helplessness—invisible in the dark. He touched Mikhail's shoulder by accident, jerked away, and said he didn't know what to do. Goebbels's orders were to deliver the glasses to Heidegger with a convincing answer to the letter. But Stumpf couldn't write an answer himself.

I'm a practical man, he said again.

A dilemma, said Mikhail.

A paradox, said Stumpf.

They made the laborious climb out of the air vent, and Stumpf told Mikhail he would give the matter some thought. He crept passed the kitchen to his shoebox of a watchtower and looked down at the Scribes, who were huddled on desks and wrestling with covers to keep warm. It occurred to him they looked like boa constrictors. Someone cried out in sleep. Someone else said to shut up. Then there was a chorus of *shut ups* and an upwelling of whispering.

Stumpf pounded on the window and shouted, *Order!*—a command that made another Scribe shout:

Be quiet! We're trying to sleep!

Stumpf watched with contempt while Scribes rearranged more blankets and papers scattered to the floor. He considered offering all five philosophers a ham and an extra supply of cigarettes in return for writing the letter. But a conspicuous bribe could lead to gossip, and gossip could lead to chaos, and there was already enough chaos in the Compound.

Just last week someone had scrawled *Dreamatorium* over the main door. Stumpf had washed it off, but it was scrawled back the next day. He considered going downstairs to wash it off again. But within moments he was asleep in his chair, his head against the glass of the watchtower.

Every afternoon between one and one-thirty it was Stumpf's job to order the Scribes to imagine Joseph Goebbels, the head of the Ministry of Public Enlightenment and Propaganda. This was to prepare for Goebbels's visit to the Compound—an event that was continually announced and postponed. The reason for the imagining, as explained to Stumpf, was so no one would be in awe of him when he did arrive and could answer his questions. Gerhardt Lodenstein allowed Stumpf to carry out the exercise so he could feel useful—an illusion that spared the Scribes from too many of his rants.

For the duration of the exercise, Scribes had to push their typewriters to the edge of the desks and put away pens and letters. Then they had to imagine Goebbels in the proper sequence, starting with his boots, on to his jodhpurs, and then to his face. There was never any mention of his clubfoot. And whoever didn't imagine in the right order would be punished.

Stumpf walked back and forth between desks, sorry he couldn't make the Scribes imagine Heinrich Himmler instead and confused about how to regulate something he couldn't see. He stared at Scribes who were trying not to laugh and gave commands:

Imagine more quickly!

Continue imagining!

Proceed in the proper order!

Nafissian was smirking. Stumpf walked to his desk and asked what he was imagining.

Goebbels's boots, said Nafissian.

What do they look like?

Black.

Are they shiny?

Yes.

Wrong. We don't know what kind of day Goebbels will have had when he visits. He could have been walking through mud. Or have a bunion and be wearing slippers.

Be prepared for anything, he continued. Goebbels could be wearing a hair net. But you won't be looking that high.

Or a housedress, said La Toya.

Shut up! said Stumpf.

The Scribes pursed their lips to keep from laughing. They never tried to imagine Goebbels. Instead they thought about a decent cup of coffee, or whom they'd try to seduce that night if they won the lottery for Elie's old room. They tried not to think about what had brought them here or what had happened to the people they left behind.

But at other times during the day—random times—on their way to the kitchen for coffee, or smoking on the cobblestone street, they saw the five-foot picture of Goebbels near the mineshaft and imagined him against their will. He was their threat and savior, the reason why they were still alive, taken from almost certain death to this place. And only Goebbels's willingness to continue this ridiculous scheme sustained the fuliginous room where they answered letters to the dead that were stored in crates.

Today, when the half-hour was over, Stumpf looked out at the Scribes. He felt—as he always felt after this exercise—relief and euphoria. He tapped on the blackboard and announced the

Compound was going to have a new member—a boy of seven who would be staying with the *Echte Jude.*

As you know, he said, we have long needed a child to answer letters from parents to children in accordance with our strict standards of *Like Answers Like.* So Fraulein Schacten is going to bring a child to the Compound. For the most part, this child will answer letters written by parents who are deemed to be pious. But if time permits, he'll answer letters from parents who haven't been deemed to be pious. So if you get a letter from a parent that is clearly to a child, put it aside for a possible collection.

Possible or probable collection? said Parvis Nafissian.

Both, said Stumpf.

What about likely? said Ferdinand La Toya.

That, too.

La Toya winked at Gitka who winked back. Stumpf caught the wink and was furious.

Wink all you want, he said. There's another mouth to feed.

(א): וְקטרפ אוה הזז; השעת אל תווצמ עבראו, השע תווצמ שש
(ג); 'ה יתלוח הולא םש שיש הבשחמב הלעי אלש (ב); הולא םש שיש עדיל
(ד); ודחייל תא ללחל אלש (ז); ומש שדקל (ו); ונממ האריל (ה); ובהואל
ומש (ח); והילע ומש ארקנש םירבד דבאל אלש (ט); והילע ומש עמשל וְמ עומשל איבנה וְמ עומשל

;ומשב רבדמה
.ותוסנל אלש (י)

＊　＊　＊

Dear Mother,

I don't know where you and father are, but I am writing
home hoping that you will get this. Marc and I are fine and there is
plenty of food. If you and father come, we will all be together again.

Love,
Pia

85

Wolfgang Maulhaufer, the Compound's engineer, had been so overjoyed about finding an underground stream to handle waste, he'd forgotten to supply the Compound with fresh water. And Thorsten Ungeheur, the interior designer, had more elegant concerns than drinking or washing.

So the Compound's only fresh water supply was the well for the original mine. It was at the edge of the forest, about nine meters from the shepherd's hut. Before Germany lost Stalingrad, twelve guards had carried the day's water supply in buckets. But after Stalingrad, every guard except Lars Eisenscher had been sent to the front. Lars and Lodenstein couldn't bring enough water on their own for everyone in the Compound. And Stumpf and Mueller thought the task was beneath them.

So in late spring of 1943 Scribes began to bring water themselves, with only Lars to watch them. This upset Stumpf, but he couldn't disagree with Lodenstein when he said the Compound was the safest place at this stage of the war, and no one would try to escape.

The first time the Scribes went to the well there had been a great sense of celebration. Sophie Nachtgarten, whose claustrophobia sometimes made her walk the cobblestone street for hours, said it was the first time in months she'd been able to breathe. Ferdinand La Toya and Gitka Kapusinki did a mazurka. Parvis Nafissian and Sonia Markova lay at the edge of the forest.

Now, almost a year later, going to the well was so routine most Scribes took fresh air for granted—except for Sophie

Nachtgarten, who bribed Lars with cigarettes so she could come up as many times as she wanted. Other Scribes carried water twice a day, usually in pairs.

But after Stumpf announced the arrival of a child, Gitka Kapusinki, Ferdinand La Toya, Sophie Nachtgarten, and Parvis Nafissian took turns holding a pail. Gitka wore a bright red scarf over a black fur coat from an indeterminate animal and smoked a cigarette from a long cigarette holder. La Toya smoked a cigar and wore a long black coat, which made him look like a piece of topiary because he was tall. Sophie wore a green embroidered scarf over a blue velvet jacket—she hated the confinement of warm clothes. And Parvis Nafissian, who combed his immaculate beard with water from the well, wore a bomber jacket and carried a mirror. They crunched over the ice and talked.

What an asshole, said Gitka, meaning Stumpf.

He had to get someone to write that letter, said La Toya. And I think it's Mikhail.

He'd never do anything for Stumpf, said Sophie.

How else can you explain it? said La Toya. Suddenly a kid's at the Solomons' and Stumpf announces it. I bet the two of them made a deal. And it started with Heidegger's wife.

How do you know? said Nafissian.

Elie told me, said La Toya. Her name is Elfriede. Elfriede Heidegger.

The name sounded funny. They laughed.

Elie says she's quite the hausfrau, said La Toya. Blond braids around her head. A Party member in good standing.

How does Elie know? said Nafissian.

La Toya shrugged. The other three understood. Sometimes Elie alluded to her past, never mentioning names. Now and then dusk would remind her of dinner with her family. Or the smell of fresh ink and paper of being a student at

Freiburg. She never told anyone her real last name. Or that she had a younger sister she missed every day. But they all knew a small part of who Elie was before she came to the Compound and were relieved they'd never read Heidegger closely and would find it hard to answer the letter.

His wife bothered Goebbels so much, said La Toya, they had a meeting. So now Goebbels has another mission here: a letter to the living.

They'd come to the well and stopped to look at the woods and drink water from the tin dipper. Sophie waved at Lars Eisenscher who was keeping watch near the forest.

How awful that the woods are so frightening, she said. When I was a child the woods were amazing in winter.

They could get more frightening if Mikhail tries to answer that letter, said Nafissian. Heidegger's no fool—he'll see through something fake. Maybe we should have tried to answer it, after all.

We would have made a mess of it, said Sophie. And Mikhail's studied Heidegger, so his letter won't seem fake.

Gitka and Nafissian stopped to light more cigarettes; La Toya relit his cigar. The wind rose at their backs as they took turns carrying the bucket to the Compound. Nafissian said it created the impression they were traveling.

Don't be ridiculous, said La Toya, nobody travels here.

If the wind blows hard enough, they will, said Nafissian.

Let's make a run for it, said Gitka, laughing.

To where? said La Toya.

To the end of the world, said Gitka.

Liebstes Bendykta,

Ich hoffe, daß dieser Buchstabe an Sie in der Zeit gelangt. Kommst du bitte schnell.

In der Eile und in der Liebe,
Albin

* * *

Dearest Bendykta,

I don't have much time to write because I have to work. Please come quickly.

In haste and love,
Lucas

Dieter Stumpf never had any intention of getting Mikhail's niece himself because if he went to a safe house, he might be recognized and shot. Besides, it was more important to be sure as many dead as possible received answers to their letters. So he asked Elie Schacten to get the girl.

Her name is Maria, he said, handing her the address of the safe house, and a note to her from Mikhail. And Mikhail will write the letter if we get her. You know Mikhail. Always a bargain.

Of course I'll get her, Dieter, Elie said.

I knew you would. You rescue everyone.

I'm only doing this for you, said Elie.

Stumpf leaned close and basked in her tea-rose perfume.

Let's keep it between us for now, he said, touching Elie's arm. Lodenstein doesn't give a damn about this letter, and he hates bargains. He might try to stop you.

Elie, who had already decided that more than one bargain was at stake, agreed. Before she left, she told Lodenstein there was an influx of mail at the outpost. Then she held out her wrist so he could tie the red silk ribbon.

Do you think this place runs by itself? he said.

No, said Elie. What makes you think that?

Because sometimes you act like it does. I wonder if you know how many notes I send Goebbels to make him happy. *Dear Goebbels: We love your stories about winning the war. Keep them up. And your denials about the Final Solution are breathtaking.*

I'll bring you something special, said Elie. What do you want?

Just for you to come back, said Lodenstein.

He walked her to her jeep, and she drove off on the unpaved road. It was treacherously slick. But when she turned to the paved road she wasn't relieved because there were other cars, and no rescue was without danger. On her last foray, Elie had hidden three children under a marble statue covered with blankets. Everything had gone smoothly until an SS officer at the Swiss border began to uncover the statue. Elie said it was for Frisch—a banker she thought he'd know. He pressed her arm, she pressed back, and an erotic current passed between them. Go! he'd said. And go quickly!

She kept looking at the rearview mirror—an endless stretch of road and cars. She felt remorse about lying to Lodenstein and was haunted by a vision of him running to keep up with her.

Maria's safe house was in a town due south of the Compound and—to Elie's relief—she had to take a road that forked off the main highway. She drove by farms and a dense forest, where she saw a man and a child dart among the trees. She thought about the Angel of Auschwitz who had bargained a laboratory for a life. She wondered if a letter could do the same.

The town with the safe house was a patchwork of commerce and neglect, like other towns that hadn't been bombed beyond recognition at this stage of the war. It dipped into dilapidated structures then bloomed into islands of prosperity. One street had boarded-up buildings throbbing with misery. Another had prosperous shops. Yet another had a train station where people held suitcases. They were dressed in good

91

coats, but Elie knew in less than a week they'd be wearing striped uniforms. She parked the jeep in a crowded section and began to walk. A jeep with a swastika in front of a safe house would attract attention.

Light snow began to fall—swirls of white on grey. The streets widened, narrowed, widened again, expanding and contracting, as though they were breathing. Nothing felt quite real to Elie—not the sky, or the air, or a coffee house where customers drank from incongruously large cups of ersatz coffee. People hurried by, surrounded by pale grey air—the only thing that seemed to hold them together. Elie passed a muddy street with a chain-link fence followed by a row of prosperous houses. The town was breaking up, and she felt she was breaking up with it. She had never confirmed anything with Mikhail Solomon, and it occurred to her now that Stumpf could be setting up an ambush or had gotten the wrong directions. It began to snow thickly, surrounding everyone in white. We're only bound by veils, Elie thought, fragile accidents of cohesion.

No one was quite visible in this snow, and for a moment she imagined she saw her sister. She wore a dark red coat and kept her hands in a white muff. She smiled then disappeared.

Near the outskirts, streets were arranged in a circular pattern. Elie passed grey row houses, brick buildings, more row houses. The last were close to where Maria was hidden. But before she made the last turn a Gestapo stopped her, said he'd lost his watch and asked the time. Her heart began to race, and her answer—*Fourteen hours and twenty minutes*—sounded like a confession. He thanked her and asked if he could help find an address. Elie said no, she was just taking a walk. He asked for her papers—she was aware of his fleshy hands—and was confused when she showed him the red silk ribbon.

What are you doing at the outskirts? he asked.

I work with Goebbels, said Elie. And I'd be shot if I told you more.

The Gestapo shook his head. Goebbels would never shoot such a beautiful woman. Only the undesirables: Shot or guillotined. Take your pick.

He laughed when he said *Take your pick* and told Elie she reminded him of his wife. Then he took her arm and walked with her far away from the row houses, to a city park where the bare branches of linden trees were covered with ice and a statue of Hitler was in the center. They walked to the statue, then slowly around the park. Eventually, the officer looked at the watch he'd never lost and said:

My God. I'll be shot if I don't get back to my post.

Elie had to retrace the circular path near dusk. She knocked on the door of a red brick building four times—the way Stumpf told her. A wiry man in dark clothes stuck out his head.

What's the code? he said.

Falling, said Elie.

He nodded and led her to a musty hall that smelled of very old carpet and mashed potatoes. It opened to a dark underground passage, and he glided her through the black maze like a nocturnal animal. Then he opened a door to another building and handed Elie a flashlight.

Go out into a hall, he said. Knock on the first door to the left, wait three beats and knock three times. Leave by this passage and keep the flashlight. I've learned to see in the dark.

Elie surfaced to another musty hall. She knocked on the door to the left, waited three beats and knocked three times. After a pause that seemed interminable, a startlingly beautiful girl answered. She had blond hair, blue eyes—delicate Aryan features, Elie thought, that had probably saved her life. She looked at Elie with deep distrust. Elie reached out her arms.

Maria, she said. You're safe with me.

Maria continued to look at her and Elie, who realized she wanted proof of her intentions, showed her the papers she carried and a note from Mikhail. As soon as Maria saw these, she smiled and held out her arms. Elie pulled bread from her bag. Maria shook her head.

I've been waiting all day, she said. And in that crawl space for months. I just want to get outside.

Elie looked at her dress—made of thin cotton. And at her shoes. They were thin summer sandals.

No one gave you a sweater or boots? said Elie. Or even a coat? Did you walk like that through the streets?

Only in a car. I'll manage with a dress and stockings.

In the snow? The SS would arrest you in a minute.

There was a closet in the hall—so long Elie wondered if it led to the street. It was filled with china, silverware, records, photographs. Deep inside, Elie found a pair of sturdy shoes, a thick sweater, a scarf, and a black coat with a fur collar. She pulled out the coat. And behind it, shrinking against the wall of the closet, she saw a thin little boy of about seven. He had large, frightened eyes and sat so still he could have been made of stone.

What's your name? Elie whispered. He didn't answer. She took him in her arms and brought him to the room.

My God, said Maria. Where did he come from?

The empty apartment had French windows covered with sheer white cloth. They filled the room with airy light, creating a sense of high altitude, even at dusk. Elie sat on the floor, still holding the little boy. He began to tremble.

What's your name? she whispered again.

He was silent and tried to bury himself in the crook of her arm.

He's scared, said Maria.

Won't you tell us who you are? said Elie.

The little boy burrowed further into her arm.

How about we give you a name? said Elie. Do you like Alberto?

To her surprise, he shook his head no.

Do you like Sergei? said Maria.

He shook his head no to Sergei—and also to Luca and several other names. But when Elie said *Dimitri* he nodded.

Is that your real name? she said.

He shook his head no and dove back into the crook of Elie's arm.

Dimitri, she said. We're going to go out now. I'll wrap you in some blankets and carry you. And if anyone asks, we'll say you aren't feeling well.

She turned to Maria. Do you understand? she asked.

Maria, who seemed glamorous in the coat with the fur collar, nodded. Of course she understood.

The town was almost in blackout when they left the safe house. Elie carried Dmitri carefully while Maria reveled in the open air. More than once she looked at her reflection in a shop window.

Don't look at anything, said Elie. And don't stare at people holding suitcases!

When they came to the jeep, Elie put Dimitri in gently and covered them both with blankets. Dimitri was as still as Maria had been under the floorboards. But Maria looked from beneath the blanket so often, Elie told her that she could come out if she crouched under the window. It got darker, the road narrowed, the pines grew thick, and Elie's fear of the dark began to grip her. She tried to quell it by telling stories she and her sister once told under a dark red comforter at night. They were about wolves who granted wishes or snow maidens who could talk. She started to feel safe until Maria said:

Do you really believe all that?

I used to, said Elie.

I never did.

Maybe you should start to, said Elie.

When they hit the unpaved road and the car began to jolt, Elie realized she didn't know where Dimitri would sleep. Or what she'd say to Lodenstein when he discovered them.

Kedves Max,

Ön talán meglepett amit En alapít kivezet út-hoz kap ez-hoz ön, de csodálatos mi egy tud csinál itt-val jobb védekezik. Legyen szíves jön-hoz él-ból kaszárnyák azért mi tud beszélgetés.

Nikotin

* * *

Dear Max,

You're probably surprised that I found a way to get this to you, but it's amazing what you can do here with the right guards. Please come to the edge of the barracks so that we can talk.

Nicolai

97

If only the landscape were rearranged, Elie thought. A wide road, telephone lines, lit houses. I could knock on any door, and people I never met would let the girl stay with them. Beyond the houses she'd find the streets of her childhood where she and her sister jumped rope and teased boys. And beyond those streets she'd find the convent where they made other girls laugh by imitating Sister Ignatius who had a nervous cough and Sister Hildegard who licked chalk from her fingers. *You're headstrong*, her father always said when they got their knuckles rapped. *You never try to imagine how things will turn out.*

That's not true, Elie thought. We were only bored. She saw her sister's face. It was attentive, alert. It held her with her eyes.

What are you thinking? asked Maria.

How beautiful the woods are, said Elie.

They are, said Maria. Even though anyone could come out of those trees and shoot us.

But they won't, said Elie.

The car skidded on ice and curved into the clearing, miraculously empty of people. The shepherd's hut was the only shape in the snow—a dark mound, silhouetted by moonlight. Elie carried Dimitri down the stone path to the hut and Maria followed. The door to the incline didn't startle her—it was clear she understood camouflage. Nor did she seem confused when Elie rushed her past the room she shared with Lodenstein. But Maria was astonished by the cobblestone street and frozen sky.

Is this a real town? she said.

I'll explain later, said Elie

Do other kids live here? she asked.

I'll explain that, too.

Maria looked at the main room curiously and smiled when Parvis Nafissian came out. Elie pushed her on to the small white house where Lars was by the pear tree. *Don't say anything*, she mouthed to him.

As soon as she saw Maria, Talia gathered her in her arms and told her how big she'd grown. She touched the snow on Maria's coat and said she'd brought real weather. Maria laughed and said real weather had come to her. She hugged Mikhail, looked around the room, and noticed a mirror.

I haven't seen myself in five months, she said.

At first Talia didn't notice the boy in Elie's arms. But when she did—in a pause that was less than a heartbeat—she hugged him, too.

This is Dimitri, she said.

Where did you come from? said Talia.

Do you want to tell? asked Elie.

Dimitri shook his head.

From a closet in that safe house, Elie said. No one came for him.

She sat on the couch and unwrapped the blanket. Dimitri tried to crawl behind her, like a mouse squeezing into a hole.

He needs to eat, said Talia.

Both of them do, said Elie.

Maria spun around, walked to the window, and looked at the frozen sky with its moon and stars. This is an enchanted place, she said.

99

Soon the atmosphere was imbued with calm—as though the children had always lived there. Talia brought potato soup from the main kitchen. Mikhail told Dmitri a fairy tale. Maria stood in front of the mirror and twisted her hair into a French knot. She wanted to know when she could see snow again and was disappointed when Mikhail said: Tomorrow.

The calm reminded Elie of her own family in the evening—knitting, reading, doing homework. While she basked in this sense of calm she thought of different things to tell Lodenstein: She'd found the children in the woods. Or in the jeep when she came back from her foray. Or a woman at a market begged her to take them. Each story seemed better than the last one.

Suddenly she heard a knock on the window and saw Stumpf's huge face at the glass. She put Dimitri on Mikhail's lap and raced outside.

What's that boy doing here! he shouted. Why didn't you take just one?

And leave the other to rot?

But we bargained for one, said Stumpf.

We bargained? I thought we were saving lives, said Elie.

I meant arranged for just one child, said Stumpf.

What do you mean *arranged?* Like the mail in your office?

Stumpf took a gulp from a bottle of schnapps and waved his hands toward the main room. This place is a rabbit warren, he said. We don't have a place to put another one.

That little boy had been in the safe house for at least a day by himself, said Elie.

All the more reason to leave him there, said Stumpf. He walked back and forth and appeared to be thinking. Finally he said:

I won't have anything to do with him. He's yours.

I wouldn't have it any other way, said Elie.

There was a thump behind him: Lodenstein dropping a chessboard.

So this is what you brought from the outpost, he shouted at Elie.

I told her not to meddle, said Stumpf.

Shut your fucking mouth, said Lodenstein.

He kicked a bench. Talia tugged at Maria, who was watching from the window.

I knew it was a bad idea, said Stumpf.

Shut up, said Lodenstein. The two of you did this behind my back.

We didn't, said Elie.

Lodenstein picked up an artificial rose bush and smashed the pot into shards.

If you didn't, he said, then how is bringing two fugitives the same as bringing mail?

Elie kicked one of the shards.

I won't talk about it now, she said. You're acting like an animal.

She went back to the Solomons, banging the door with such force it rattled the artificial pear tree.

I did it for Elie, said Stumpf when Elie left. And the deal was for just one child.

What do you mean deal? said Lodenstein.

I mean it was for Elie, said Stumpf. She's good-hearted, but she doesn't think. Here—have some schnapps.

I don't want schnapps. I want to know what's going on.

Elie went to that town and got them. I'll make her bring them back.

You're a liar and a moron.

Don't shout! said Stumpf. It's our private business.

Business, my ass. Lodenstein picked up the chessboard and held it over Stumpf's head.

I could crack your skull with this, he said, and no one would know. That's how stupid you are.

The tick above Stumpf's eye began to skitter.

Please! he said. The walls can hear!

And indeed all the Scribes were listening. Nothing was better than a good fight. Maybe Lodenstein would murder Stumpf, and they could bury him in the woods.

I told you there would be a mess, said Ferdinand La Toya.

Maybe it's not a mess, said Parvis Nafissian.

Believe me, it's a mess, said La Toya. We should have tried to write a letter after all.

Soon banging pots could be heard throughout the Compound—Stumpf, eating more than his share of sausage to quell his anxiety. Elie buried her face in the Solomons' couch.

What is this place? said the girl.

Someone's invention, said Mikhail.

But do people really live here? said Maria.

In a manner of speaking, said Mikhail.

Where do they sleep?

Mostly in a big room, said Talia. But you'll sleep here.

Can I see that room? Maria asked.

Tomorrow, said Mikhail.

I wish I could see it now.

Talia and Mikhail looked at each other with disappointment. Maria, who'd been nine when they last saw her, now reminded them of Aaron before they went to Lodz – fascinated by the world, whatever that world was – and not very interested in them.

Elie turned to Dimitri. Do you want to see the room, too?

No, he said. It was the first word he'd spoken.

Elie, who was pleased that he'd said something, kissed him and said: Why not?

Because this is so soft, said Dimitri, patting the couch.

Talia and Mikhail looked uncomfortable. Then Talia said: He's so little. You two can sleep on the couch for tonight.

I don't mind sleeping in that big room, said Maria.

And there's always room for another Scribe in there, said Elie.

Mikhail laughed. Always room for another Scribe? he said. You're talking like the Reich.

But I'm not thinking like the Reich, said Elie. She hugged Dimitri and told Talia and Mikhail to bring him to her if he got scared.

Don't lose sight of Maria, Talia mouthed.

I won't, she mouthed back.

While they walked down the cobblestone street, Elie pointed to the frozen canopy and told Maria not to worry about the groans of pulleys and gears—it was just the sky changing from night to day and back again. Maria said the only sounds that worried her were gunshots.

103

No one new had arrived for almost a year, and Maria got a standing ovation from Parvis Nafissian, Niles Schopenhauer, and a man named Knut Grossheimer, who never talked to anyone. When the clapping stopped, Elie took Maria back to the street and asked if she knew about French letters—common slang for condoms. Maria said she'd gotten some from a soldier who snatched her from a line to the gas chambers; but she only needed to open one.

So that's how she saved herself, Elie thought. She brought Maria to her desk, showed her where to find them in the top drawer, and told her to open every single one she needed. Maria nodded and looked at the wall.

What's all that stuff? she asked.

A jumble-shop, said Elie. She pulled out a blue coat and held it to Maria's face.

Look, she said to her. This coat is the color of water. It would look lovely on you.

But Maria –as if suddenly transported to when she saw her parents led to the gas chambers –said she didn't want anything lovely. She suddenly looked very young and as though she was going to cry. Parvis Nafissian came up silently, swept the coat from Elie, and put it around Maria's shoulders.

You're more than lovely, he said to her.

Parvis, said Elie. She's been through enough.

I agree, said La Toya.

What business is it of yours? said Gitka.

He's robbing the cradle, said La Toya.

That cradle would be in a death camp if it hadn't been robbed before, Gitka said.

She opened her fur coat and showed La Toya a black lace camisole—delicate, filigreed. La Toya turned away and Elie remembered—not without hurt feelings—that she'd gotten

Gitka's camisole from the best corset-maker in Berlin—a favor for smuggling her son to Switzerland. She pushed aside the telescope and pulled thick fur coats to make beds for her and Maria.

Where do all these coats come from? said Maria.

Elie hesitated. Then she said:

From people who weren't so lucky.

The Scribes were getting ready for the night. A few who hadn't won the lottery for Elie's old room began to push desks together so they could make love in cramped tunnels. There were sounds of scraping, bumping, paper cascading, and shouts of *Damn! But better than a bed at Auschwitz.*

Elie eased into layer of coats and sat by the opulent junk-shop against the wall, with her arms around Maria. One lamp after another went out until finally the room was dark.

;השעת אל תווצמ עבראו, השע תווצמ שש—תווצמ רשע ןללכב שי
םש שיש הבשחמב הלעי אלש (ב) ;הולא םש שיש עדיל (א) :ןטרפ אוה הזו
(ז) ;ומש שדקל (ו) ;וננממ האריל (ה) ;ובהואל (ד) ;ודחייל (ג) ;'ה יתלוז הולא
עומשל (ט) ;והילע ומש ארקנש םירבד דבאל אלש (ח) ;ומש תא ללחל אלש
.ותוסנל אלש (י) ;ומשב רבדמה איבנה ןמ

תווצמה לכ רואיבו
.ולא םיקרפב ולאה

* * *

Dearest Joseph,

I want you to know that I'm okay. The food is decent—
better, they say, than at home. And there's a woods where they keep
angora rabbits. Most of all, though, I miss our walks, our dinners—
and seeing your face in the morning. I think of you all the time. I can't
imagine life without you.

All my love,
Ernestine

106

Late that night, Elie left the Scribes asleep on desks and in tunnels, and knocked on the Solomons' door. Dmitri was sleeping on the velveteen couch, half-covered with a white afghan. Talia was asleep in the alcove. And the eternal crescent moon was shining outside a window. Elie adjusted the afghan so it covered the small boy and once more felt a sense of peace. Then she saw a chess game on the piecrust table.

Was Gerhardt here? she asked Mikhail.

Good for five moves before he got furious, said Mikhail. He said he would have gotten Maria if I'd asked him. Is she asleep?

I wouldn't have come here if she weren't, said Elie. In fact, she got a standing ovation. You should be glad she's beautiful. It saved her life.

I know, said Mikhail.

Gerhardt's right, she said. He would have gotten her if you asked.

I know that too, said Mikhail.

But you made a deal with Stumpf instead, said Elie.

What makes you so sure? said Mikhail.

Because Stumpf asked me to get Maria. And he told me everything.

Mikhail adjusted a lantern and leafed through a German dictionary.

Is that all you're going to say? said Elie.

I had to save my niece, said Mikhail. So I put teeth into my bargain.

More like fangs, said Elie, when you mess with a fool like Stumpf.

They looked at each other evenly, not without resentment: Elie, forced to travel, unable to stop saving people; Mikhail, in seclusion, hardy able to save his niece. Elie walked over to the window and lit a cigarette. Then she said:

I was happy to save Maria. But now I want a favor.

In return for saving a *child?* What's come over you?

Elie went on as though Mikhail hadn't spoken. I want you to write the kind of letter Asher Englehardt would never write, said Elie, as though Mikhail hadn't spoken. A letter to Martin Heidegger that doesn't make sense.

Those weren't the orders.

You've never been Goebbels's puppet, she said. So don't be Englehardt's ventriloquist.

This is a letter, not a circus act.

A circus act is exactly what the Reich wants, said Elie.

I won't insult Heidegger's intelligence, said Mikhail. Or mine either, for that matter. Do you know what he wrote? *You see a crooked picture and fall right out of the world.* That's a remarkable mind, even if he is a Nazi.

I know all about those crooked pictures, said Elie. But I brought you Maria. And if you write something Asher Englehardt would never write, Heidegger will see through it and make a fuss about finding him.

Since when have you lived in Heidegger's brain?

Elie hesitated. Then she said: You mustn't tell. But I knew him at Freiburg. And everyone knew that he and Asher Englehardt were good friends. Asher had a son. He must be seventeen by now.

So, still a kid, said Mikhail.

Close to Maria's age, said Elie.

She reached into her pocket and showed Mikhail the photographs of Asher Englehardt's shop and Heidegger and Englehardt in the Black Forest. The mountains and open air looked incongruous in the cramped, dark room.

Don't ever tell, she said again.

Mikhail's eyes grew soft. Of course, I won't, he said. But everyone knows a famous crackpot in the Party. I could name a hundred, and they didn't help anybody. Heidegger's not any different. And the Party doesn't exactly love him anymore.

He still gets his way, said Elie.

Maybe, said Mikhail. But this letter you want me to write could blow up everything.

The letter you promised Stumpf you'd write could blow up everything too.

Elie held a glass paperweight by a lantern and watched light scatter on the walls. Then she told Mikhail about the Angel of Auschwitz. The story filled the room with a nearly totemic presence—but only for a moment.

There were rumors like that in Lodz all the time, said Mikhail. They came to nothing.

But I brought you Maria, said Elie. She's sleeping in the main room right now.

You could save Maria because they hadn't found her yet, said Mikhail. But getting someone from Auschwitz is a dream.

Maria wouldn't be here if it weren't for me. And now we could use these orders to save two lives.

She walked to the bookcase and picked up a photograph. It was a picture of Mikhail's son Aaron.

Everyone is worth saving, she said.

Not if they're already dead, said Mikhail.

There was a knock on the door—it was Lars, ready to take Mikhail out to see the sky.

You cannot rescue the world, said Mikhail getting up.

Elie walked alone under the frozen stars and looked in on Maria, who seemed younger and smaller beneath the pile of coats. Then she took the mineshaft to her room with Lodenstein. He was drinking vodka and manhandling his game of solitaire by throwing cards on the floor. Elie stood at the door watching him. After a moment she said:

So you're not talking to me.

Why should I? said Lodenstein. You went behind my back with Stumpf and brought two fugitives. You put us all in danger.

I'm sorry, said Elie in a low voice. I didn't have time.

But time for me to tie your ribbon. I was good for that.

Gerhardt, please. I rescued two children. That's what matters.

Then why was Stumpf part of it? He doesn't care about rescuing anyone. Why didn't you ask me? Why did you leave me out of it?

Elie sat on the bed and put her hand on his arm.

Because it happened too quickly, she said.

Lodenstein tore one of the cards.

You never answer, he said. I never know who you are. Maybe there *are* two Elies.

It's Mikhail's niece, Gerhardt. He was frantic. And the little boy was all alone in the safe house.

You still lied to me, Elie. And if I'd called the outpost because I thought you were there, it would have been a disaster.

He got up and emptied a bureau drawer. Ties and camisoles and socks scattered around the room. When the drawer was empty, he yanked it from the bureau and threw it against a wall.

How could you connive with that asshole? How could you even think of it?

It wasn't like that.

What was it like then?

Mikhail was frantic.

You've already said that.

Lodenstein threw the mattress on the floor. The grey quilt crumpled next to it. He opened a weather-beaten trunk, took out a wool carder, and broke it over a chair.

Don't! said Elie. That's for our house after the war.

What house? We'll all be shot for hiding fugitives.

No one's going to find out.

And suppose they do?

We can hide the children. And they weren't your orders.

Whose then? Stumpf's? He can't give orders. Did you blackmail him so you could do another rescue?

Are you crazy?

Then why didn't you tell me?

I can't explain.

You never can.

Elie began to drag the mattress to the bed and stopped.

I'm sleeping downstairs, she said.

You don't have a bed there.

We don't have one here either. I'll sleep on coats.

Take mine. It's warm.

I don't need your fucking coat. I don't need your anything.

Pieter,

Tu per esempio sei bene , solo nessuno vero indirizzo poich, tu - giusto un ufficio in Berlino. Pregare mi dica dove sei,

Amore tu ed io perdere tu,
Eleanora

* * *

Pieter,

You say you are fine, but there's no real address for you—just an office in Berlin. Please tell me where you are.

I love you and miss you,
Eleanora

Mikhail might have never written the letter Elie wanted him to write if more nightwalkers hadn't shown up a week later. This was the name for fugitives who walked under cover of darkness at night and slept in safe houses during the day. They abandoned everything they had except jewels that they could sew into their clothes, and walked on unmarked paths to ports where a ship might take them to Denmark. A town near the Compound was by the sea. Now and then Elie arranged for nightwalkers to sleep in the old officers' quarters.

It was five-thirty in the morning when a dozen bedraggled people emerged from the mineshaft. Mikhail, who was in the kitchen making tea, watched them stare at the sunrise—a maneuver Hans Ewigkeit never got right, so the yellow sphere groaned and wobbled on a pulley, and its silver rope was illuminated until floodlights wiped out the stars. The nightwalkers huddled near the mineshaft.

You can sit on those, Mikhail said, pointing to the benches.

In this inferno? said a woman wearing two hats and three scarves. We could melt.

Mikhail sat on a bench, and when they saw it didn't melt, the nightwalkers sat down, too, and began to unpeel layers of clothes. They wore coats under other coats, three or four sweaters, extra trousers, skirts, blouses, socks. A few people checked waistbands where they'd sewn jewels.

Because there was a warning about the SS on their trail, the nightwalkers stayed an extra day while Elie found a guide with an SS uniform. They played chess, learned words from *Dreamatoria*, and drank schnapps Stumpf forgot to hide. On their last night, there was a modest feast: Elie lit candles. La Toya cooked spicy potato soup. Lodenstein made a toast.

After dinner, people stayed in the main room talking. At first they talked about the war—how hard it was to find forgers and how astounding that people still believed gassings were a rumor. Eventually they began to talk about friends who disappeared without warning and children who never came home from school. One man talked about seeing his daughter beaten to death on a city street.

You mustn't think about these things, said Sophie Nachtgarten.

Who are you to talk? said the woman who'd called the Compound an inferno. You lead a charmed life down here.

Not that charmed, said Sophie.

Charmed enough, said the woman. My uncle was seventy years old, and the SS threw him right against the glass of his shop—he looked like a bird falling against a window. Then they shot him.

When the guide with the SS uniform arrived, the nightwalkers left, and the Scribes scrambled to sleep. But Elie and Mikhail stayed on, watching the candles. When they started to sputter, Mikhail put his hand on Elie's arm.

I'll write the letter you want, he said. For Asher Englehardt's son. And I'll write it for Aaron. I'll write the letter for Aaron, too.

Matka i Ojciec,

Ja potrzebował (chciał; potrzebny) pisa list (litera) przez jaki czas ale one pozwalaj mnie urzeczywistniaj (praktykowa) mój podpis. Wy mieli cie przybywa , te , i zatrzymywa (pozostawa ; pobyt; przystanek) z mn . przepuszczam (by nieobecnym) was i Lucia wiele (wielka ilo ; du o).

Miło ,
Leokadia

* * *

Dear Mother and Father,

Did you see me leave with all the other children? I hope you did. Have you seen Lucia? I can't feel you anywhere.

Love,
Leokadia

115

When Mikhail told Talia he was going to write the letter Elie wanted him to write and she ought to practice Asher's signature, Talia was annoyed. She was an expert forger and had made identity cards early in the war, but resented being part of a hare-brained scheme.

What makes you think a letter would get anybody out? said Talia. Or even that they're alive?

I have to write it anyway. Stumpf keeps bothering me about it, and if I don't, he could turn Maria over to the SS.

You can't get people out of Auschwitz, said Talia. Look what happened to Aaron in a town square. And it was hard enough to get Maria.

Lodz was a ghetto, said Mikhail. And maybe the story about the Angel of Auschwitz is true. Anyway, I have to write something. And Elie will bring the letter.

Elie's no Angel of Auschwitz.

She got Maria, said Mikhail. And she has a way with people.

Don't I know it, said Talia.

She fussed with her hair, which theoretically should have been an Orthodox wig but never had been and certainly wouldn't be now. She unleashed the clasp and let her hair fall on her shoulders in long red curls.

So you'll do what she wants, she said.

Suppose a letter had saved Aaron?

But it didn't, said Talia. And no piece of paper can stop a bullet.

While Talia studied Asher's signature from the prescription for Heidegger's glasses, Mikhail began to think about Heidegger's happiness—or, more exactly, about what would annoy him. These thoughts began to consume every minute of his day. When he went to look at the stars, he hardly talked to Lars at all. And when he came downstairs, he reread Heidegger's letter to Asher, and used a German dictionary to unravel the etymology that Sophie Nachtgarten said was nonsense.

Stumpf had given him the dictionary. He'd said it had more words than any other dictionary in the world, and Mikhail became so obsessed with every word of Heidegger's letter, he'd begun to believe him: Heidegger played with the word *entfernen*—to distance—as in *I distanced myself from the controversy*. From *entfernen* he had invented *ent-fernen*, which Mikhail took to mean *to get rid of distance*. It amused him that Heidegger played with words. It reminded him of arguments in the Talmud.

Tonight Mikhail looked at the paralyzed horizon outside his window and saw Aries and Chiron and the North Star in a sky that wasn't real. It gave him the same sense he'd had when he'd once seen a potato cart overturn in Krakow, transforming the street into a vegetable bin. There had been a moment when he couldn't remember what streets were for—a moment without signposts or moorings. It must have been how Heidegger felt when he hadn't recognized his glasses.

Mikhail lit a cigarette and waved smoke from the couch where Dimitri was sleeping. How many people had given thought to this matter the way Heidegger had? And did

117

Heidegger have any idea about the gas chambers when he ranted about people not understanding the Being of machines and technology?

He stayed at the window for a long time, trying to imagine the kind of letter Asher Englehardt would write and the kind of letter Asher Englehardt would never write. The first would be thoughtful and intelligent. The second would be nonsense.

He wanted to write the first—if only to reach another mind across his unbearable sense of isolation. But he knew he had to write the second because it could save Asher's son, who—if he were alive—must be terrified. He remembered Aaron's eyes right before he'd been shot and replaced it with a memory of Aaron at nine after he'd thrown dirt at Mrs. Mercier's porch. He was trembling when he got home, and Mikhail told him: *Don't be scared. Mrs. Mercier likes to yell.*

In addition to the dictionary, Stumpf had given him a typewriter—an Adler. Mikhail began to type, avoiding etymology because he didn't want to make nonsense out of *entfernen.*

While he wrote, Mikhail heard incessant rustling in the main room. It seemed to be talking to itself, as if resuming an interminable conversation it couldn't have during the day. Maybe it was complaining about the smell of ink and earth. Or maybe it was troubled about the Compound's mission. He also heard mumbling that sounded like a séance. Stumpf had told him he was going to invoke a button dealer from the 19th century: *One of the respectable dead,* as he'd put it.

Mikhail debated when he came to the part of Heidegger's letter that talked about the Being of machines. In Krakow he'd had an old Renault that was always breaking down. The car ran his life instead of him running it.

But he couldn't mention a car because he didn't know if Asher Englehardt ever owned one. And the only other thing he could think of was the gas chambers. So he didn't write about machines. Instead he indulged himself by writing something about etymology. Then he invented an imaginary text from the Talmud—but crossed out most of it because even though he didn't have faith in anything anymore, he thought he should leave the Talmud out of it.

When he was finished, he read the letter over and saw that it was appropriately ludicrous. *The hidden letter,* he wrote in his coded notebook. *The words we only dream.*

What a piece of nonsense, Talia said when she read the letter.

It could save a child, said Mikhail.

I'm tired of saving other people's children, said Talia.

She pulled the letter away and duplicated Asher's signature. She didn't include his last name, because Heidegger had only signed *Martin.*

While Talia wrote, Mikhail was aware of Dmitri's quiet breathing on the couch, the rustling in the main room, and mumbling from the séance. There was a sudden blast of artillery and a chorus of *shut ups* and *use your fucking pen for God's sake.* It was La Toya, who meant to publish his memoirs after the war.

Then there was silence and no more mumbling. Undoubtedly Sonia's delectable bum had distracted Stumpf, and it crossed his mind that he wouldn't show him the letter at all but bring it straight to Elie. On the other hand, Stumpf had been hovering constantly. And he'd helped save Maria, even if Elie had done all the legwork.

What nonsense, Talia said again when she was finished.

Mikhail said he meant it to be nonsense and took the letter up to the shoebox. He heard the click of seven latches and entered a room rife with incense. Stumpf was so pleased by the letter's utter incomprehensibility he abandoned Sonia and walked with Mikhail to the cobblestone street. Lars, who was going to take Mikhail to see the stars, raced over to them.

It's okay, Mikhail said. I'll go with Stumpf tonight.

Mikhail and Stumpf walked across the clearing, ice cracking under their shoes. Stumpf lumbered up to the watchtower and Mikhail followed. The stars were uncannily bright.

What do you see? said Stump.

A world to fall out of, said Mikhail.

What do you mean? said Stumpf. The world is here. He gestured beyond the platform. The woods are all around you. Germany—the fatherland.

He kept pointing towards the woods as though he owned them. Then he said:

It's a wonderful letter. I think I'll deliver it myself.

Not yet, said Mikhail, taking it back. Talia has to sign Asher's last name. Otherwise Heidegger won't believe it.

But they were friends, said Stumpf.

Mikhail ignored him and walked back to the shepherd's hut, hurrying down the incline, with Stumpf heaving after him. After they'd walked down the street and were navigating the pear tree, Stumpf lifted the dictionary off the bench.

You made good use of this, he said.

Mikhail nodded and opened the door. Within moments he felt the dictionary crash on his head and the letter pried from his hands. By the time Stumpf ran to the main room and grabbed the box of glasses off Elie's desk, Mikhail had lost consciousness. He didn't hear Dimitri scream. He didn't know that Lodenstein ran after Stumpf to try to stop him from driving off down the long narrow road.

The Black Forest

Dear Martin,

I have read your letter with great interest and have been giving some thought to the word Ent-fernen. You are obviously still preoccupied with the element of distancing from objects in order to see them, and, of course, I shared your preoccupation. When we don't see things as there for our use, we see them differently, perhaps as someone from another culture would see them. And for this purpose there is nothing more interesting than the word Ent-fernen.

Yet I fear you are playing with leaves on trees when you should be looking at the forest. (And you, of all people, should know about forests!). The mystery of Being found in falling through the paths is of utmost importance in these times. And paths can become abstract unless they are real paths, and you are walking through them. I must tell you that recently I have come upon an ancient text (in the Zohar of all places!) that talks about the Mystery of the Triangle and for some reason it's caught my attention. The text reads as follows:

The triangle is the most paradoxical of human situations. It is the secret of all covenants and a cause of betrayal. Indeed, it's a great challenge to the human heart because it has the power to create incredible good and cause incredible grief, as well as induce states of ecstasy and lunacy. Making a triangle with integrity is in the service of God.

Even though it's an archaic text, I think it speaks to the need for a clear understanding between people, especially during troubled times. If there are two things, there has to be a third thing to be sure they balance. This third thing is to keep the first two things in place but it should never interfere with the spirit of their interaction.

As for poetry, it can evoke. And I think that poetry often brings people to the heart of experience. But references to etymology, as wonderful as roots are, often escape people.

And you want them to understand so they can arrive at a perilous edge from which they dare to leap into new understanding. This is what happened with your glasses, didn't it? (Your new pair is enclosed, by the way.) You experience them—as much as anyone is capable—as things in themselves and we must do this with everything, particularly with each other.

Your faithful friend,
Asher

Stumpf drove recklessly, screeching over the ice, and skidded into a snow bank several kilometers after leaving the Compound. Three large tanks of petrol crashed around in the back of the jeep. He didn't have a shovel, was terrified Lodenstein would follow him, and lugged stones under the back tires. Then he spun them mercilessly until the car heaved free. *An auspicious sign,* he thought. *Goebbels must want me to deliver everything tonight.*

But when he reached the main road he felt panic and dismay. In his hurry to leave, in his exuberance about snatching the letter and finding the glasses, he'd forgotten that the Black Forest was six hours away. He'd imagined it an hour away—a peaceful drive in the moonlight. But it was more than six hours away on a dark, empty road where snow was beginning to fall.

He reminded himself that Germany was a vast country, about to become even more so, and he should feel privileged to be able to drive such a long distance. But the sheer emptiness of the road unnerved him. And he kept thinking of Mikhail lying face down on the floor after he'd hit him with the dictionary. He saw Mikhail's head, half-covered by his skullcap; his arms stretched slack on the Oriental rug. He was sure he hadn't killed Mikhail. He was sure he hadn't even hurt him. Nonetheless he distracted himself by imagining the best way to deliver the letter and the glasses.

Should he say *Heil Hitler!* before or after he knocked at Heidegger's hut? And suppose Heidegger invited him in? Should he say he had to leave or share a glass of schnapps? He'd forgotten the orders were to deliver everything without a trace of where they came from and kept recycling the same alternatives: To come in or leave. To announce other missions or be mysterious.

Goebbels would probably want him to drink with Heidegger. He spent at least an hour a day in the marketplace talking about Germany's victory and approved of mingling with the people. On the other hand, Stumpf had forgotten his SS jacket, and it was sheer luck he'd been wearing boots instead of his wooly bedroom slippers when he hit Mikhail on the head and ran out of the Compound. It would be best to say *Heil Hitler!* and leave. And not to imply that he had other missions.

Towards dawn, light began to leak from the sky, and pines hulked on the side of the road. The cold, grey morning came too close, and Stumpf pulled over to get his bearings, careful to avoid snow banks. He leaned back, began to nap and startled awake when he heard crackling in his pocket. It was Mikhail's letter—too creased to deliver without disgracing the Reich. Thank God he'd been holding the German dictionary when he left; it would smooth out the creases in the letter. But when he saw the cover splattered with blood, he had visions of Goebbels's rage in case he really had killed Mikhail, who was, after all, an *Echte Jude*—so important to the cause.

Stumpf put the letter in the dictionary without looking at the blood and pulled back to the main road. When the sun rose higher and more cars appeared, there was much waving and honking because of the swastika on the Kubelwagen. This waving and honking raised Stumpf's spirits, and he was sure Goebbels would commend him. *Very good,* he heard him say. *Very good work indeed.*

Yet, his spirits sank two hours later when he reached the Black Forest and found no directions to Heidegger's hut. He'd expected a sign that said *Todtnauberg* as soon as he turned off the main road. Yet the more he drove, the taller the pines and dimmer the light, until he was in a canopy of darkness. Stumpf remembered a story about a road that led to a place where it was always night. There had been two peasants who'd walked down that road and were never seen again. He turned around—a treacherous maneuver. But the open road disappointed him too. He'd been expecting quaint huts surrounded by small trees. Instead there were large huts far apart, on knolls bereft of trees. The people who lived in them were unimpressed by his hat when he knocked and gave him vague, stingy directions to Todtnauberg. He drove higher into fields of snow until he found a monstrous Alpine hut with two attics, dark wood trim, and deep overhanging roofs. This was where Heidegger lived.

Well done, he heard Goebbels say again, as he drove closer. But his voice was barely audible. Stumpf blew his nose and opened the dictionary. Yet two hours between all those words hadn't smoothed out the creases in Mikhail's letter. They were as deep as lines of an ancient palm. And since no respectable member of the Reich would ever deliver a letter in such miserable condition, Stumpf decided to leave everything outside the hut and drive away as quickly as he could. He rummaged through the box of glasses, certain Elie had shown him a pair marked *für Martin Heidegger.* But he couldn't find them and settled on a pair that looked familiar and didn't have a white tag like the others. Then he tiptoed to the house, his feet making little imprints in the snow. There were three slippery

129

steps before the hut's dark door, and Stumpf decided not to risk them. Instead he left the glasses and letter on a stone and turned away. But then a voice called out:

What are you doing outside my hut?

Stumpf turned around and saw a short stolid man in black boots and thick black overalls. Without a doubt this was Martin Heidegger. Heidegger had a walking stick and waved it in front of Stumpf's face.

Explain yourself, he said.

I'm making a delivery, said Stumpf.

What delivery? said Heidegger.

An important one.

Why did you sneak away if it's so important? said Heidegger.

Because I have other deliveries, said Stumpf.

That's not a good reason to leave, said Heidegger. He pointed towards the hut as though Stumpf were a dog. It was dark inside—a cavernous hole that could swallow him up. Stumpf backed away and picked up the glasses and the letter.

Stop standing like a moron in that snow, said Heidegger. He grabbed Stumpf's arm and yanked him to a cramped, cold room filled with coats, gloves, umbrellas, boots, and scarves.

Put everything there, he said, pointing to a three-legged milking stool that belonged in a barn.

I can't, said Stumpf. It's too important.

Then we'll go to the kitchen, said Heidegger, steering Stumpf towards a room with low beams and a bed behind the stove. There was a table by a window that let in pale, peaked light. The table had a loaf of bread, a few forks, and Aristotle's *Metaphysics*. Heidegger picked it up and waved it at Stumpf.

Nothing like the Greeks, he said. I'm going back to the source.

Don't let me interrupt, said Stumpf.

You already have, said Heidegger. And once before, too, at a conference about the nature of Being.

I never went to anything like that, said Stumpf.

Then your people did, said Heidegger.

I'm not with any people, said Stumpf.

What's that then? said Heidegger, pointing to the insignia on Stumpf's hat.

Something delivery people wear, said Stumpf, who realized he shouldn't have worn the hat in the first place.

Since when does the SS have its own postal system?

Stumpf was about to say it always had. Then he realized he should say it never did. Then he heard Goebbels tell him not to say anything. He put the letter and glasses on the table and turned to leave. But Heidegger clapped a hand on his shoulder.

You have to come for a walk with me, he said. I want to know what you people are up to.

Stumpf said again he had to leave on another mission. But Heidegger laughed.

Don't think you can leave without explaining yourself, he said. Don't think you'll get away with it.

He steered Stumpf back to the cold room and rummaged for a jacket, a green pointed hat with a feather, and boots. They were all for Heidegger—not Stumpf, who now realized Heidegger's overalls were actually a ski suit. *Who except someone dangerous and strange would wear a ski suit indoors?* he thought. *No one safe enough to walk with.*

They left the hut and Heidegger led the way up a snowy hill.

Now tell me about your mistake, he said.

What mistake? said Stumpf.

You know what mistake. The fucking interruption.

I don't know about an interruption.

Of course you do, said Heidegger. You're one of the herd, and every single animal in the herd knows what the rest of the animals are doing.

They'd come to a slight rise. Stumpf held a pine branch to keep from falling.

I don't know what you mean, he said.

The Gestapo interrupted me, said Heidegger. They led me to the hall. They made a fuss. At an important international meeting.

I don't know about international meetings.

Then why is the Gestapo watching me? said Heidegger.

Stumpf, who had forgotten the Gestapo was watching Heidegger, was now sure they were hiding under mounds of snow, ready to leap out at him. He decided not to affirm or deny anything.

The fucking herd, Heidegger continued. Of course you don't understand because you're one of them. A bunch of noses following more noses. You've forgotten your roots. All you can do is graze.

Stumpf had no idea what Heidegger was talking about and panted to keep up with him. They came to a cluster of pines that gave him a momentary sense of shelter, but after a few steps the pines grew thick and the air almost black. They came to another clearing—much too bright. And now they came to more woods, where Heidegger shook pine branches, drenching Stumpf in snow. He rambled on about the meeting and Stumpf kept saying that the only meetings he knew about were meetings of the Party.

Every time they came to a clearing, Heidegger said it was like finding one's way in philosophy. Every time they came to a cluster of pines, he said it was like losing one's way. Then he said:

We always walk on paths that lead us back to getting lost.

Stumpf wondered vaguely if this was a paradox and grunted. Twice, the feather on Heidegger's hat caught on a branch, and Stumpf had to untangle it. He wondered what Heidegger did about the feather when he walked alone.

Eventually Stumpf couldn't go on. He'd wanted to rest when they came to a clearing, but his breath gave out in the darkest part of the forest. He looked around for wolves that might be hiding in pine trees. Heidegger hit him on the knee with his walking stick.

You haven't told me about that meeting, he said.

I've told you everything I know, said Stumpf.

What about the Gestapo?

Stumpf tried to remember why the Gestapo was watching Heidegger: He was sure it had something to do with Heidegger not respecting the goals of the Party, but he knew if he said this, Heidegger would get furious. So he looked at the pines and wondered if there were other creatures besides wolves hiding there: elves, for example, who would make him say just the wrong thing. He listened and only heard wind. Heidegger got up and kicked the snow.

You're a useless civil servant, he said.

By the time they got back to the hut, the whole world was filled with shadows. Stumpf said he had to leave on a mission, but Heidegger pulled him to the kitchen where a blond woman with a crown of braids stirred soup.

Look at this, he said, pointing at Stumpf.

Stumpf said *Heil Hitler!* And Elfriede Heidegger saluted without turning. Then she looked at him and squinted.

Who is he? she said to Heidegger.

Some asshole from the Party, said Heidegger.

You shouldn't talk that way, said Elfriede. And you shouldn't wear that hat in the snow. She took it off and stroked the feather. It will get ruined, she continued. Don't wear it again until spring.

Don't bother me about the hat, said Heidegger. But look at this. He showed her the glasses and the letter. Elfriede Heidegger squinted again.

What do you people do? she said to Stumpf.

We deliver things, he answered.

Who's we? she said.

An office.

You said you weren't with an office, said Heidegger. He picked up Aristotle's *Metaphysics* and walked towards another room.

You figure him out, he said to Elfriede.

Elfriede made a clucking noise and turned back to the soup.

Please sit down, she said to Stumpf.

Stumpf didn't want to sit down. The dark wood furniture and the peaked light from the window made him feel outside of ordinary time—not the dreamlike time of séances but the tilted, malevolent time of fairy tales. Yet he felt under a spell, just like unlucky people in fairy tales, and sat on another three-legged stool that also should have been in a barn. He looked at the beams, which he thought could fall on his head.

Elfriede kept stirring the soup. Which office are you with? she said. I know all of them.

None.

Then why are you dressed that way?

Protocol.

Elfriede Heidegger shook her head.

There's no such thing as protocol, she said. A uniform's a uniform.

She rummaged in a cupboard, set a bin at Stumpf's feet and handed him a knife and five potatoes.

Please peel these, she said.

Stumpf peeled anxiously and messily—half the peels landed on his boots. While he peeled, he looked at Elfriede's blond braids and thought she looked just like a woman named Frieda, whom he'd almost married.

Frieda was probably making soup, too, he thought—but in an ordinary house with pleasant furniture. Why had he let her go and become so entangled with the Offices? And how could he be entranced by Sonia, who sometimes, in the semi privacy of the shoebox, did leaps, pirouettes, arabesques, twisting her body into shapes that looked like the alphabet, startling him into thinking that the letters were nearly human; both heels on her shoulder for M, slithering for S, a backbend for O, one leg on her forehead for D. Sonia could become any letter in the world, even the Cyrillic alphabet. But when he looked at Elfriede, Stumpf realized he kept forgetting Sonia was a Russian Jew—not at all like the woman he once wanted to marry.

While he peeled potatoes, Elfriede Heidegger talked about Party meetings he'd never heard of because he was sentenced to the life of an underground creature, forced to live in the Compound. He thought again of Frieda making soup in a kitchen that didn't have a bed. He was sure she went to more Party meetings than Elfriede and had at least four children.

Elfriede Heidegger put the potatoes in the soup and swept the peels off the floor. Did Goebbels send you? she asked.

That's exactly what I want to know, Heidegger yelled from his study.

Stumpf said he wasn't able to divulge information but helped out as a private envoy. He was simply a connection between people of great importance: a messenger, a link, a go-between.

Andrezej

Wci adnych wiadomo ci o Ewa i dziecci. Ale Ja otrzymał
co zapytamy. Tak (wi c) prosz przybywał do zwyczajnego miejsca
jak (poniewa) szybko jak (poniewa) wy mo e dzi wieczorem.

Januz

* * *

Andrezej,

Still no news of Ewa and the children. But I've been
talking to someone who can travel freely and I have other news.
Meet me at the edge of the barracks.

Januz

The soup was potato soup with dark bread. It was thick, but not nearly as good as the soup the Scribes made: Stumpf thought about Parvis Nafissian banging pots, Niles Schopenhauer peeling potatoes, Gitka Kapusinki sprinkling spices, Sophie Nachtgarten adding bread, and one of the Russians always saying *don't stir the tea with your dick.* La Toya always put in something outrageous, like vodka and cinnamon, which made the soup taste better, and Elie surprised them with sausage or extra cheese. And all at once, like a child too far from home, he missed the dank mineral smell and subterranean comfort of the Compound. He even missed the Scribes making fun of him and the word games he didn't understand. At the very same time, he missed the increasingly imaginary Frieda, dishing out soup in a pleasant ordinary house with ordinary furniture. In other words—he missed everything at once, and this crescendoed inside him like a bleating lamb, even though he couldn't cry. He tried to elude the invitation to spend the night and was dismayed when Elfriede led him from the oblong table to the bed behind the kitchen stove. She said that they went to bed with the birds and got up with them, and he could be on his way early in the morning. Stumpf climbed into the bed and realized the smell of potato peels bothered him more than the dank smell of the mine. The shadows of the pots and pans looked like bears, ready to bite because he had hit Mikhail on the head when he'd gone to great trouble to write a letter.

Stumpf hadn't slept above ground since he'd been to his brother's farm in the fall. For a while he lay in the small bed without moving, listening to the Heideggers cough, and worrying that the rustling pines were the SS, spying on his catastrophic visit. He crept to the window and couldn't see anything. But he didn't trust this dark and saw advantages to sleeping below the ground. It was what the Führer was doing right now.

He let himself drift and began to imagine Frieda in a large bedroom without her husband: he'd gone to the front like every other sensible German. Unfortunately he'd been killed, and Frieda was lonely. Stumpf was in the process of inching his hand towards her breasts when he saw light from the dining room and heard a great pounding. Then he heard Heidegger shout:

I can't see out of these glasses!

Stumpf sat up and bumped his head on a pot. For some reason these two people who went to sleep with the birds and woke up with them, were awake in the middle of the night.

He crept from behind the stove and saw both Heideggers at the table in bathrobes. His was dark brown, hers light blue. He was reminded of a frieze in Himmler's office of two Greek gods who worked in tandem. Stumpf asked Heidegger if he was sure he couldn't see out of the glasses, and Heidegger said of course he was sure. How could he not be?

Now, said Elfriede. Tell us where you got them.

Stumpf said he couldn't say.

Then where did you get the damned letter? said Heidegger.

An office, said Stumpf. They give us smaller things.

You think this stuff about *Ent-fernen* is small? Or this ludicrous business with triangles?

The Reich doesn't think anything is small.

Then you *are* with the Reich.

Stumpf repeated he was an envoy. And then, as though he'd forgotten what he needed to conceal, he said Asher Englehardt had lost his shop, and people who lose their shops sometimes do strange things: maybe Asher made the glasses with the wrong prescription. Or written a crazy letter.

Heidegger didn't register that Asher lost his shop, but Elfriede Heidegger did.

How do you know? she said.

We got word from an office, said Stumpf.

Who's we?

I can't tell you.

They never tell you anything, said Heidegger. He shoved the letter in the soup tureen. It floated on the surface then sank in the potato peels. Stumpf pulled it out and blotted it on his sleeve.

Someone you work with? Elfriede said.

I'm not at liberty to say.

Of course you are! said Heidegger pounding a fist.

Stumpf was about to go into more detail about people losing their shops. He was going to talk about the confusion of papers—mismatched files, bulging mailbags. But Heidegger's pounding and the rattling tureen made him want to go far away from this dark, gloomy hut, to a street with soft lights where people wore fur coats and the aroma of tea-rose perfume permeated the smell of earth. He could smell the tea rose as if he were in the Compound. He could see the lamp on Elie's desk and her white arm with the red ribbon as it reached for the chocolate she always gave him. And he could smell the aura that surrounded her in winter—real weather, perfumed snow. *Dieter*, he heard her say. *Elie.* Her name flew out of his mouth. Elfriede Heidegger widened her eyes.

Elie, she said, as though the name quivered on a special scale. *Elie*.

Stumpf held his chins. Heidegger glared at the soup tureen.

I wonder if it's *that* Elie, said Elfriede.

What Elie? said Heidegger.

The little tart that came to my party, said Elfriede. She got my recipe for *bundkuchen*.

I don't know whom you're talking about, said Stumpf.

There was an Elie at Freiburg, said Elfriede, who was there one day and gone the next. She didn't even tell her landlady. One of those Aryan-looking Poles with blond curls and blue eyes. Everyone said she went underground.

Lots of Elies have blond hair and blue eyes, said Stumpf. And this Elie is from Latvia.

Not so many who disappeared, said Elfriede. And not so many who snuck around.

Stumpf's head felt unbearably heavy. He rested it on his chins. Heidegger took the letter.

Now tell us about Asher Englehardt, he said.

I can't.

Is he dead?

No, said Stumpf, who had no idea whether or not he was.

What about this other envoy? said Heidegger.

Stumpf didn't answer. Heidegger held Stumpf's chair by the rush bottom seat and pulled it off the ground.

I want you to take me to Asher Englehardt, he said. I want to hear from him if he wrote this absurd letter.

I can't. Believe me, I would if I could, but I can't.

Then Elfriede is going to report you. And this Elie person too.

Threats were the order of the day, as they'd been throughout the war. They came in the form of nods, snubs, notes, a revolver in one's ribs, even a wink.

Stumpf reviewed Heidegger's threat while Heidegger held up the chair. He was sure Mikhail had written a wonderful letter, and anyone could have taken the wrong glasses. On the other hand, he was the only person from the Compound the Heideggers had seen and could be shot for exposing the project. And even though there were times when Stumpf thought he wouldn't mind being shot, he always thought he would be the one to decide where and when it would occur. So he found himself saying what he never imagined he would say—the unthinkable, the unutterable.

I'll find a way to take you to Asher Englehardt.

Heidegger lowered the chair.

When? he said.

I can't tell you, said Stumpf. These things don't happen like clockwork. Meanwhile I'll get Asher to sign a statement that he wrote the letter.

I don't trust statements, said Heidegger. I want to hear it from him. And I want my glasses.

We'll wait two weeks but no longer, said Elfriede.

Two weeks, I promise. Can I have the letter back?

No, said Elfriede, tucking it in her bathrobe. We'll keep everything until you bring Martin to Asher. He was a wonderful man, by the way. You'd have no idea his father was Jewish.

The plan agreed with Heidegger. He began to talk about the Being of lost objects—in this case his glasses. Or maybe they weren't lost, he said. Maybe they were only *wrongly categorized*—in a drawer with buttons and bric-a-brac and letters. And perhaps, so was Asher Englehardt. Mentioning Asher Englehardt made Stumpf worry that Heidegger knew about the camps. Mentioning letters made him worry that he knew about the Compound. But letters and camps weren't his point. Heidegger meant the glasses were somewhere in the world— brute objects, not part of human life, the way he'd seen his glasses when he hadn't recognized them.

Heidegger speculated, Elfriede touched her crown of braids, and Stumpf remembered he had over twenty pairs of glasses in his jeep. One of them might be Heidegger's. But the thought of waiting while Heidegger tried them on was unbearable, and he left as soon as he could, taking a brown bread Elfriede forced on him, saying *Very soon!* and *Less than two weeks!*

At last Elfriede closed the door, and Stumpf walked down the path so quickly he dropped his hat. He picked it up without looking around, as if the mere sight of the hut would enchant him or turn him to stone. At his Kubelwagen he was surprised to find the ill-fated box of glasses and dictionary spotted with blood. It was as though he'd come from a realm where ordinary objects didn't exist. He had to drive slowly on the unplowed road—back through the pines, which seemed even more ominous since he'd been bewitched. By some miracle the main highway was plowed—a sign of redemption, he was sure. He breathed freely and drove with speed. All he wanted was to get back to his crystal balls and Sonia dancing letters of the alphabet. But when he remembered he'd promised to take Heidegger to Auschwitz, and telling them Elie's name, he drove so slowly the Kubelwagen dragged along the road.

The Angel of Auschwitz

Marietta.

*My po prostu (dopiero co) poznaj my mo e '*t* udaj si
pod. Ludzie (lud) w frakcjach, zawsze dyskutuj cy (wnioskuj cy;
dyskusja). Ale wszelki (wszyscy) zgadza si co w niewielu miesi cach,
Warszawa b dzie widzie podnoszenie lubi nikogo kiedy .
Prawdopodobnie jed z USA b dzie ywy potem, ale to wygrał
(wygrany; zwyci ył; zwyci ony; wona) '*t* sprawa dlatego e nikt
USA s rzeczywi cie ywa teraz. posyłam ten (to) wy z moj miło ci,
jak (poniewa) zawsze.*

Miło ,
Gustave

$*$ $*$ $*$

Dear Marietta,

*I think of you all the time, and sometimes imagine I can
see your face looking at me from the apartment opposite one of our
walls. Thank God you left. People are in factions, always arguing
and everybody agrees that in a few months, this ghetto will see an
uprising. None of us will be alive afterwards, but it won't matter
because none of us are alive now.*

Love,
Gustav

146

Twenty-seven hours after Stumpf assaulted Mikhail and left the Compound, Gerhardt Lodenstein began to straighten the room he had trashed for the second time in ten days after an explosive fight with Elie where he'd called her a meddler and a traitor. She'd locked herself in Mueller's old room.

Maybe, he thought, *it's only my illusion that I'm Obërst. Maybe my life really consists of destroying this room and putting it back together again.* He started by putting things he'd thrown back in his trunk—an enormous trunk he used to stockpile keepsakes.

The trunk was from the Navy, and he kept it for memorabilia because ever since he'd come to the Compound something had happened to his sense of time: ordinary things he touched, heard—even Elie—seemed to go through a slipknot and become part of a memory of *having happened.* One instant a pen, a scrap of paper, a face, would simply be itself. The next moment it became part of the past and reverberated like memories from childhood—the sound of street games, the rim of a skate. He wondered if this was because he was afraid he might not survive the war or worried that Elie would be killed on a foray. Or did the war itself warp time, pulling objects and events into wormholes? He held a white velvet rose and remembered the smell of summer lilacs.

Elie made these roses for women in the Compound because she couldn't find fresh flowers, except feverfew, which grew during summer. She assembled the velvet into petals so they thrust up like real flowers, sprayed them with tea-rose perfume and offered them with the same abandon as she offered fur coats. Now and then she gave a rose to Lodenstein. She'd given him this rose when he persuaded her to sleep upstairs again—after their fight about the children.

The trunk was filled with objects: used typewriter spools, a glass lamp, photographs, Elie's empty perfume bottles, a crooked whisk, a typewriter, fingerless gloves. He picked up pieces of the wool carder and put it back in the trunk carefully, next to a pair of glasses with a white tag marked *für Martin Heidegger.* Then he retrieved two maps. One was the original blueprint for the Compound. The other was a duplicate map— his private record that showed how it was really used. He'd named Elie's old room *Fraulein Schacten's Gift to the Scribes* and had drawn a skull and crossbones where the Compound dead-ended in the tunnel. On Stump's watchtower he'd crossed out *watchtower* and written *séances, shoebox, invocations to the dead.* He'd changed *guards' quarters* to *nightwalkers* and Mueller's room to *site of mysteries.* He'd marked the water closet where people held conferences *place of asylum.*

Now he wrote *Elie's hideout* over Mueller's old room and *hutch of fiascos* over Stump's watchtower. He considered writing *backstabber* over the Solomons' house. But Mikhail and Talia had endured enough aspersions before they came to the Compound. Instead he picked his way across the room to get another rose. He put it in the trunk.

During the twenty-seven hours since Stumpf left, a pall had come over the Compound: Mikhail had a huge welt on his forehead and stayed inside *917*, as did Talia, who said to him, *This place is as bad as Lodz.* Lars, who blamed himself for not guarding Mikhail more carefully, kept watch outside the house. Elie almost never left Mueller's old room. Scribes used the kitchen quietly.

Only Dmitri was happy because Elie was now downstairs. Since he'd come to the Compound, she took him with her almost everywhere. And if she didn't, Dimitri shadowed her, popping up near her desk so often, the Scribes nicknamed him *the little mouse.* He loved to look at the stamps on the letters as well as pictures of animals Elie found in books. And early that morning, Elie had taken him to the well and a thin calico cat walked out of the forest. The cat delighted him. He named her Mufti.

As for Lodenstein, even solitaire upset him. Games that once amused him, like Beleaguered Castle, or Forty Thieves, now had aching resonance—about Elie's schemes, Mikhail's collusions, and the letter on its way to Heidegger. He'd capsized the bed and had to play on the floor. Cards kept slipping under socks.

He thought about trying to play another game, then noticed two pieces of paper he'd found in the main room. One read: *Who in the hell is bothering to write to* us? The other read: *If Lodenstein thinks this is all horseshit why does he go along with imagining Goebbels?*

Both sounded like La Toya. He folded them and saw light in pale bands through the oblong windows. It was already dawn. He'd slept only three hours.

All at once he heard an engine roar into the clearing and boots crack the ice. The door to the shepherd's hut opened, and Lodenstein felt wind and cold weather on his face. Then he saw

Stumpf tiptoeing past his room. Lodenstein walked over the smashed ivory box and experienced a moment of piercing repulsion, a sense of visceral recognition that happens after someone who's familiar has left and then comes back: all the things he'd done to airbrush Stumpf were out of reach.

Stumpf didn't know he was being watched. It gave Lodenstein vicious pleasure to put his hands around Stumpf's thick neck.

You evil fucker, he said. I should shoot you in front of everyone.

Please, said Stumpf, in a wheezing voice. I didn't do anything.

Then why was Mikhail unconscious? And why are the glasses gone?

A terrible thing has happened, said Stumpf. Yes. Terrible.

What in God's name are you talking about?

Please don't shoot me, said Stumpf.

What happened?

I don't want to tell you.

Stumpf's eyes were points of dread in his enormous face. Lodenstein's stomach lurched.

What did you do? he said.

You don't want to know. Believe me.

You have to tell me.

I can't.

I have to know.

Stumpf looked down. Tears fell in the crevices of his face.

I promised to take Heidegger to Auschwitz, he said.

What?

I have to take Heidegger to Auschwitz.

Lodenstein pushed Stumpf against the wall so hard the bread Elfriede gave him fell from his pocket. Lodenstein picked it up and ground it into Stumpf's face.

You fuck up everything you touch, he said.

Then he pounded Stumpf's chins and neck and heavy shoulders and slammed his head against the wall, as if he could pummel out everything Stumpf had done.

I can't believe you're real, he said.

Stumpf began to wail.

Heidegger is a living link! he sobbed. A living link to the Compound!

Don't bother to spell it out. You've told me enough.

But Stumpf spelled everything out: How Elfriede Heidegger had made him peel potatoes. How Martin Heidegger had made him walk in the Black Forest. How planks could have fallen on his head. How he'd had to sleep behind a stove. How he'd brought the wrong glasses. How Mikhail's letter had fallen in the soup.

He went on and on until Lodenstein put his hands around Stumpf's neck with such force his chins rose around his face.

I want you to tell me about Elie, he said.

They don't know anything about Elie.

But Lodenstein knocked him to the floor again, and Stumpf's teeth cut his lips, oozing blood.

Tell me, he yelled.

Stumpf wiped the blood with his sleeve.

They know about Elie, he said.

Caro Cipriana,

Non li ho visti per due giorni Dove siete? .se venite alla recinzione, vi mangerò il pane supplementare per. Ogni giorno conservo poco un più dalla mia razione.

Amore,
Mirella

*   *   *

Dear Cipriana,

People are stealing shamelessly from each other—not just food, but shoes and coats. Still, every day I save a little more bread for you. Please come talk to me.

Love,
Mirella

Lodenstein hit Stumpf on the mouth where it was already cut, oozing more blood. Then he shoved him down the incline into the mineshaft. When it thudded to the earth, he threw Stumpf to the ground and pounded on the door of Mueller's old room.

Let me in, he shouted to Elie. You have everything to lose if you don't.

Elie unlocked the door and shrouded her face with her hair so Lodenstein couldn't see she'd been crying.

Tell me something, he said. How many lives would you risk to save a child?

None, said Elie.

But you did, said Lodenstein. And now Heidegger has to go to Auschwitz.

I don't understand.

Ask Elfriede Heidegger. She says you're a little tart.

Elie flinched.

She doesn't know me.

Yes she does. How many Polish women in Freiburg got her recipe for *bundkuchen*?

What do you mean?

I mean Stumpf told her your name.

Elie took off her scarf and wrung it as though it were a neck.

How could he do that? she shouted.

Because he's Stumpf, said Lodenstein. And you've set him up to do everything he's so good at.

I wish I'd changed my first name too.

Are you insane? Your name's not the point. You went behind my back twice. And now we're all in trouble.

Stop.

Why should I? I always stop. From asking what you do to get people across borders. Or why the SS are so nice to you.

I don't want to hear anymore.

You have to.

Elie went outside and sat on one of the wrought-iron benches. Lodenstein followed her.

You flirt all the time, he said. With forgers. With bakers. With anyone who could help.

Elie began to cry.

I told you I was going to see Heidegger myself, she said.

And then what were you going to do?

Manage it, said Elie. She heard her voice reverberate throughout the Compound. It sounded hollow, like a voice from the dead.

You mean manage Martin Heidegger, who loves the Reich but pissed them off so much the Gestapo's watching him? You mean manage Elfriede Heidegger, who doesn't like you at all? You mean getting her to go to Auschwitz and pick up Asher Englehardt the way you'd pick up someone at a train station?

You're relentless, said Elie.

So are you, said Lodenstein.

It was barely six in the morning. The Scribes woke up and listened with concern. Mikhail Solomon opened his door.

You better come inside, he said. And for God's sake, talk quietly. You'll wake Dmitri.

154

Elie and Lodenstein sat far apart on velvet chairs. Mikhail touched the welt on his forehead. Talia looked at her hands.

Did any one of you ever think about how dangerous this was? said Lodenstein quietly, noticing Dimitri asleep on the couch.

We did it to save Maria, said Mikhail.

You knew I'd get her if you asked, said Lodenstein.

That doesn't matter, said Elie. I would have brought Heidegger the right glasses.

Who gives a damn about the right glasses? said Lodenstein. You had no business messing around. Besides, Elie, if you were going to manage everything, why didn't you write the fucking letter yourself?

I don't know enough philosophy to mess it up, said Elie.

Ah! Our linguist from Freiburg. Why bother to write a letter at all? Why not just talk to Elfriede Heidegger? Because it got involved with saving Maria, said Elie.

That's ridiculous, said Lodenstein. Stumpf's a fool. So now Heidegger knows about Elie.

My God, said Talia.

What else did you expect? said Lodenstein. And there's even more: Stumpf's promised Heidegger he could see Asher at Auschwitz.

But that's not possible, said Mikhail.

But he has to, said Lodenstein. Because if he doesn't, Elfriede Heidegger will tell Goebbels that he knows about the Compound. Did you ever think that almost sixty lives were at stake? Or who would have to fix this?

No one answered. Mikhail and Talia reached for cigarettes.

While they smoked, the crescent moon made its last mechanical descent—the gears creaking and groaning as if a giant were in agony. Lodenstein walked to the window and wondered if everyone woke up to a life they hadn't chosen or whether he was the only one who'd been singled out. Was this a punishment for joining the Party without giving the matter much thought? Or for not helping Elie with Heidegger's glasses in the first place? No matter. He kicked an ottoman and left the room. Elie followed.

Where are you going? she said.

To see Goebbels, he answered.

You can't. It's too dangerous.

I have to, Elie. They know your name.

But Goebbels is crazy.

You should have thought of that sooner, said Lodenstein.

He went to the mineshaft too quickly for Elie to get in, locked the door to their room, and played Imaginary Thirteen and Half & Half. A few Scribes were in the clearing, and he didn't want to run into them in the SS uniform he had to wear for trips to Berlin. So he couldn't leave and felt imprisoned, as if time was solid, and he was standing next to it. He played more solitaire and got perverse satisfaction when Elie tried to open the door.

It's dark, she said. You can't drive there at night.

Of course I can, he said.

Gerhardt, please. I'm sorry I started this.

It's about saving you now. And everyone else in the Compound.

He pushed away the clutter and managed more solitaire. It was awkward on the floor, but he viewed the upturned furniture as a token of his anger and felt setting it right would be a concession—especially to Elie if she saw he'd straightened the room.

Near midnight he put underwear, socks, his gun, and playing cards into a duffel bag. He checked for bullets, knotted the black SS tie, considered taking the compass and then decided not to. Then he rummaged in the trunk for the rose Elie gave him when he asked her to sleep upstairs again. He found it by the broken wool-carder—soft, fragrant, like a rose in a summer garden. He held it for a moment then pushed it to the bottom of trunk. But within moments he was rummaging again. The rose was still perfect when he found it, buried under photographs and lamps. He picked it up and put it in his pocket.

Дорогое Дасюа,

мы не имеем никакую мысль наших жизней, больше.
Мы как раз знаем мы не может препятствовать нашим детям,
нашим друзьям, нашему супругу, нашим супругам,
вспоминает нас как идущ вниз.

Влюбленность

*   *   *

Dear Dasha,

We have no thought of our lives, anymore. We can't let our
children, our friends, our husbands, our wives, remember us as
going under.

Love,
Nicolai

158

Gerhardt Lodenstein let himself out of the shepherd's hut a few minutes after Mikhail and Lars came back from the watchtower. There had just been a snowfall, and his boots carved a path—one he hoped Elie would see in the morning. A week ago she'd taken his jeep to buy cigarettes and left a red scarf on the seat. He threw it next to his duffel bag. Then he began to drive on the long, narrow road.

The fresh snow was piled in drifts, and every few minutes he had to get out and shovel a path. He shoveled angrily, lifting huge mounds of snow and throwing them into the forest. While he shoveled, he remembered Elie parodying the Nazi salute when he began to throw their dresser drawers on the floor for the second time. She had kicked shirts and camisoles and said he was a fucking Nazi. He'd overturned the mattress again and told her she was lucky because only a fucking Nazi could fix this mess. The images exploded in his mind along with regret: He should have let Elie in when she cried outside the door. They should have made love before he left. He didn't want to think, but thought anyway, that he might never hold Elie again.

He drove and shoveled and drove and shoveled until he came to the junction that led to the main road. It was miraculously plowed at this stage in the war—a long, dark arrow pointing to Goebbels and the Offices of the Reich. He got out of the jeep to look at the sky. Orion and his hunting dogs were glittering due south, the Great Bear had pine branches nestling in his paws, and Lepus, the Hare, was arcing over the forest. Everything was in order.

For a moment he thought about disappearing—like the other officers who left without a trace: The admiral who had helped Wilhelm Canaris rescue Jews vanished in Denmark. The SS officer who gave his uniform to the nightwalkers hid in a barn near Dresden. A former assistant to Himmler was in England. These officers were scattered like stars. The SS hunted them tenaciously. The Resistance protected them in return for their uniforms, identity papers, and information. They lived for days seeing no one, afraid of being caught—like any other fugitive. Images of such a life burst before his eyes like grenades. But he knew if he disappeared he couldn't save Elie. Or the Compound.

He got back in his jeep and drove slowly on the smooth, wide road. Near dawn he stopped at an inn where he used to drink on his way to Berlin—over ten years ago, when he'd been reading for law. The innkeeper didn't recognize him and apologized for the ersatz coffee. Then he made jovial conversation about the war while his wife stood behind him smiling. Lodenstein left without bothering to salute.

By the time he got to Berlin snow was falling. It dusted streets like sugar on cakes no one could make since the war turned, including—he thought bitterly—Elfriede Heidegger and her *bundkuchen.* He remembered once loving this city and his exuberance on the wide, open streets. He remembered nights in beer halls where people talked about books that had no doubt been burned. Now the Gestapo was everywhere.

Yet houses were intact, and winter vegetable gardens looked prosperous—not like the bombed-out city of Hamburg, where another SS officer hid, or the town where Elie had rescued the children. The only evidence of war was a line outside a butcher shop snaking around a corner. A beet-faced man in a white apron opened the door and shouted:

We don't open until ten. And no sausages today!

The line scattered, and Lodenstein ignored the butcher when he saluted the swastika on his jeep. He wanted to leave this city as soon as possible, yet he drove slowly. Everything was gone for him here—even the Brandenburg Gate. He'd once loved its Doric columns—part of Athens floating in the north. Now it was hung with Nazi banners and led straight to the Offices of the Reich.

Lodenstein drove past the Kaiserhof Hotel—a huge stone music box dripping with banners and flags. Before Hitler came into power, he'd occupied a whole floor and anyone who mattered—diplomats, officers, mistresses, wives—still stayed there. The front of the building was clotted with SS, as well as civilians who wanted to bask in its façade. Lodenstein recognized a diplomat.

As though it had a will of its own, the jeep drove the length of the Kaiserhof until it reached the Reich Offices: a grey monolith that extended for two city blocks and reminded Lodenstein of a stalag. He would rather have found Goebbels through a small side door, but his jeep was forced to drive into the Honor Courtyard.

The courtyard was the main entrance to the Offices and designed to broadcast immensity. As soon as Lodenstein drove in, his view was focused on the main building. It was gargantuan, with steep steps, flanked by two identical statues of muscular men in black marble. One carried a torch to represent the Party and the other a sword to represent the Army. Two other buildings surrounded this building. All three had Greek columns.

While Lodenstein waited for someone to park his jeep, he watched officers walk up and down the steps. They looked as if they'd been ratcheted with screws and would fall apart if anything came undone. They often had expressions of awe because they'd just left, or were about to enter, the Great Mosaic

Hall—a one-hundred-and-fifty-foot crimson corridor with a gold-rimmed skylight and mosaics of Greek battles. Lodenstein had never liked this hall. It made him feel drenched in red.

The officer at the desk didn't recognize him and asked him to empty his pockets. He was glad he'd left his duffel bag in the jeep and sorry he'd taken Elie's rose. He was led through more crimson halls and left in Goebbels's antechamber.

Elfriede Heidegger must have waited here to meet Goebbels as well. Lodenstein imagined the overstuffed chairs and polished wood tables would have pleased her. There was a huge photograph of Goebbels and Hitler shaking hands, another of Hitler kissing a child. He leafed through some propaganda pamphlets—all about Germany's victory.

After nearly an hour, he heard boots tapping on the marble. Generalmajor Mueller stood in front of him, looking prosperous.

My good man, he said, shaking his hand. How nice to see you in these winter months.

I thought you were going to the front, said Lodenstein.

Not a chance, said Mueller. There were more important projects. And Goebbels is always in the marketplace. Can I tempt you with lunch until he gets back?

Lodenstein didn't want to spend a minute with Mueller, but he knew the offer wasn't a choice. They went through more crimson corridors to the dining hall where tables were set with white cloths and crystal goblets.

Amazing news about the war, Mueller said after they'd ordered rabbit stew. Last week everyone celebrated in the Lustgarten. What a fest! Even in ice! He wiped his moustache and lowered his voice.

You're lucky you got switched to the SS, he said, because Wilhelm Canaris is about to be put under house arrest. Maybe even sent to Auschwitz, so he can see who he's trying to save before he's hung.

I'm sure he's a double agent, said Lodenstein.

It's a pity you were ever in the Abwehr, said Mueller.

They finished their coffee—real coffee—and walked down winding stairs to a room with a hunter-green sofa and white walls.

It's quieter here, said Mueller. Better than all that bustling. And here's Goebbels's latest pamphlet. I'll get you when he comes back.

Mueller shut the door, and Lodenstein noticed a distinct quiet, as though the room were wrapped in swaddling. He touched the walls and discovered they were brick. The door was cold, metal, and locked. He opened the pamphlet, and the list of everything he'd surrendered at the door fell out. This made him sure he was in a cell, and Goebbels had ordered his arrest as soon as he arrived. The Reich would never jail an officer without giving him a list of his possessions.

Liebe Leonie,

Ich habe kein Papier, also schreibe Ich diesen Brief auf eine Wand. Sonstig Volk bist schrieben zo. Ich muß schnell schreiben.

Ich liebe dich,
Niklaus

*   *   *

Dear Leonie,

I have no paper so I'm writing this letter on a wall. I must write quickly.

I love you,
Niklaus

Lodenstein listened more closely and heard clattering keys. This must mean other people were in this underground jail. He'd heard about such cases—officers in disfavor, thrown into cells and forgotten until they turned into bodies so bereft of food and water no bacteria was left to make them rot. The bodies were completely clean. They were folded a few times over like paper and thrown away.

Now he could see the cell was only thinly disguised as a waiting room. The sofa was a narrow bench. The brick walls were painted white. There was an overhead light and a cement floor—clean except for one dark drop he didn't want to look at too closely. Now and then the rattling keys grew louder. Sometimes they sounded like knives. Sometimes they sounded like sleigh bells. Now and then an oblong-shaped slat in the door opened, he saw a pair of eyes surveying the room and the slat shut as quickly as a guillotine: someone checking to see he hadn't done himself in.

Lodenstein did fifty push-ups, avoiding the spot on the floor. He lay on the bench and played three games of solitaire in his head. He read the list of everything he'd surrendered, and made up theories about why they hadn't taken his belt or shoelaces. He read and reread the list until it began to float in front of him.

One map, one deck of cards, three cigarettes, one box of matches, one piece of white velvet.

His mouth was dry, and the room was cold. He started to shiver. He thought of how, during his training, the Abwehr had glossed over torture: they were a rarified group that ciphered codes. He wondered what he'd be able to endure. If he'd break quickly. If it would hurt. If they'd use Elie as a hostage.

His hands were in fists. He forced himself to unclench them. But he clenched them again when he realized it had been a while since he heard keys. Suppose he was the only person here? In that case he'd been singled out for inquisition, torture, and hanging. He played more solitaire in his head, but he couldn't keep the different games straight. Royal Parade merged with Citadel. Citadel merged with Above and Below. Stonewall turned into Flea. The cards unfurled, the white bricks undulated, and the cracks between them assumed infinite depth. Inside the cracks, like jewels in crevices, Lodenstein began to see letters of the alphabet. He didn't read them but looked at the floating list, which told the story of a man with a deck of cards, three cigarettes, a box of matches, and a velvet rose. This man set out for Berlin in mountains of snow, drove to a huge grey building, and was thrown into a cell.

At some point the list detached from the paper, and the letters flew into the bricks. The room assumed a dreamlike radiance. And Lodenstein flew up to the ceiling. He could see the entire room—including a man who looked just like him, lying on the hunter-green bench.

The man he saw knew a secret: namely that writing to the dead wasn't the Thule Society's idea but a clairvoyant's. The clairvoyant was the extraordinary Erik Hanussen, who was also a mind reader and hypnotist. He had predicted Hitler's rise to power and taught him to mesmerize crowds just by raising his hand. But he'd also disguised the fact that he was Jewish, lent too many officers money, and knew about their affairs. And when he predicted the Reichstag fire days before it happened, it was clear he knew the Reich wanted an excuse to erect the very building where Lodenstein was jailed. In the winter of 1933 Hanussen was shot and left in a field.

Through a series of accidents (or was it the prescience of Lodenstein's father, who was still in the Abwehr?) Lodenstein, who was reading for law in Berlin, had a seat in the audience when Erik Hanussen revealed his secret key to the Reich's world domination. The year was late 1932, months before Hanussen was shot. The place was Hanussen's black and gold Palace of the Occult in Berlin, a ghoulish cabaret attended by members of the Nazi Party every night. The cabaret had a crooner, a chorus line, a strongman who lifted stones—and Hanussen, who appeared at the end of every show in a tuxedo. He called women in furs and diamonds to the stage, put them in trances, branded their hands with burning coins and was triumphant when they didn't feel pain. Once he told a Party member to send fire trucks to his house because of a faulty electrical system. The trucks arrived and saved the house from burning.

In addition to the cabaret, the Palace had a gold and black marble room for séances. It was in this room that the meeting about Hanussen's secret key was held.

Lodenstein sat in the back, surrounded by smoke and members of the Nazi party, and looked at the stage where Hanussen held séances. It had a round marble dais with a round marble table where black triangles pointed to an empty center. This was where Hanussen focused his mind so he could travel to realms other people couldn't see. His travels had served him well: a judge once pardoned him from a swindling case because he knew where a criminal was hiding.

More Nazi Party members crowded the hall. When Himmler and Goebbels arrived, everyone stood. Then the lights went out, and Hanussen appeared in a tuxedo. There was a moment of silence when he looked at the audience with eyes that seemed to know everything they hid in their pockets, as well as their souls. Then he unveiled a picture of an enormous globe filled with cracks. The cracks oozed letters and envelopes.

Unsightly, he'd said. But *real*.

Hanussen then explained that the letters stood for all the unanswered correspondence in the world, and the dead who'd written them were still waiting for answers. Every unanswered letter, he said, was like a brick in a building without mortar. They left perilous seams and created dangerous gaps in history. To ensure that the mortar was firm, all letters written by the dead must be answered down to the very last query from a haberdasher.

And why was this situation urgent? Because the dead would be upset unless they got answers. Indeed, they were already agitated in their pale green cities, able to penetrate this very room, demanding answers to their letters. Hanussen himself had to turn many away. And if the Reich wanted absolute power, they should answer all possible letters to fill in these seams. Then Germany would seal the globe and gain world-domination.

While Hanussen talked, Lodenstein had a distinct sense of the world falling out of itself. The stolid officer to his left asked him for a piece of paper and drew a duplicate of Hanussen's globe—as though he could stuff every crack with letters. Other people took out paper and wrote down names of the dead who might be waiting for answers. The amphitheater was filled with scratching pens and rustling paper. Lodenstein's legs began to twitch—a sure sign that he wanted to leave. But he realized someone might report him; so he took out paper and looked as though he were trying to remember the dead in their pale green cities. When Hanussen turned on the light, the room was full of questions.

If the dead don't have an address, how can we send them letters?

The letters don't have to be mailed, said Hanussen. It's enough to store them in boxes. The dead will know when they've been answered.

Where can we find the letters?

Everywhere. In attics, old ships, offices, museums.

But it's impossible to find all of them.

An astrologer will tell you when you've found enough.

Can we confiscate these letters?

When the time is right.

The last question came from a short, heavy man in front of the amphitheater, sitting between Himmler and Goebbels. He held two glasses of water, and every few minutes one or the other snapped his fingers, and the heavy man handed him a glass. At one point he stood up, and Goebbels jerked his sleeve—but it was too late. Hanussen had noticed him.

Can we answer all the letters in German? he asked.

Only if they're written in German, said Hanussen. The dead can read, but they cannot translate. Never forget this. *Like Answers Like* should be your motto. And answer faithfully.

There was loud applause. Every member of the Reich, including Himmler, Goebbels, and the short, squat man went to the dais to greet Hanussen. Lodenstein had watched, fascinated by the folds in the heavy man's face. Later, when he met Stumpf, he recognized him as the same person.

Marek,

Tardy) znajdowa co pisa z. Albo wiatło (lekki) pisa przez. Wszelki (wszyscy) wydaje si jest pisz cy (pisanie) sobie. wiat (wiatowy) pełny listów (litera) stale s pióra. Wy mieli cie poznawa wszystek na czas obecny, wł czaj cy fakt co dwa z ci gn ł zdumienia.

Il widz was wkrótce.
Urajsz

* * *

Dear Marek,

Letters are being passed all the time and prisoners have managed to bribe pens from guards. Even in this unspeakable place people write to each other constantly. God willing, I'm going to see you soon.

Love always,
Urajsz

Before Lodenstein came to the Compound, the SS officer who evaporated in Denmark told him the idea of answering letters from the dead had been the object of conversation for days after the meeting at the Palace of the Occult. But when Hanussen was shot, anyone who mentioned his name or referred to his ideas was shot too. It was a mere stroke of luck that no one made a connection between Hanussen's vision and the Thule Society's obsession with answering letters written by the dead. Maybe Hitler had forgotten. But Lodenstein doubted Goebbels had: Goebbels remembered everything. And Goebbels had condoned Stumpf's post, knowing Stumpf was much more interested in answering the dead than in record-keeping. Stumpf's appointment must have been Goebbels's concession to the Thule Society, in spite of his own disdain for the occult. And he had allowed Hanussen's motto *Like Answers Like.*

Now the man on the hunter-green bench retrieved every detail of Hanussen's speech at the black and gold Palace of the Occult. He retrieved them from the jewel-like letters between the bricks, which he could now read. After he'd read everything, the walls stopped undulating, and Lodenstein came down from the ceiling and slid inside the man who looked just like him. He put his hands in his pockets and realized the letters of the alphabet weren't in the wall but on a piece of paper. He stood up and felt his legs, his arms, the cramped enclosure of the cell. And when the little hatch opened again he cleared his sandpaper throat and shouted the name *HANUSSEN!* so loudly, the face stepped back, and he heard keys drop to the floor.

HANUSSEN! he said again in a hoarse voice. Tell Joseph Goebbels that Lodenstein remembers Hanussen.

The sound of the keys grew fainter, and Lodenstein was alone. He wondered whether he'd be shot for mentioning Hanussen, or grilled about the meeting at the Palace of the Occult. When the keys jangled again his legs trembled, but the officer gestured toward the winding steps that led to the Mosaic Hall, and once more he was enveloped in crimson marble. He heard an accordion in the officer's cabaret. It must be evening.

The officer led him back to the antechamber and opened an enormous door. Goebbels sat behind a desk, still propped up by books to look taller. He was exactly the way Lodenstein remembered him—a thin face with dark, heavy-lidded eyes—circles Elie once called *bizarre, almost romantic eyes*. The desk was piled with pamphlets, two copies of *Mein Kampf*, a tin of biscuits, a bottle of wine, bottles of water, and fluted glasses.

Goebbels waved away any mention of Hanussen and listened to Lodenstein talk about Stumpf's visit to Heidegger. When he was finished, Goebbels speculated whether he should kill Heidegger as well as Stumpf and every single Scribe, since who really cared about records concerning people who died? But what if, he continued, Heidegger was exonerated after the war and no one could find him? Then his murder might be discovered, and the Compound of Scribes might be brought to light.

While he talked, he drank water from one of the fluted glasses. After his third glass, he lit a cigarette.

I should have Stumpf hung, he said.

When the right times comes, thought Lodenstein.

Heidegger, too, said Goebbels. I have no idea why that woman bothers with him.

Lodenstein supposed he meant Elfriede Heidegger, but didn't ask. He folded his hands, which felt like dry wood, and waited while Goebbels looked to the left, to the right, at a fresco of Hercules on the ceiling, and at his desk. He shuffled papers and picked up a photograph of his wife and five children—a perfect family and a perfect wife. He drank more water and pushed a glass towards Lodenstein, who lunged for it. It hurt to swallow.

Goebbels watched him drink with a look of contempt. Then he said:

People have visited Auschwitz before. And Heidegger won't talk because of his wife. He's a ludicrous country bumpkin, and I'm sure she knows it.

Lodenstein stared at the glass.

Never mind, said Goebbels, who'd once hugged Mrs. Heidegger at a meeting for housewives and had been delighted to see her again when she'd come to his office.

He leaned back in his chair, looked at the ceiling, stared at Lodenstein, and looked away. Then he slapped a hand on his phone, called Auschwitz and asked if the Jew named Asher Englehardt was still alive. Ten minutes passed while someone looked up his number.

These are strict orders, Goebbels said into the phone. Have him make glasses for the officers. And give him enough food and a place to rest during the day. What do I mean? I mean he's a lens grinder, and the officers' clinic has made a mess of that. Better for them to have new glasses than pick through piles of Jew-glasses. And be careful of his son. Heil Hitler!

After he hung up he looked at Lodenstein for the first time.

You can take Heidegger to Auschwitz, he said. And deal with the consequences. But you'll have to stay here—no getting a room at the Kaiserhof or messing around Berlin. And you'll go to Auschwitz with Heidegger in the dark—I mean true dark—on a night when there isn't a moon.

Lodenstein pointed out that every month there was only one night with no moon and a trip to Auschwitz took two days.

Don't split hairs with me, said Goebbels. And not a word about Hanussen.

Then he crawled to the top of his desk and looked down at Lodenstein. His eyes became slits. and if pupils could manipulate the world, they would have flattened everything in the room, including Lodenstein.

Blackmailer! he said. Naval scumbag! Pervert! Asshole head of a hovel!

His voice rose to emphasize his point, creating a circle of dramatic air. Lodenstein let him go on. He had no choice. He also hoped that if Goebbels spit out his venom, he'd never take revenge, and the Compound would remain a strange, safe haven in the middle of a failing war.

When Goebbels finished, he crawled back to his chair, sat on his pile of books, and rang a buzzer.

This is Obërst Lodenstein, he said when an officer appeared. Give him the best food, the best wine and—he winked—the best women.

Lodenstein gave the Nazi salute and followed the officer down the crimson hall to the cabaret, amazed that his legs were holding him up. A woman in a tight black bodice was playing the accordion, and an officer was singing Lorelei into her ample bosom. Lodenstein sat near the door and ate venison and potatoes. He left the cabaret, went to his room, and threw up.

Soon he was in bed—vast, unfamiliar, much larger than the bed he shared with Elie. He fell into half-sleep and woke when he heard rustling outside his door. He was afraid Goebbels had sent a woman. But when he opened the door, he found an envelope filled with everything he'd surrendered, including the white rose, which still smelled of Elie's perfume. He slept with it for almost two weeks. Then Heidegger arrived on a moonless night, and they set off by train for Auschwitz.

Lieber Gretchen,

Muß ich Du sehen.
Sorgen Du sich nicht. Niemand können herausfinden.
Freunde halten uns sicher. Ich suche Du durch die Gatter. Ich suche Du durch Felsen. Ich muß mit Dich sprechen, Du Gesicht zu sehe, glaube Dich Armen, Dich Ofnung. Kommst Du schnell.

Liebe,
Paul

* * *

Dear Gretchen,

I need to see you.
Don't worry. No one can find out. Friends will keep us safe. I look for you by the gates. I look for you by rocks. I need to talk to you, see your face, feel your arms, kiss you. Come quickly.

Love,
Paul

Asher Englehardt, a terse man with shrewd blue eyes, had been surprised to be pulled from a job lugging rocks in the snow.

Over here! said a guard, grabbing him by the shoulder.

Nobody stopped working because they would get shot, as Asher was certainly about to be. He put down the stone, thinking at least he wouldn't be lifting something that weighed almost as much as he did, and stepped from the line. An Uberoffizier was standing next to the guard, and an Uberoffizier often meant a hanging—worse than a swift bullet near the red brick wall of the jail. Hangings happened in the evening when the whole camp assembled for roll call. Daniel would watch him die.

The Uberoffizier motioned Asher to his Kubelwagen and drove along the unpaved road. He was so pleasant Asher assumed he wanted to put him at ease since panic made it hard to cooperate with a noose. They drove to the camp through the side entrance, rather than the main gate where Asher saw *Arbeit Macht Frei* every morning when he left for work. Instead of going to the jail, they went to a small room in the officers' quarters where another officer brought in soup, huge slices of rye bread, and beer. It was the first table set with food Asher had seen in over four months.

Eat slowly, said the Uberoffizier. It takes time to adjust if you haven't eaten for a while.

Asher hesitated. It occurred to him that he might be part of one of the ghoulish experiments the camp gossiped about—performed by Mengele, the doctor who greeted transports and decided who would live or die. He performed experiments, the prisoners said, on people with or without disease. And perhaps this one, Asher thought, would be about the rate of digestion of starving people after a full meal. There would be one needle to knock him out and another in the heart: Not bad. But did he want Reich food in him when he died?

The Uberoffizier pulled up his chair and offered Asher a cigarette, which he took without thinking. The Uberoffizier lit one for each of them and said:

Cigarettes. The common bond around here.

Asher laughed, then wondered if he shouldn't have. People got killed for thinking the wrong things were funny.

Listen, said the Uberoffizier. Things at the clinic are a mess. We need you to make glasses.

Asher didn't ask what kind of mess he meant, and the officer didn't explain because there was a blast of motorcycles from a battalion that was revved up to drown out screams when people were gassed. The officer left the room for over ten minutes. When the motorcycles stopped he came back.

No one's getting the right glasses, he said. And it's chaotic to sort through the heaps.

Asher understood that heaps referred to the piles of glasses that belonged to people who'd died in the gas chambers.

So we really need you, the officer concluded.

Asher didn't believe him. But knowing there had just been a gassing filled him with a conviction he sometimes had when he knew there had been an atrocity—namely that he was lucky to be alive, even special. This made him decide to eat while he still could. The soup was thick. The rye bread was fresh. The beer tasted like manna. The Uberoffizier looked relieved and said he'd be back in a few minutes.

And now it's going to happen, Asher thought. A couple of needles. Maybe even from Mengele himself.

But Mengele didn't appear. The Uberoffizier came back with real shoes, thick socks, a warm sweater, and a woolen cap and gloves. Then they walked to the officers' clinic, past the winter quarters for the angora rabbits. Many camps had rabbits tended by the prisoners to prove to the Red Cross that there were pleasant pastimes at the camps. The Uberoffizier tried to hurry him past Mengele's quarters, but not before Asher saw two twins strapped to gurneys.

Beste Petra,

Schrijf ik om u te vertellen dat u en Miep hier zou moeten komen. Er is overvloed van voedsel. En de tweelingen worden zeer goed behandeld. Herinnert u niet hoe vier van ons om op de speelplaats gebruikten te lachen en te zeggen dat de tweelingen speciaal waren? Goed, waren wij juist! Iedereen is goed aan Sylvie en me. En ik weet zij aan u goed zullen zijn en Miep.

Liefde,
Ania

* * *

Dear Petra,

Do you remember how the four of us used to laugh on the playground and say that twins were special? Well, we were right! Everybody is good to Sylvie and me. And they'll be good to you and Miep.

Love,
Ania

The room in the officers' clinic was like Asher's shop in Freiburg shrunk to a fourth of its size. In this miniature version of his old room, he saw an optometrist's chair, an illuminated eye chart with gothic letters, and tools for grinding lenses. A man with a green armband was cleaning instruments and said he would be his assistant, since he knew how to weld frames.

Asher still wondered if this were a prelude to death, but after two days, he didn't care because life was a little more bearable. After morning roll call, a guard walked him through the snow to the warm quiet halls of the officers' clinic. Every time Asher opened the door he thought he might find Mengele and instruments of torture. But he always found an optometrist's room—calm, quiet, efficient. The officers who came for glasses answered questions politely—so politely Asher almost forgot he was a prisoner.

He was pulled from heavy labor in mid-February: a few mornings later he looked from the window of his workroom to a snowfall that covered everything in a bridal-veil of white—even the rune-like barbed-wire fences, and the corpses that hung from them like sheets. By noon there was a shooting, and a red stain bloomed in the snow. The stain faded to pink, and by dusk it was a rust-colored blotch.

A few days later there was another snowfall, veiling the camp in white all over again. It occurred to Asher—not without irony—that as long as there was snow, whatever happened in Auschwitz was reversible. He liked looking from the paned window of his workroom. The snow reminded him of winter childhoods when he played with his sister, who'd been smart enough to move to America. It had been a time when the woods were safe for children, and they believed in snow maidens who came to life and wolves that could grant wishes. He and his sister had lain in the snow, waved their hands, and left imprints that looked like angels.

Now and then he worked late and saw the night sky. The searchlights made it preternaturally bright and obscured the stars. Once he saw the moon and was surprised it was still in the sky. Sometimes he saw shipments of boxes outside Mengele's quarters—one labeled *Furniture,* another labeled *Bones.* At least once a day he heard motorcycles.

One evening he saw a transport. People were in clotted groups. Children were crying. A floodlight illuminated the figure of Mengele. He was an elegant man with his right elbow on his left arm, gesturing with a gloved index finger that moved hardly at all. The night Asher and his son arrived Mengele had sent a tailor from Freiburg to the left and Asher's son to the right. After pausing, he'd also sent Asher to the right. He hadn't known what this meant until he'd whispered to a prisoner in the five-by-five bunk above him. Then he understood the tailor had been gassed.

As soon as Asher Englehardt began to make glasses, more and more officers wanted them. They didn't like rummaging through the collection from the gas chambers—a haphazard junk shop, annoying some and upsetting others, because they'd looked too long in the eyes of women and men and children who'd waited in the quaint little woods that concealed one of the gas chambers.

Some officers said that they liked the new frames made from melted Jew-gold. Others said they liked the way Asher asked questions—as though everything they said had significance. But there was also something else that brought them to that room, and this was the aura of calm Asher emanated while he tested the eyes of people who had killed his friends. It was a deep and almost audible sense of peace that Asher himself didn't understand—especially since his son Daniel was digging trenches in air so cold your tongue would stick to anything it touched. He saw Daniel at night when he brought him bread and extra food. The guards looked the other way. They knew about Goebbels's orders.

After a week, a bed appeared in his workroom so Asher could nap during the day. He slept, not caring if he'd be murdered. Since coming to Auschwitz, he hadn't been aware of dreams. The barracks were filled with stench. People were moaning and begging for water. At least one person was in the process of dying.

But now, in this quiet white room, Asher dreamt of his wife playing Schubert on the piano. And of Daniel playing with blocks on their living room floor. When he woke up, he still smelled burning flesh. He was still surrounded by barracks and bloodstained snow.

From time to time he thought of Martin Heidegger, who came for glasses every year and had visited him a few days before the shop was raided. The October day had been warm, and Heidegger wore lederhosen and an alpine hat. The SS man who was Asher's friend had just told him there wouldn't be enough coal to get through the winter and that they were cracking down on people with Aryan mothers and Jewish fathers, making Heidegger's visit strained and splitting Asher into two people—one an optometrist who joked and talked about philosophy, the other a terrified man who thought he and his son were about to die.

Heidegger sat in a high-backed chair looking at the alphabet while Asher changed lenses and made notes. He went along with Heidegger when he said—as he often did—how ironic that the first person he'd told about a revelation caused by his glasses became an optometrist.

Usually Asher could ignore his terror. He could joke that Heidegger's glasses were the only reason he'd become an optometrist—as though it had nothing to do with losing his teaching job or his father being Jewish. But on that particular day he struggled to remember what to say.

Heidegger's eyes were somewhat worse, and Asher said maybe he should switch to an Aryan optometrist—because these days you never knew. Heidegger waved him off and tried to cheer him up by telling him how disappointed he was in the Nazi Party.

I've warned them that they don't understand that machines have their own Being, he said. No vision. No guiding principles.

Vision always trumps machines, said Asher.

Heidegger nodded and told Asher he'd fallen out of the world as recently as a week ago. Elfriede Heidegger had been dishing out stew, the handle had broken, and the ladle fell into the pot. Without the ladle the handle became a ludicrous stick and eventually the whole kitchen felt tilted. Elfriede got irritated that he wasn't helping.

Martin, Asher said—as he always did—we're always in the world. So there's nothing at all to fall out of.

I know, said Heidegger.

Then why not just live here? said Asher.

Because no one can all the time.

Yet Asher had done it since Krystallnacht. After that night of broken glass, he'd never been able to sink into a soft, pillowy sense of comfort—however illusory. When he saw Daniel sleeping, he thought *he's safe for now*. When he got a loaf of fresh bread, he thought *this might be the last*. And when he saw people at the train station holding suitcases, he thought *Daniel and I might be next*. In this state, many things were soaked of meaning. Suitcases and bread were oblong shapes. A wrench didn't look that different from a spoon.

Asher tried to forget this last conversation with Heidegger the way he tried to forget all the conversations with people he couldn't talk to anymore. He tried to forget angry conversations with his wife, who'd joined the early Resistance and blamed him for not paying attention to the rise of the Party. And animated conversations with a woman—lovely, blond, compassionate—who became his lover when his wife disappeared. The woman had disappeared too.

As Asher ground lenses, he wondered if his eternal conversation with Heidegger about death was prescient because in Auschwitz people were pushed so closely against death they couldn't fall away from an awareness of mortality. The sweet smell of burning flesh permeated the camp. Shots blasted every few minutes.

Even the SS men walked rigidly, as if trying to not to hurtle into death. The whole camp reminded Asher of a ghoulish Black Forest of Being, a bizarre amusement park, with barracks instead of trees.

The only person who didn't seem to feel on the precipice of death was Asher's assistant, Sypco Van Hoot—a large, compassionate man who'd been a successful bank robber in Holland. His generosity confirmed the opinion at Auschwitz that bank robbers were the most trustworthy and straightforward of criminals because they'd always been honest about their motives. Sypco told Asher he'd gotten used to living with danger, so what was the difference now?

Sypco, who knew how to weld, took the lenses and Asher's instructions to another part of the camp to make frames. He always stopped at a place called Kanada, where inmates, most of them women, most of them beautiful, sorted possessions from new arrivals. Now and then Sypco brought Asher gifts from Kanada—a watch, a pair of shoes, a sweater. Asher gave them to Daniel, so he could use them to barter for food.

Two weeks after he'd been transferred to the clinic, Sypco brought him a suit and a fedora.

So they're going to shoot me in style, said Asher.

They never shoot anyone in style, said Sypco. It's too much trouble to take off good clothes.

Gas me in style, then.

They'd never give me anything from Kanada for someone who's about to die, said Sypco. It's too much trouble to sort again.

That night no one came to take him back to the barracks. Asher sat at his worktable, sure he was about to be shot. He was astonished and resentful that his instruments still gleamed and kept thinking about his son. After what seemed like hours, an officer brought him beef, potatoes, warm milk, a loaf of bread, and beer—another last meal. Only this time Asher was so used to food, it didn't occur to him not to eat. The same officer came back and helped him into the suit. When he put the fedora on his head, the officer looked at it critically, adjusting it until he was satisfied. Then they left the clinic.

Asher had seen Auschwitz many times at night, but now he imagined how his own blood would stain the snow. The searchlights would turn it black. By morning it would be pink.

By afternoon it would fade to rust. No one would give it any thought except Daniel, who would realize what happened when his father didn't answer roll call.

The officers' quarters was filled with drunken singing. One officer walked up to them, raised his stein, and spilled beer on Asher's shoes.

For God's sake, said the officer escorting him. If you can't hold your liquor, can't you at least hold your glass?

The other officer bowed and wiped Asher's shoes. They kept walking until they came to a large mahogany door.

You're honored, said the officer. This is where the Commandant entertains visitors.

Asher entered a wood-paneled room with leather armchairs and a fireplace with a fire—the first fire in four months he was sure wasn't meant for burning people. The Commandant stood in front of the fireplace, a man in an SS uniform to his right, and Martin Heidegger next to him. He wore a ski outfit and an alpine hat.

What on earth are you doing here? said Asher.

My friend, said Heidegger. I had to see you. He walked over and put his arms around Asher. My God, he said. How do you spend your time here?

Making glasses, said Asher.

You came all the way for that?

Yes. But it was worth it.

They laughed, and entered a realm no one else could follow—the realm of old friends and private jokes.

For a moment there was a festive feeling in the room. But when the Commandant told everyone to sit down and poured brandy, the air was imbued with silence. The silence continued until the SS officer pointed to a 17th-century painting of a man with a ruched collar.

That's a wonderful Rembrandt, he said.

The Commandant nodded. We went to a lot of trouble to get it.

Everyone should go to trouble to find roots in the past, said Heidegger.

Exactly, said the Commandant.

To Das Volk, said Heidegger, raising his glass.

Well put, said the Commandant.

The Commandant cleared his throat and Heidegger took a paper from his ski suit. It was covered with dried soup and strands of potato peels.

Did you write this letter? he said.

Asher looked at a letter he was sure he hadn't written. But he saw his own signature. Had he written it in his sleep? The letter was about poetry and the mystery of the triangle and the word *to distance* as in *I distanced myself from the controversy.* He never would have written such a letter. Yet his signature was there. And the wrong answer could get him shot.

I can't say, he said.

For God's sake, said Heidegger. I need to know. Because if you wrote this, the whole world has gone mad.

The Commandant laughed. Let's drink to that, he said. The sanity of the world depends on who answered a letter.

You don't understand, said Heidegger. This man was my colleague. He brought Leibniz to the modern age. The two of us *think.*

I don't do that anymore, said Asher.

You mean you *did* write the letter?

At this point three shots rang out. The Commandant walked to a gramophone and put on Mozart's piano concerto in C Major.

I'm sorry for the commotion he said, turning the handle of the gramophone as though it were a meat grinder.

Well did you? said Heidegger.

What? said Asher.

Write the letter.

It's been so long.

But you can't have, said Heidegger. You have a remarkable mind. Believe me, he said, turning to the Commandant. You have no idea who you're talking to. It's not just a question of whatever little thing you might have read in school about whether trees make a noise when they fall in the forest. This man understands Leibniz.

The Commandant raised his fists to either side of his head and pulled his hair. Then he poured Asher more brandy.

You can talk freely here, he said to him. You're a privileged person. Believe me—he addressed the SS officer—this man has been given everything. And he makes wonderful glasses.

I know, said Heidegger. I always go to him. And I never got the last ones he made.

Well, now he makes glasses for officers, said the Commandant. And they're very pleased with them. He has every assurance of continuing.

Every assurance of continuing could mean *is just about to be shot.* Asher wondered if his status as a philosopher made his death deserve a witness like Heidegger. The SS officer seemed to share his mistrust because he said there was probably one thing Asher wasn't sure about at all and this was being able to go on living.

No one gets that anymore—not even me, said the Commandant.

There were more shots outside the window. The Commandant turned up Mozart.

You see? he said. I can't even ask for quiet.

Then why did you bring me here? said Heidegger. We're in a room with a fireplace, and my friend looks like a ghost. There are gunshots outside, and we can't even hear. This whole place is tilted.

How could anything be tilted? said the Commandant. We're in a pleasant room. We've just made a toast to the past. There's no place that's safe to talk anymore.

I can think of other places that are safer, said the officer.

Where? said the Commandant. That ridiculous alpine hut where this pontificator lives? Or the street in Holland where they wiped out twenty people for hiding two fugitives?

No one spoke. The phone rang, and the Commandant didn't answer. When the ringing stopped, he said:

I understand you gentleman have matters that are best talked about in private. So we'll leave you in peace. Help yourself to brandy.

He left with the officer, and Asher faced Heidegger alone. The Mozart concerto intensified his sense that he was in Freiburg: his wife had played this piece many times. But he kept himself from lapsing into a feeling of well-being and looked carefully at the man sitting opposite him. Was this really Heidegger, or someone pretending to be? And would a philosophical discussion be a prelude to death?

But this person was so bulbous in his ski suit—indeed it seemed as though the chair was about to extrude him—Asher decided he was really Martin Heidegger.

190

Martin, he said, leaning over and touching his shoulder, you came all this way.

I had to, said Heidegger. You didn't answer my letter.

I never got it.

But why did you leave in the first place?

To make glasses.

Did you ever make mine?

Yes, but I don't know if you got them, said Asher. Don't you remember I told you to find another optometrist?

I thought you were joking.

I wasn't.

The Commandant stuck his head in the door and wanted to know if they'd finished their conversation. Heidegger said not at all. The Commandant disappeared and Heidegger fell silent. Then he said:

What were we laughing about when you first came in?

I can't remember, said Asher.

Something about *but it was worth it,* said Heidegger, looking around as though he could find the joke. But it had vanished beyond the walls. So he reached for something else.

Did you know I'm not teaching anymore? he said.

You told me, said Asher.

I miss it, said Heidegger.

But you said you were writing.

Not every minute of the day. And it's hard to escape mortality without teaching.

I thought not trying to escape was the highest calling, said Asher.

It is, said Heidegger. But no one can do that all the time. The hut is darker than it used to be. I can even smell the darkness.

You should write about that, said Asher.

I already have, said Heidegger. What else is there to say?

But Asher didn't want to explain. He'd lost the marrow of friendship during Heidegger's visits to his shop. And whatever was left had been destroyed by what he'd seen at Auschwitz. So instead of elaborating he leaned forward and said:

Martin, I hope you understand that your interest in man's awareness of mortality has a different kind of meaning in a place where just wearing the wrong pair of shoes can get you shot.

I don't know what you're talking about.

I'm amazed you don't, said Asher. I'm amazed you don't know that people here are forced to remember their mortality in the most horrible conditions. And no one ever asked them if they wanted to think about it in the first place.

How am I supposed to know about things like that? said Heidegger.

The rising timbre of his voice made the Commandant open the door.

Have you gentlemen come to a conclusion yet?

Heidegger said they hadn't and the Commandant left. Heidegger stood by the fireplace.

What's the real reason you didn't you answer my letter? he said.

I told you. I didn't get it.

Don't they mail letters here?

No.

I've never heard of anything so stupid. Letters should be mailed. That's what they're for.

The Commandant opened the door.

You're shouting, he said. We don't allow that.

I don't care what you allow, said Heidegger. You can't even deliver a letter.

The phone rang again. The Commandant pulled his hair. When the ringing stopped, he turned to the SS man and said:

He's making a nuisance of himself. The next thing he'll be yodeling. And the Jew's heard too much. So take him where you came from, or we'll deal with him some other way. But whatever you decide about the Jew, this alpine asshole has to go. And understand you're on your own. All I can give you is a Kubelwagen to the station.

The SS officer nodded, and they shook hands. The Commandant looked sadly at Heidegger.

I'd like to have him shot, he said. But after the war they might make him a national treasure.

He has immunity, said the officer dryly.

Indeed, said the Commandant. And I happen to have some good news for you, he said turning to Heidegger. You and your friend can talk in peace.

Where? said Heidegger.

On the way to the train. Without this damned noise.

I can't leave without my son, said Asher.

My God, said the Commandant, pretty soon you'll be asking for caviar. What's his cellblock?

Asher told him. It was different from his.

You inmates, said the Commandant. Every night's a talkfest, and we keep working.

He opened the door and collared a guard:

I'll send you to the front, if you don't get me this prisoner in five minutes, he said.

Then he filled his glass with brandy, not offering it to anybody else.

Nothing has gone the way we planned, he said. I told them not to make any noise for once, but they never listen. Those fucking disorganized transports.

There was a huge map of Germany on the right side of the fireplace. The Commandant walked to it, unmasked a vault, and began to pull out food. Asher saw enormous hams, bottles of champagne, cases of wine, gargantuan rounds of cheese, heavy blocks of chocolate. The Commandant pulled randomly, threw everything into a duffel bag and shoved it at the SS man.

Take it. Take it all, he said. And keep the fuck quiet about this.

Then he opened the door and yelled: Where's that goddamn kid in the cellblock?

The cellblocks were far away from the officers' quarters, but within

minutes the guard brought in a boy. He was thin, with shrewd blue eyes like his father. The Commandant threw him a coat.

You're about to travel, he said. Put this on.

Daniel's face went white.

Put it on, said the Commandant. You're going with your father.

Asher looked at his son. For over four months he'd been a shadow, reaching for food by the barracks in the dark. Now he was in a warm room, not unlike the room he'd grown up in, with music his mother once played. Who knew what would happen? Who knew where they were going? Still, Asher mouthed the words: *you're safe.*

A door opened. A Kubelwagen appeared. They entered a snow-covered field without searchlights, guards, or fences. Asher had a vague sense that he was part of something that was never supposed to happen. But all he could see was his son.

194

Heidegger grew small as the train gathered speed, and Lodenstein watched him disappear. He was alone in the station, illuminated by one light from the platform shelter. Heidegger paced back and forth, jabbed the snows with his walking stick, and lectured to the dark, still without his glasses. Eventually he became a speck, and then the station disappeared. Lodenstein turned back to the car, which was mysteriously empty. Perhaps the Commandant had ordered it that way, so no one could hear Heidegger's rants or see two skeletons from Auschwitz. With Heidegger gone, only Asher and Daniel were left, asleep in near-darkness. For a moment Asher woke up, and Lodenstein handed him sausage. He shook his head and went back to sleep.

And now a porter appeared and asked Lodenstein if he was thirsty. He ordered lemonade and the porter seemed startled—no one ever drank lemonade in winter. But he brought it to him quickly—the SS uniform impressed him—and Lodenstein gulped it down, wishing it would go to his blood like an instant transfusion. He felt empty, like a bag of flour that's been pummeled and pounded, and neither he nor the train seemed quite real. He'd had to listen to Heidegger's rants since leaving Auschwitz and was more than glad to see him exit at the last stop—barreling off the train, gesturing with schnapps, still pontificating. Lodenstein couldn't believe Asher had slept through the whole thing. But now everything was quiet, and the train rumbled through the dark with a soft, comforting rhythm.

The lemonade reminded Lodenstein of summer, and he wished he could slip back into a summer childhood, where the only evidence of war was trenches he built with his friends. At dinner, his mother had fits about his muddy shoes, and his father tried to convince him that deciphering codes was far more exciting than battle. But he couldn't slip away into anything because the past three weeks felt ground into his body like glass.

He was seared by his memory of the cell, where he'd floated to the ceiling, and Goebbels's eyes and the Commandant's hair-pulling and gunshots and blood on the snow—all of which he'd endured to save Elie Schacten's life.

For a moment, his actions seemed opaque, as if he were watching someone he didn't understand. He looked carefully at Asher and Daniel, who were close together, as if carved from a single stone. They seemed like an ordinary father and son on the verge of starvation. But they weren't just a father and a son. They were two more fugitives on the way to the Compound.

Lodenstein kicked the duffel bag the Commandant had given him then realized it had enough food for almost two weeks. La Toya could make soup from the sausage. The chocolate would delight Dmitri. Everyone would enjoy real coffee. He understood Elie's excitement about bringing extra loaves of bread, an abundance of ham. He'd always worked to keep the Compound safe—written ridiculous letters to Goebbels, been civil to Mueller, who probably wanted him shot. He'd even let Stumpf make Scribes imagine Goebbels, because it would soften his rants. But bringing food to the Compound and helping cope with hunger—this was new. He'd started to think like Elie.

Yet in truth, he could hardly remember her. She was a haze of blond curls and tea-rose perfume. He imagined reaching for her in the dark, telling her about being thrown in jail, and talking to Goebbels. And then about the shots at Auschwitz and Heidegger's rants on the train. He was holding her while he talked. And she was listening. But whom would he be telling this to? The Elie who flirted with officers? The one who'd once knew Heidegger? Or the Elie he made love to under the grey quilt? He'd always tried not to think about what Elie did to get what they needed on forays. He tried to make whatever she did outside the Compound into motes that barely touched her. Elie did, too: he could feel her shaking them off with her coat when she came back.

Lodenstein kicked the duffel bag again. Daniel and Asher made whimpering noises in their sleep. It was the whimpering of people who'd been beaten, abused and didn't know if they'd wake up the next day. Yet the sound annoyed him, as did the odor of sausage from the duffel bag and the warm air in the train.

He walked between the cars and looked out to the snow and pines. Now and then he saw a house leak light from blackout curtains just like cracks in Hanussen's globe. He supposed the train had crossed from Poland into Germany but wasn't sure. He could be anywhere.

Before he'd left Heidegger had shoved Mikhail's letter at him, and he was still holding it—a catalyst in this absurd chain. It had traveled from the Compound to the Black Forest, then to offices in the Reich and to Auschwitz. It had been stolen, crumpled, shoved into a soup tureen. It was creased, covered with dried soup. It looked as if it couldn't survive another journey.

Lodenstein raised the letter to the light and tried to read it, but the words made no sense at all. Indeed each letter of the alphabet looked like a tiny person in Hanussen's theater. Some were crowded in the middle, others were alone at the end of the aisle. But a few tumbled into a string of words:

The triangle is the most paradoxical of human situations. It is the secret of all covenants and a cause of betrayal. Indeed, it's a great challenge to the human heart because it has the power to create incredible good and cause incredible grief, as well as induce states of ecstasy and lunacy. Making a triangle with integrity is in the service of God.

He found the letter bizarrely true, as well as ironic, because the letter itself was the essence of betrayal. By Elie. And by the Solomons, whom he'd always trusted. It was the reason he'd traveled to Berlin, seen Goebbels, gotten thrown in jail. It was the reason he'd taken Heidegger to Auschwitz and heard gunshots accompanied by Mozart. It was the reason he'd trashed his room and for all the fights he'd had with Elie. It was the reason for everything. This letter would never get an answer. It should never have been written in the first place.

He opened his hand and let the letter loose. For a moment it was pinned to the car by the wind. Then it fluttered in the dark until the train gained distance and it disappeared.

Fugitives

Chers grand-maman et grand-papa,

j'ai été ici pendant juste une semaine et déjà je remplis hors de mes vêtements. Il y a des bois à jouer dedans, beaucoup de neige et un endroit spécial où ils conservent des lapins avec de longs cheveux. J'ai même obtenu de les alimenter une fois. Il y a abondance de l'eau et un bon nombre de gens intéressants. C'était un long voyage à cet endroit merveilleux. C'est le meilleur endroit au monde.

Amour,
Rene

* * *

Dear Grandma and Grandpa,

I have been here for just a week and already I am filling out my clothes. There are woods to play in, lots of snow, and a special place where they keep rabbits with long hair. I even get to feed them. There is plenty of water and a lot of interesting people. It was a long journey to this wonderful place. It's the best place in the world.

Love,
Rene

One afternoon, blond wasted Gitka leaned over Maria's desk and offered her a white velvet rose.

We're both Poles, she said, and we know how to sleep our way in the world.

Maria had never told anyone she was Polish. She spoke German without an accent and only answered letters in Italian and French. It frightened her that Gitka read her like an X-ray.

I want to teach you about silence, Gitka said.

I have to work, said Maria, who was in fact reading.

No one works here, said Gitka. And Die Gnädige Frau is sewing.

This was how she referred to Elie, who was in fact leafing through her dark red notebook. Her face was pale, and she bit her lower lip. Dmitri sat on a high stool next to her, sorting stamps.

You see? said Gitka. She doesn't eat. She doesn't sleep. And she never laughs unless she's talking to the little mouse. All she thinks about is him. And she never cared if we worked anyway. So let me teach you something.

She led Maria to a room on the back wall of the main room—the room where Elie had lived before moving in with

Lodenstein. It was dark, cavernous, cool, surrounded by the mine on three sides.

This is the first place that's soundproof, said Gitka. Except it's never empty.

She opened the door wider, and Maria saw Niles Schopenhauer on top of Sophie Nachtgarten.

The point is, my little friend: never come here to talk.

I never did, said Maria.

Good, said Gitka. So now you never will.

She led Maria from the large mahogany door, past the wrought iron benches and the kitchen. It was mid-afternoon, and the artificial sun listed towards the west, dappling the artificial pear tree and the rose bushes in front of the Solomons' small and peculiar house. Lars, who was standing by the door peeling an apple, waved at them. They walked further down to the dead-end of the street where there was a wall of earth. Gitka guided Maria's hands around the *trompe l'oeil*—a perfect arch that camouflaged the tunnel. She traced one of Maria's fingers around the metal key hole.

It's a door, she said, when Maria looked confused. And it leads to the second place where everything is silent. But it's locked, and no one has the key. Besides, who'd ever want to? It leads to a tunnel where the Gestapo take people from town and shoot them.

You don't scare me, said Maria. I came from a place much worse.

But her fingers were trembling as she traced the door. Gitka smiled and didn't answer. She turned around and stopped at a door opposite the Solomons'. It opened to a small room piled with wooden crates stamped *Geantwortet.*

This place is soundproof, too, Gitka said. But they store the letters here, so no one tries to fit inside.

I never knew it was here.

Well, now you do. Forget you saw it.

Then Gitka took Maria to the smallest water closet and opened the vent above it. She pointed to a stool and told Maria to climb into the opening. Maria said she didn't understand, and Gitka said *if you get up on the fucking stool, you'd see what I mean.* Maria got up on the stool, and when they had settled themselves in the jagged dark Gitka said:

This is where you come when you need to say something you don't want anyone to hear.

Maria said, Fine, thank you, and was about to climb down when Gitka came so close Maria smelled her cigarette-breath, her incongruously expensive perfume, and the slightly mildewed odor of her fur coat. Gitka touched her with her hand and Maria felt her nails. They were long, and Maria could almost see the red nail polish in the dark. Wait, said Gitka. Because I have this soundproof thing to say to you. You can have Parvis Nafissian. But stay away from Ferdinand La Toya.

I never thought of going near him.

Good. Keep it that way.

Someone came into the water closet and took a long, languid piss. Then someone else came in and began to climb up into the vent.

It's occupied, said Gitka.

I'm sorry, said a voice. It was Elie Schacten. After she left, Gitka lit another cigarette.

I bet she's lost ten pounds since he's gone, said Maria. All she does is worry.

All of us do, said Gitka. Believe me. She's not the only one. She exhaled, and the air filled with smoke. So—are we clear about Ferdinand?

Yes, said Maria, who didn't say she hated his cigars.

Good. Then we can leave.

Gitka ground her cigarette into a wall, and they climbed down back into the water closet. Gitka pulled her coat around her shoulders and put another cigarette in her long black holder.

Not everybody wants young ginch, she said.

After Elie Schacten was banished from the vent, she walked down the cobblestone street with Generalmajor Mueller who had arrived just fifteen minutes ago, unannounced, to—in his words—see how Elie Schacten was doing. Elie was panic-stricken. She pulled Dmitri to the coats against the wall and whispered to a Scribe to hide him at the Solomons.

Mueller had been lucky, he'd told Elie: he hadn't gone to the front, but stayed in the Reich Chancellery working on a special project. When he mentioned the project, he closed his eyes, exuding intrigue. He worked in an underground library, where precious documents were stored. And that was how he'd heard Lodenstein was in solitary confinement: no, not in the regular jail, but in a cell that looked like a waiting room. Goebbels threw him in the minute he showed up. And then he'd let him out so he could take that fool of a philosopher to Auschwitz. But now two prisoners were missing. And it was all over the Reich that Lodenstein had taken them. Who knew what would happen if they caught them? And this is why Mueller came to the Compound, when he knew Elie was alone. He wanted to console her.

Who knows where they went? said Mueller. I don't think he'll ever come back here.

Maybe they're only rumors, said Elie.

Goebbels doesn't spread rumors, said Mueller.

But why didn't the Commandant stop him? said Elie.

Mueller pulled his eyebrows together.

Goebbels and the Commandant have a score to settle. So probably nothing will happen. Yet.

Elie suggested they go to the vent to talk in private. She planned to climb up first and shoot Mueller through the eyes so he would never discover Dmitri or threaten anybody in the Compound again. While they walked down the cobblestone street, she remembered what Goebbels had told her about shooting people. *You're hand is just talking to the trigger. It's only the gun that's doing it.* She thought this while she hurried him past the Solomons' house and into the water closet. But the vent was occupied, so they had to retrace their steps. Elie let Mueller hold her arm.

They passed the Solomons' house again. Dmitri, who was by the lead-paned window, ducked, and Elie pointed to the cumulous clouds in the sky. Her hands were shaking.

What was that? said Mueller, looking at the window.

The Solomons' cat, said Elie.

Since when did those Jews have a cat?

Months.

What's it called?

Mufti.

A cat with a name like that should stay outside, said Mueller.

They'd come to the end of the hall. He sat on a bench near the mineshaft. He patted the space next to him.

Sit down, he said. I want to know how I can help you.

Elie forced herself to sit down, and Mueller pressed his ring against her shoulder—so hard it felt like he was stamping her flesh with it. La Toya stuck his head out from the main room, and Mueller glared at him.

Who can talk near this joke of a workplace? he said.

No one, said Elie. Let's go upstairs.

And this time, she thought, *nothing can stop me from shooting you.*

Mueller hugged her in the mineshaft and walked up the incline, holding her hand, saying they were doing a minuet, and it was a shame the bed made the room too small to dance. But when they got to the door his face crumpled like a paper bag, and he leaned against the lintel.

My good man, he said, as though he were talking to the air. I thought you'd left us forever.

Elie turned and saw Gerhardt Lodenstein standing by the clerestory windows, staring into space. She had thought she'd never see him again. Yet now he stood in front of her—intact, vibrant—like people who've died and appear in dreams. He hadn't shaved and was wearing his rumpled green sweater, which he'd rummaged for quickly, scattering socks on the floor, throwing his compass on the bed. This delighted Elie, who normally hated clutter. It convinced her that he really was back. She raced over to him, he took her in his arms, and she started to cry. Mueller fussed with a medal on his coat. Eventually he said:

I hear you had quite a journey.

Lodenstein looked at Mueller as though he was about to say something dangerous. But he managed to smile and shake Mueller's hand.

It was good of you to come, he said.

How could I not, with poor Fraulein Schacten alone and you going through such dreadful things?

You mean the rumors that fly around like crows? Nothing was dreadful. Even that green waiting room.

Mueller plucked at his medal again, and Lodenstein picked up the duffel bag Mueller had brought in anticipation of spending the night.

I wish I could offer you brandy. But they want you back in Berlin.

What do you mean?

I don't know. It's secret, like all your missions.

Elie heard the conversation as if she were in a trance. She walked outside with the two men, and they crossed the stone path, their boots making sharp noises. A wind blew fresh snow in their direction, and Elie held Lodenstein's arm, afraid he'd disappear into the snow if she didn't hold on to him. When they came to Mueller's Kubelwagen, Mueller grabbed the duffel bag from Lodenstein and threw it on the ground. He took out his knife. Elie put her hand on her revolver.

Are you satisfied, my good man? Mueller said.

With what? said Lodenstein.

The results.

No one's satisfied these days, said Lodenstein.

Really? Mueller took out a handkerchief and began to polish his knife as though he were buttering toast. People just aren't themselves anymore, he said.

Goebbels seemed to be.

That's because you don't know him as well as I do, said Mueller. By the way, he said, an extra cat's not a problem. Or maybe even a kid – although that could turn out to be serious. But two fugitives are different.

That's why we don't have them, said Lodenstein.

Good, said Mueller. Because one of these days Goebbels really will visit. Except he might send someone who looks just like him. Or there will be ten people who pretend to be him. What I mean is—you're asking for trouble.

209

I don't know what you mean.

Maybe you can play Persian Patience. But you don't know how to bluff, said Mueller. So I think you do know.

He held his knife up to the sun—Elie could see light quivering in the blade. Then he put it away, moved closer to Elie, and took Lodenstein by the sleeves: Elie saw his greased hair and smelled his loathsome pomade.

The Reich's just like any other office with a mission, he said. In the long run, people die when they show up in the wrong places. And so do the people who hide them.

Only a fool doesn't know that, said Lodenstein.

Then there are some fools around here, said Mueller.

Lodenstein smiled and shook Mueller's hand. It seemed twice as large in its leather glove.

Have a safe journey, he said.

Mueller took off, his Kubelwagen rumbling over the road like a dangerous beast. Elie and Lodenstein watched it turn the bend. Then, Lodenstein rushed her back to the hut, saying it was cold, and walked over to his jeep. It was just starting to be dusk, and the light had shifted to a milky haze; a time of half-sleep, where the edges of the world begin to lose their hard outlines. Elie saw a confusion of blankets in the jeep, unearthly cloth that seemed to move by itself. Then she saw two figures emerge—so thin and insubstantial, they could have been smoke or shadows. Lodenstein shrouded them in more blankets. Then all three walked towards the shepherd's hut. Elie began to shake when she heard the ice crack. It was as though a spring had uncoiled inside her, as though every moment she'd ever lived was coming together at once. The figures came to the door.

Elie Kowaleski, said a voice in the cloth. Is that you?

Elie couldn't stop staring at Asher's face while he sat on the cobblestone street, staring at the pretend sky. It didn't look like a real face, but grey skin stretched over bones, an assemblage of angles and hollows, a vehicle for exhaustion and starvation— but not a face. The skin stretched over it was taut. The flesh beneath it was gone. His eyes were the only thing that seemed alive. Yet she could see everything in that face, as if his entire life were etched in the lines. She could sense every gunshot he'd heard at Auschwitz, every moment he'd seen people die, every day he'd lived in terror. And the person she'd known at Freiburg, she could see that too: The man who worried about his wife and gave exhilarating lectures about Leibniz. The man who read at night in a room full of books.

She and Lodenstein were pulling crates from the storage room Gitka had shown Maria hours before. It would be a bedroom for Asher and Daniel. They bent and swayed with the rhythm of people who are used to working together, as though they'd never been apart—and this surprised Elie. She suddenly remembered Lodenstein's great strength. Crates seemed weightless when he lifted them. And the characteristic way he pushed back his hair, quickly, as if he didn't have a moment to waste. The stack got top-heavy, and he moved crates near the *trompe l'oeil* that led to the tunnel. Elie found mattresses, blankets, lanterns, and a Tiffany lamp for the one wall socket. She stopped at the Solomons to look in on Dmitri. Then she and Lodenstein went to the kitchen for water.

My god, I missed you, said Elie handing him a glass.

I missed you, too. You don't know how much.

Are you upset that he knows me?

Not now. I'm just glad to see you.

Are you saying that to be nice? Or do you mean it?

For the most part, said Lodenstein.

Asher began to cough, and Elie brought him a glass of water. Daniel was still in the street looking at the paralyzed sky. Asher had moved to a mattress in the storage room.

Don't ever say my last name here, she said to him. I'm Elie Schacten now.

Asher smiled. So you found yourself an alias. Like everyone else in this war. Did you just get new papers—or were you baptized?

Elie said she'd gotten new papers, and realized she couldn't remember the way she and Asher used to talk. It was a language of nuances, irony, and double meanings. Now she spoke a language of crisis that was urgent, truncated, and literal. Sometimes it surged with intimacy and shared revelations, the way people confide when they're never going to see each other again. But beyond moments of peril, suspense, and exhilaration, she'd never spent much time in the company of someone she'd helped rescue. Finally she said:

Was it safe for you on the train?

I doubt it. I tried to sleep, but I kept wondering if we'd all be shot. The only thing that made it bearable was Gerhardt Lodenstein. I think he's some kind of angel, and I don't even believe in them.

I do too, said Elie. And I don't believe in them either.

But where did he bring us? To a heaven that's run by pulleys?

He brought you to a place where we answer letters from people who are probably dead by now.

Asher flinched. They must have a lot of work then, he said.

Elie wished she could remember how to joke, if only to erase the look she saw on his face.

They only write to people whose letters are returned, she said. These—she pointed the crates—are where they put the answers.

Returned from where? said Asher.

From the camps, said Elie.

Did you ever get a letter from me?

No, said Elie. But we got a letter for you, along with your prescription for Heidegger's glasses. It's a small part of why you're here.

They were interrupted by Stumpf, who walked past them with mincing steps and arranged crates near the *trompe l'oeil.*

Asher noticed Stumpf's uniform and edged toward the wall. You have guards here, he said.

He's a lackey, said Elie. No one to worry about.

I don't think so, said Asher. I think this place is just like Thierenstadt.

He was talking about a camp in Czechoslovakia with a few pleasant streets and decent houses that were facades for visits from the Red Cross. Children sang in an opera and were sent to Auschwitz to be gassed the next day.

Nobody dies here, said Elie.

What a comfort.

Elie looked at Asher directly. And there they were: the same blue eyes she'd seen at Freiburg.

Did you really go to Auschwitz? she asked.

Asher stared at her the way he once stared when Elie said she was sure his wife was safe. Elie looked at her hands. They were dappled with red and white light from the Tiffany lamp, and she turned them at different angles until Lodenstein arrived with two bowls of soup. Only two bowls of soup? Where was the sausage and Knäckebrot?

I'll get your dinner, she said to Asher with relief.

That night, Elie and Lodenstein stayed in Mueller's old room so they could be close to Asher and Daniel, who were resting in the room that had once stored the crates. They were near the main part of the Compound, and could hear Scribes cry out in sleep—a sound Lodenstein once found eerie and now found comforting because they were familiar and human, not the clinking of a jailer's keys or the shots at Auschwitz. He'd felt close to Elie when they said goodnight to Asher and Daniel. And he felt close to her when they said goodnight to Dmitri. They'd spoken softly, the way they'd say goodnight to children. But now he felt an uncanny tension, as though the air between them was vibrating with taut string. He leaned over and opened the duffel bag he had brought back from Auschwitz.

Elie, I have a surprise for you. You know all the food you get? I've finally gotten some too.

My God, said Elie. You do enough.

Lodenstein uncorked a bottle of wine and handed it to her.

The best, he said. And now people who deserve it can drink it.

Elie smiled and leaned against him.

I'm sorry I never told you my real name.

It's a long name, said Lodenstein. I would never have remembered it.

Are you trying to be nice?

Only a little. But I just want to know—were you two ever lovers?

Elie hesitated. Then she said:

At Freiburg. His wife was gone. The Party was starting. And both of us were lonely.

Lodenstein took a long drink of wine and rubbed a hand over his face as though he were trying to erase something.

It doesn't matter anymore, he said finally. What matters is we saved two people.

He reached for Elie in the dark. But Elie sat up and hugged her knees.

That's not the least of it, she whispered.

The least of what?

The least of anything. Mueller knows.

What do you mean?

Mueller knows that you left Auschwitz with two fugitives. He says it's all over the Reich. He says people are gossiping.

People gossip all the time, and nothing comes of it, said Lodenstein. Don't think about it. Have some more wine.

But he even saw Dmitri.

Don't worry, said Lodenstein. Dmitri's safe. Asher and Daniel are safe. All of us are safe.

He set down the wine and repeated the words—*Don't worry, Don't worry*—so often they began to seem like a lullaby. Elie opened the covers and he fell against her. It had been so long since he'd felt her supple strength. And so long since he'd felt that sensation of light, binding them together. And making love felt like the long culmination of all the moments when he'd thought about her—in the brick-laden jail, in the vast bed in the Reich holding her rose, traveling on an empty train from Auschwitz. Elie fell asleep. He stroked her hair and began to drift off, feeling the tension from his body ease out onto the floor. But just as he came to the edge of sleep, he clamored awake. In his exuberance at being with Elie—hearing her voice, sharing wine, making love—he'd forgotten they were in Mueller's old room. But now he saw the posts of the rosewood bed like masts of a ghost ship on dangerous seas. He saw Mueller's knife. He felt his huge leather glove. He heard his voice talking about fugitives. *An unspeakable act of treason,* he could hear him saying. *An arrow of death pointing to everything below the ground.* Lodenstein threw off the covers. Here, in the heart of the Compound, he suddenly felt buried under ten meters of dirt. He'd gone to jail, weathered Goebbels, traveled to Auschwitz, endured Heidegger, rescued two people. But the danger was boundless, infinite. He had no idea what to do. He only knew he had to breathe.

Lodenstein took the mineshaft and passed Lars, who looked young and untroubled asleep on a pallet, into the freezing night. At that moment he despised everything about the Compound: the fake hut, the cobblestone street, the playing cards from people who'd been gassed. He despised the front path with stones broken purposefully because Hans Ewigkeit wanted them to look old. He despised the fact that something that never should have been there in the first place had been made to look like it belonged.

He heard his own boots break the ice that filled the brittle field and climbed the narrow ladder to the watchtower. It was dark, and the stars were faraway, small white flies he could never touch. He looked for cigarettes on the platform of the watchtower and found a stub. Thank god he had matches.

All at once he became aware of his hands, his legs, his whole body. He hadn't been alone since he'd driven to Berlin, and the sensation was both familiar and unsettling. His breathing slowed. His heart ached a bit less. He touched the wooden railing and looked at the wide night sky. It was clear, with a panoply of stars. He looked down at the clearing where mounds of snow billowed in the moonlight. He looked back at the sky, still shot through with distant light.

It occurred to him that stars had always fallen in and out of the world. Sometimes they were lights. Sometimes they were angels, animals, or gods. Sometimes they were dazzling. Sometimes he couldn't see them at all. He took a deep breath, watched thin smoke float from his mouth, and decided that Heidegger probably understood what it felt like to fall out of a world made safe by human meaning. A fragile world, he thought. Poised to fall apart.

This sense of union with Heidegger's philosophy, however tenuous, and however much he disliked Heidegger, made him feel sure nothing would ever get worse than it already was. But his sad sense of tranquility was destroyed as soon as he finished the cigarette. He pawed the wooden platform for more discarded butts and only got splinters in his hands.

The woods rustled—a deer darting through the pines. Lodenstein looked at the stars again and wished he could believe they were angels so he could ask them to keep everyone here safe. But he'd spent enough time in the Compound to know that everyone had a moment of believing in something or other, and was sure he could only believe in what he thought would probably happen: The SS would take them by storm, discover Asher, drag every Scribe and fugitive to the cobblestone street and shoot them, one by one. He and Elie would be forced to witness every death before they themselves were shot because they were the most responsible.

He looked for more cigarettes, couldn't find any, tore a rotting beam from the watchtower, and hurled it below. Every pine tree was a Gestapo. Every clearing a minefield. Every stone a torpedo. He climbed down from the watchtower, tripped on the plank, and hurled it to where Mueller had parked his Kubelwagen. He wished the plank were a gun, and he could shoot Mueller between the eyes.

When he came downstairs, Elie was sitting up in bed.

Are we safe? she said.

No, he said. We aren't safe at all.

Marianne,

Non so se otterrete questa lettera in questa casa pazza. La gente è sul bordo di fuoriuscita, allora perde il cuore, prova per fuoriuscire comunque, solo essere colpo. L'altra gente di giorno due ha buttato giù due uomini degli ss, messo sopra le loro uniformi ed ha eliminato in uno dei loro camion. Osserva come lo ha fatto attraverso il bordo. Con tanta gente che va, ho razioni del supplemento e ve li conservo tutte per.

Amore,
Luca

*   *   *

Marianne,

I don't know if you'll get this letter in this mad house. People are on the verge of escaping, then lose heart, then try to escape anyway, only to be shot. The other day two people knocked two SS men out, put on their uniforms and drove off in one of their trucks. It looks like they made it across the border. There were ten hangings from their cellblock. With so many making plans, I was able to sell my extra shoes for a loaf of bread. So I have more for you.

Love,
Luca

Ever since he'd been brought in, shrouded under blankets, Asher Englehardt hadn't known what to make of the Compound. The frozen sky and the enormous room where over fifty people in fur coats and fingerless gloves spent hours answering the dead or writing in an imaginary language—not to mention bizarre word games, lotteries for half-smoked cigarettes and cries during the night—was the stuff of purgatory. What was once obviously a mine now contained a cobblestone street, gas lamps, and wrought-iron benches. Even the sky was confused: The moon was always a crescent. The sun groaned when it rose and set. The stars were always the same, night after night.

At times it was hard for Asher to know whether the people here were alive, dead, or in a limbo. A woman with whom he'd once had an affair and hadn't thought about in years had mysteriously reappeared and now left food outside his door. Letters to the dead sat outside his room in crates. The guard with the SS uniform wore wooly slippers.

And two people and a wraith of a child lived opposite his makeshift room with a Tiffany lamp in a little house with a number, even though the street didn't have a name. Asher made a point of avoiding them because Daniel, who heard gossip, said the woman had forged his signature, and the man had written the utterly ridiculous letter to Heidegger—a letter that might have saved his life, but nonetheless had frightened him at Auschwitz. He made furtive trips to the kitchen for coffee and steered clear of the water closet that concealed a secret cavern in its ceiling. He never went to the main room where the Scribes talked and slept and instead kept to himself, reading the detective stories Lodenstein brought to him.

Daniel, on the other hand, discovered the main room on his third day and began to look human after two weeks of eating everything Elie brought him. He also learned how to fix typewriters and sometimes showed them to Asher, littering the floor with keys, spools, carriages—amazing Asher with his ability to take them apart and put them back together so effortlessly. He'd also begun to sleep with Maria, creating a scene with Parvis Nafissian, who yelled at him and called him a *putz*.

Daniel told Asher that the other Scribes were in awe of him and viewed him as nearly mythic. He'd come from a place they'd managed to avoid and was proof that such a place existed— and proof that some people could survive there and return.

At first, the Scribes asked Daniel if he'd seen any of their relatives and friends. They mentioned name after name, places and cities halfway across Europe, described faces in detail. When they realized he'd never met them, not even one, they began to ask about the camp. Invariably, they asked the same question:

Were there real chimneys with real smoke?

Yes, Daniel would say. There were real chimneys. And the smoke coming from them smelled sweet.

He complained to his father that no one ever asked about beheadings by candlelight or people getting shot every morning at roll call. Asher said this was because chimneys used to be part of something safe and every house with a fireplace had one.

So if there are chimneys, he concluded, people understand how something safe can turn into something dangerous.

It had been almost a month since they'd arrived at the Compound, and it was the first time they'd talked about Auschwitz. For over three weeks, it had been enough to share real food, gossip about the Solomons, go to sleep knowing there wouldn't be roll call, and not wake up to find that eating utensils had disappeared —stolen by another prisoner.

You should come out of this room and tell them about the chimneys, said Daniel.

Never, said Asher, dipping some Knäckebrot in soup. I'm sure this place is like Thierenstadt. It looks nice so people can be gassed without knowing it, until they can't breathe.

It's not like that at all, said Daniel. People are friendly.

I don't want to be part of an exhibit.

You wouldn't. You'd like it.

I've been too many places people told me I'd like, said Asher.

You could learn *Dreamatoria*, said Daniel.

I'd much rather read.

Daniel stood in the doorway, half-lit by the kerosene lamp. His hair had begun to grow—lank and blond like his mother's—and he wore a dark green trench coat that could have belonged to one of their neighbors. He smiled at Asher.

Sometimes I think you don't want to see the woman who met us at the door, he said.

What are you talking about? said Asher.

Elie, said Daniel. Elie Schacten. The one who's always with that little kid. Is she the one who helped saved us? Who is she?

An old student, said Asher. Someone I knew at Freiburg. And I'm happy to see her. I'd just rather read. He paused and took a deep breath. Then he said:

I notice you don't sleep in this room much these days.

I like the main room better, said Daniel.

Is there someone there you like too? said Asher.

You already know there is, said Daniel. Are you angry?

Asher shook his head. Suppose Daniel didn't survive the war? This would be his only chance to lie next to someone in the dark and share the intimate durations of sleep. His only chance to feel the warmth of another body.

Just be careful, he said. The last thing this place needs is a baby.

Daniel looked insulted: It was the Compound of Scribes. There were French letters everywhere.

A few minutes after Daniel left, Asher heard a knock and opened the door. Talia Solomon stood in front of him with some resentment in her eyes—after all, she'd forged his signature without ever being thanked. But in a moment she smiled and said:

How would you like to come over and play chess?

On a Friday evening? Aren't you Orthodox? Or—Asher smiled—maybe you don't bother anymore.

I'm asking you to play chess, said Talia. Not have a hair-splitting discussion.

Asher hesitated. On the one hand, he loved chess. On the other, he didn't want to be part of a world where people lived in an eternal limbo, and the Solomons were clearly among them, especially since they'd written the letter to Heidegger.

Lodenstein said to ask, said Talia. He says you live like a mole.

223

Asher reconsidered when he heard that name because Lodenstein was the only member of the Compound he was sure to be among the living. He'd come to Auschwitz, seen Auschwitz, and had driven him and Daniel away from Auschwitz. So he followed Talia. But when he saw the Solomons' living room, he was in shock all over again: It mimicked an earlier century with velveteen chairs, antimacassars embroidered with nonsense in Hebrew, and portraits of men in skullcaps who would never have posed in the first place because they thought graven images were blasphemy.

There should be a piano, he said to Talia.

Why? she said. Neither of us plays.

Because. It would complete the picture.

What about a harpsichord? said Mikhail.

That would be too much, said Asher.

A violin then?

No. A piano. With some sheet music.

Not Wagner.

No! Scarlatti.

They all laughed. Talia and Asher began to play chess, and Mikhail played Beleaguered Castle—a game of cards Lodenstein had taught him. Just before Talia took one of Asher's bishops, she told Asher he might not realize how much Elie had worked to save him.

What does this have to do with chess? he said.

Nothing, said Talia.

Asher took Talia's knight.

Why did you mention it then?

I was just thinking of Elie, said Talia.

Asher took another knight. He was sure they wanted to tell him about the letter and then ask if he really had known

Heidegger. No matter where you were in this war, there was gossip. It was a trivial part of life that kept everyone going.

But no one said anything, and Asher was the one left to think about Heidegger in the Commandant's room wearing a ski outfit and an Alpine hat, while Mozart's concerto drowned out gunshots and Solomon's letter waved in front of him. Asher suddenly had a vivid sense of Auschwitz—corpses like sheets on the barbed wire fence, melting snow that revealed blood, stench, and dying in the barracks, his daily and heartbreaking fear over Daniel's safety. The idea that everything was infinitely reversible seemed far away, just as Heidegger's agitation about never getting his glasses seemed absurd. As did his visits to the optometry shop in Freiburg and his incessant joking about the irony of Asher becoming an optometrist. He thought about the real laughter between them when he taught at university, and the hills and valleys around Heidegger's hut—the walks they would take in the Black Forest, their moments of joy and exhilaration. But that all felt remote, a world he no longer believed in. He thought of how he would never walk there with Heidegger again.

Armesto,

Internet je na taj na in odavno I've pp od see te i zatim oni ono što je kazano taj zatvorenik sa nesretan mnoštvo jesu trgovanje identies sa zatvorenik sa sretan mnoštvo in izmjena za kruh. Ugoditi oporaviti se vojarna at no i Da vidim naprodikovati te.

Hatar,
Tahari

＊　＊　＊

Armesto,

It has been so long since I've seen you and now they say that prisoners with unlucky numbers are trading identities with prisoners with lucky numbers in exchange for bread. But how can you know what number's lucky or unlucky? And who can change luck when those numbers are on your arm forever?

Love,
Tahari

To the left of the window, hidden from Lars, Elie was watching Asher play chess. On the one hand, she felt illicit because watching people who didn't know they were being watched felt wrong. On the other hand, she felt innocent because she wanted to be sure this emaciated man really was Asher Englehardt—the one she had known. The lead-paned glass on the window was thick, making the interior seem cast in waves, adding to the sense that perhaps nothing that occurred inside it was real. She'd hidden behind the artificial pear tree, and its dappled light shifted as the sun rose in its jagged ascent. For a moment she thought the pear tree was moving and inched closer to the bench.

Without question this man played chess the way Asher had—appearing to be indifferent but not indifferent at all. He didn't seem to concentrate on the board and surrendered pieces with abandon. Elie saw him look amused when he checkmated Talia, just as he once checkmated her, then challenge her to another game—which Talia accepted with some annoyance. Asher was drinking tea—a procedure Elie watched with great absorption. He held a piece of sugar in his mouth and stirred first to the right, then to the left. He once told her that his grandfather drank tea by holding sugar in his mouth—a custom that belonged to peasants—and he liked to think about the tides when he stirred because he was sure that one day scientists would discover them in something as small as a teacup. Watching him was like reading a book she hadn't opened for years. She leaned closer to the window and stepped back when she heard footsteps in the hall. They belonged to Lodenstein and Stumpf—who both looked ponderous –and Dimitri, who ran ahead. She kissed him and told him to go inside.

I have such regret, she head Stumpf say in a mincing voice. If I ever can do anything….

You can never stop being a fool.

Stumpf slunk away like a dog that's been hit on the nose. As if a more formal appearance would undo the disaster he'd helped create, he'd begun to wear his black SS jacket in the Compound. It was too tight to button and billowed behind him when he walked. He still wore his woolly slippers, however, which make his appearance even more incongruous and out of sorts. Elie watched Stumpf walk sadly to the kitchen. Lodenstein walked up to her, and she felt unhinged, as though she had traveled back to Freiburg, played chess, gone to Heidegger's lectures. She hadn't believed there would be a war, then. She'd even told Asher she was sure his wife was safe. Yet someone she herself thought had been killed in that war was now walking towards her.

Alain,

Tu na aucune idée comment je désire ardemment pour tu et comment parfois j'imagine tu. Tu ne faites jamais n'importe quoi remarquable—allant au réfrigérateur pour le lait, ou laissant chez le chat. Avec l'espoir que toi obtiendrez ceci.

Amour,
Sylvie

*   *   *

Alain,

Sometimes I imagine you. You are never doing anything remarkable—just going to the refrigerator for milk, or letting in the cat—yet I find these memories precious just because you are yourself. I do not know if I'll see you again.

Love,
Sylvie

In the dark, under the soft grey quilt from Rotterdam, Elie and Lodenstein still found each other in bed. They made love as if at any moment the Gestapo would break down the door, and they must hold each other so tightly nothing could separate them. During these times Goebbels, Mueller—the whole notion of danger itself—became the stuff of inflated fears. But during the day, when sun shone through the clerestory windows and light seemed to chase them, they worried. Lodenstein interrupted games of solitaire and patrolled the forest, terrified that a group of SS or Gestapo were advancing and using the pines as camouflage. Elie made lists of names, people who might help Asher, Dmitri, and Daniel find a boat to Denmark, and burned them in the forest. Once, Lodenstein found her burning names under a pine tree. He stamped the fire out and hurried her to the shepherd's hut.

Don't burn those anymore, he said. You never know who's watching.

You shouldn't be out there, either, said Elie.

I always carry a gun.

I do, too.

But I'm patrolling. And you write the same list over and over. Why torture yourself?

Because it calms me, said Elie.

They both felt paralyzed from taking action and talked in circles. If what Mueller said was true, the entire Compound would be implicated for harboring fugitives. Perhaps Maria was safe—she could blend in with the other Scribes during an inspection. But they had to get Dmitri, Asher, and Daniel to Denmark. Elie often repeated what a Resistance fighter once told her: *A fugitive is like a puppet with a red string. The Reich can trace it to the end of the world.* To which Lodenstein replied: *We can't think like that. It's like focusing sunlight on paper on a hot day. If we do it long enough, there will be a fire.*

They would then decide that Goebbels was too preoccupied to care. The Russians had penetrated Silesia. Allied troops were close to the Rhine. And the Germans hadn't been able to split the Allied forces in the Ardennes. Furthermore, there hadn't been any mail from the outpost since Asher and Daniel had arrived.

These rationalizations soothed them both. But only for a while. And the next time they were caught by daylight, they found themselves terrified all over again—not just for Asher, Daniel, and Dmitri—but for everyone in the Compound. The Reich had become more brutal with every failure. There was talk of a scorched earth policy, and more plans to blow up the gas chambers.

As if the artificial sun could comfort them, they sometimes went downstairs where they sat on a wrought iron bench and tried to strategize—about finding money to offer a bribe for safe passage to Denmark that no one could resist, or discovering a place they could hide Asher, Daniel, and Dmitri. One day, Stumpf came out of his shoebox to join them. He sat on the very edge of the bench, as if he didn't deserve to take up any space in their presence. Then he said:

If only I'd brought the right glasses! I could have left without a trace, and Goebbels would be happy.

Elie said he should never have meddled in the first place and Lodenstein stayed quiet, quelling the words inside him. Why bother to mention that Elie should never have gone behind his

231

back? But when Stumpf talked about Elie getting Frau Heidegger's recipe for *bundkuchen*, he shouted to him:

Go back to your fucking shoebox! I never want to talk about this again.

Then he went to the kitchen and poured a glass of schnapps. Elie followed.

You're angry with me too, she said.

Maybe, said Lodenstein. But I don't love Stumpf.

You're still too hard on him.

At this very moment, Asher and Sophie Nachtgarten came from the main room and walked to the mineshaft. Elie began to stop them from going upstairs, but Lodenstein held her waist.

Nothing will happen today, he said. Let him get some air.

As if you were sure, said Elie.

She watched Sophie and Asher disappear into the mineshaft and felt a tug at her heart – not jealousy, but pain. Seeing Asher with Sophie made her think about other people she'd seen him with, people she could never bring back.

Lieber Tessa,

Ein Soldat, der sagt, daß Sie ihn kennen, hat mich gebeten, Ihnen eine Anzeige zu geben: Wenn der Krieg rüber sein, kommen Sie treffen mich. Geben Sie, Tessa acht. Sie wissen nicht, was mit den Leuten geschieht nach rechts und die nach links verlassen.

Liebe,
Lottie

* * *

Dear Tessa,

A soldier who says you know him has asked me to give you a message: When the war is over, come meet me. But be careful, Tessa. You don't know what's happening with people deserting right and left.

Love,
Lottie

Asher had come to the main room that day, after a month in which the only people he saw were Talia and Mikhail. He resented their writing the letter to Heidegger, and yet the Solomons were a link, a tether to Auschwitz and superstitiously— although Asher despised superstitions—he was afraid if he forgot Auschwitz completely, some unexplained force would send him back there. He also loved chess and the illusory justice of detective stories where every criminal was punished. But one day, he closed a book and realized he'd been immersed in a world of antiseptic murders, as well as tiny conquests on a wooden board.

I'm restless, he said to Talia. And that's the only virtue of living in fear. There's no such thing as monotony, tedium, or ennui.

He was surprised he'd confided in Talia, and Talia caught his surprise. She smiled and took his bishop.

You must be very bored to think of all those words, she said. And you've just lost two games in a row. Why don't you spend some time with the Scribes?

They'd ask questions, said Asher.

Don't answer them. Amuse yourself.

Talia smiled again, and he smiled back, realizing he'd forgiven her and Mikhail about the letter to Heidegger which— even if absurd—had saved his life. He carried a detective story and a treasured coffee cup—a blue and white mug from Holland—to the main room where he got a desk as well as pillows so he could sit in a corner and read. The Scribes saw the numbers on his arm, and remembered, as they had with Daniel, how close they'd come to that place themselves and how willing they'd be to come close again just to keep him safe. They also decided not to annoy him by asking about chimneys. Except for Paris Nafissian, who wanted to annoy him because he was still angry with Daniel for taking Maria away from him.

Of course there were chimneys, said Asher. They were the hardest workers at Auschwitz. They were alert, even lively.

Sophie Nachtgarten smiled at him.

Lively chimneys, she said. Now there's an interesting idea. By the way, you should get a coat so we can go outside.

From people who are dead? said Asher. Do you answer their letters now? *Dear Frau So-and-So, not only is your husband fine, but I happen to be wearing his coat!*

Listen, said Sophie. There's not one of us who hasn't scrambled and clawed our way to get here. There's not one of us who hasn't lied or faked languages or done whatever we could to stay away from where you've been. So what if we wear gloves and hats and scarves that belong to people who are dead or have lice eating into their skin?

He watched her grab at the coats with increasing fury and heard tears in her voice:

I lost my entire family, she said. My mother and father, my two brothers, their wives, and my four-year-old niece. I think I should be allowed to choose a coat.

While she spoke, she'd been rummaging through the coats until she found a leather jacket with a fur collar.

This might be interesting on you, she said. Once more her voice was calm.

After what you just told me? No.

Just try it, said Sophie.

Asher put on the jacket, and Sophie stood back to look at him.

It fits you, she'd said. You can pretend you're a bomber with the Allies.

Not unless I have a scarf, said Asher.

Then I'll get you one, said Sophie, pulling a white scarf from a burlap bag.

Perfect! she said. You can pretend you're a British pilot on his day off.

Should I play cricket? said Asher.

Cribbage would be fine, said Sophie. She took his arm. Please take me for some air. Please take me to the well.

Asher refused. As much as he distrusted this compound in purgatory, he thought his upsetting version of eternity might be better than being shot, or hung, in the forest. Besides, his very presence in the Compound put everyone at risk. He needed to remain hidden below the earth.

I owe it to all of you to stay inside, he said.

But there was an upwelling of nos and Niles Schopenhauer said he had come from a place they'd all barely escaped, and they owed it to him to make sure he got fresh air.

Asher said they might not be so heroic if they'd actually been to Auschwitz, and he followed Sophie to the cobblestone street, avoiding the miserable little group on the bench, and walked into the mineshaft. The lift rumbled as it took them from the earth, and the sounds reverberated like gunshots.

Sophie led Asher up the incline, through the shepherd's hut, to the snow-covered clearing. Asher followed slowly, looking at the forest. Sophie urged him on. It was the first time he'd seen real sky in months. It was an extraordinary blue with white clouds that moved swiftly, miraculously. Not long ago he'd felt like a scrap covered with rags, lighter than the wind. Now he could feel his body had weight, substance, gravity. He felt taller than the trees. He touched his arms, his legs, and his face.

Sophie kept beckoning until he got to the well. And even though his face quivered in the water, Asher could see that it was no longer the face of a skeleton, but the face of a living man. Sophie handed him the big tin dipper.

Drink! she said.

Asher drank. Water had never tasted so good.

Diane,

Usted sabe probablemente sobre la insurrección. Algunos de los presos que reparaban cargadores robaron los armas. Entonces la sincronización estaba apagada y tuvieron que ponerlos los días de back. Two que los robaron más adelante otra vez. Todos fueron matados, incluyendo el oficial que le dije alrededor. Me preocupo de mis padres pero es una relevación a no ir a su sitio. Mientras tanto, no he visto que usted y yo nos preocupamos. Viene por favor la charla a mí.

Amor,
Homa

* * *

Diane,

You probably know about the insurrection. Some of the prisoners repairing uniforms found a way to break into the armory. Then the timing was off and they had to put the guns back. Two days later they snuck them again. All of them were killed, but before they were killed they shot the officer I had to sleep with. He was protecting my parents, so I worry—

Love,
Homa

When he came back from the well, Asher barely looked at Elie, who was sitting at her enormous desk. She was part of what came before his life snapped in half, and he didn't want her to be part of it now. Indeed—in some odd boomerang of the mind—he wondered if their affair had something to do with his wife joining the earliest Resistance, which later resulted in her death. And even though he'd met Elie after his wife disappeared, he decided it had, and he didn't care if Elie had anything to do with his being in this dungeon instead of Auschwitz. He stared at her over his detective story and remembered everything about their affair that had been unpleasant: Sneaking to cafés where people from the university couldn't find them. Impaling himself on a filing cabinet in his office when they made love. It had rained a lot during that time, and they were always taking cover under awnings. Once Elfriede Heidegger walked by and saw them. Ever since she had treated him with disdain.

He also wondered why Elie Kowaleski deserved adoration when other people were dying like flies. And how a discreetly rebellious student of linguistics had been reborn as a star in this underground world. When she came back from a mission, people applauded. And sometimes, for no apparent reason, people toasted her. What had she done to deserve it? How did she get so much food?

Yet when Gerhardt Lodenstein sat by Elie's desk—as he did now—Asher watched their every move. They often seemed passionately worried, and the intensity of their absorption made

Asher realize he was lonely because it had been a long time since he'd been intimate enough to share worry with another person. And even though he'd long forgotten Elie, he began to feel jealous of Gerhardt Lodenstein—a feeling that upset him because Lodenstein had saved his life, Daniel's life, and had nearly been killed himself in the process.

Now he got up and stood near Elie's desk, pretending to be fascinated by the jumble shop against the wall. He couldn't hear what she and Lodenstein were saying but listened to their tone. It was clearly passionate, with a timbre of anxiety, even anger.

He turned around and met Lodenstein's eyes. Lodenstein smiled—a smile of truce and good will. *Of course he knows*, Asher thought. *And what's more, it doesn't matter to him that much.*

He hardly ever thought about the past during the war because he was so preoccupied with Daniel's safety and his wife's disappearance. But Elie's face opened a floodgate to times long before the war, times when something as simple as a walk could make him happy. He remembered his wife reading in the evening, light against her face, and Daniel crawling into bed to hear a story. He remembered snow on the skylights, warm air after winter, the first lectures of the fall. Everything was a pathetic stand-in for what his life had been since then—even this underground world. And every time he saw Elie, he was pushed against this earlier world that he wanted to forget because he had been happy.

He barely smiled back at her and returned to his cluster of pillows, where he buried himself in another detective story and thought about the time he'd been relegated to *before* the war: He thought about his wife playing Mozart. Daniel doing homework instead of this absurd preoccupation with typewriters. And he thought about his house filled with plants and books. He felt irritated with the Scribes, who behaved like children—writing in secret codes, inventing languages, exalting in a spirit of privilege and discontent. He was tired of seeing Lodenstein's rumpled green sweater and the eccentric compass he often carried. He even hated Mikhail and Talia Solomon and their preoccupation with chess, which seemed ponderous. As well as Dmitri, who liked to collect stamps.

Mijn beste zuster,

Waar bent u wanneer ik aan de prikkeldraadomheining bij nacht kom? De mensen zeggen u fijn-juiste bezig bent het voeden van de konijnen. Maar ik wil u zien.

Liefde,
NAME TK

*   *   *

My dearest sister,

Where are you when I come to the edge of your cellblock at night? People say you're in charge of feeding the rabbits, but I've heard of hangings by candlelight, especially of women under twenty. I need you to be outside so I can see your face.

Love,
NAME TK

One day, when Asher was in the throes of such mean-spirited thoughts, La Toya said he wanted to discuss something where no one else could hear them. Asher said he would never go to the vent above the water closet where people sat in a dark cave and heard others piss and shit. So La Toya suggested the well.

It was early spring, and the snow was melting. Asher saw that grass was already in the clearing, and the ash trees had buds. There was no more snow that could make things infinitely reversible. It was a different world, one without camouflage. They navigated mud puddles, and La Toya asked what was going on between him and Elie Schacten. Asher tightened his hold on the pail.

Nothing. What makes you ask?

You seem angry with her, said La Toya.

I'm not.

They say you knew her at Freiburg.

Who's they? said Asher.

Everybody.

La Toya pointed to the sky. It was blue, filled with the cottoned traffic of clouds.

Would you have seen this at Auschwitz? he asked.

I have no idea. Why?

Because Elie saved your life.

That's not true. Lodenstein did.

Then why do I think she fought for you?

I don't know what you mean.

Then I'll tell you, said La Toya. She was going to find a way to go to Heidegger and tell him where you were. She thought his wife would get you out.

Elfriede never liked her.

We've all heard the business about the *bundkuchen*, said La Toya. But Elie is persuasive. Where do you think we get fresh bread? And good sausages? How come there's always cashmere for people who want blankets? Or plenty of schnapps? Do they fall from the sky? No. They come from the shit Elie puts up with and the favors she does for people.

Maybe they do, said Asher. But we hardly knew each other.

That's not what people say.

What then?

You can imagine. People know everything, just the way they know about the camps.

But they keep asking about chimneys. Why can't they stop?

Because, said La Toya. There's a difference between knowing something and believing it. They know about the chimneys but don't believe in them until they've talked to someone who's seen them.

They'd come to the shepherd's hut without spilling a drop of water. La Toya said it was a job well done, and Asher said at Auschwitz you learned not to waste anything. But he wasn't thinking about water. What La Toya had said stayed with him long after he returned to the Compound, and late that afternoon he walked up to Elie's desk. She slammed her dark red notebook shut and looked at him as if she expected someone else—no one in particular, just not him.

I want to thank you, he said.

244

But Elie didn't hear him because someone had created a word for *Dreamatoria* the Scribes found hilarious.

What? she said, while the laughter closed in around them.

Asher suddenly felt embarrassed by his own gratitude, as if it could destroy a necessary shell. He told her he needed more typewriter ribbon.

I don't know why you need it when all you do is read detective stories, said Elie.

Oh I'll get around to using it, he said. The dead can't wait to read my answers.

Spare me, said Elie. But she smiled at him, making him remember the first time he'd met her at Freiburg—at a party at the Heideggers, over an impressive table of desserts. He went back to his desk and remembered how his wife disappeared without a trace, telling him she was going to Berlin to help a piano student, kissing him, hugging Daniel, racing down the steps.

After Asher had gotten a ribbon he didn't need, he began to think about what would have happened if he'd stayed with Elie. He imagined different lives—one in which they'd taught at Cambridge and taken long walks on village greens. And another where they escaped to Argentina and set up a dry goods store. Yet another where the boat to Argentina sank. *Parallel lives* he scribbled on a piece of paper, *a hat trick that makes life and death reversible.* It was the first thing anyone had ever seen him write.

Gitka said: That corpse is beginning to lighten up.

NEW NAMES TK—
Diana,

En la noche, un protector en el cuarto del oficial. Él dice que él me ama. Pero él me da el alimento adicional. Y se cerciora de mirar hacia fuera para mis parientes. Venga por favor a la cerca. Nadie está mirando eso de cerca. Te quiero y yo fáltele.

Homa

*   *   *

Diana,

At night, a guard and I make small talk. He says he loves me. And gives me extra food and makes sure to look out for my parents. I think he's trying to find out more about the insurrection. Please come to the edge of your cellblock. No one is watching very closely.

Homa

Asher proposed a new phrase for *Dreamatoria*— *infinitely reversible.* It reminded him of fresh snow at Auschwitz that covered pools of blood and corpses and nooses as well as the old snow that melted and revealed everything. It reminded him of himself as well: how he'd been given a life, denied it, and given part of that life back again. The Scribes applauded, and Asher won two cigarettes. He offered one to Elie.

Oh no! she said. You won it fairly.

Then smoke one with me, he said.

Well, maybe a fourth of one, said Elie.

They went to the hall and sat on a wrought-iron bench. Asher said it was nice that dead people could get answers in such a charming atmosphere.

You haven't lost your sarcasm, said Elie. You don't even sound glad you're here.

I am, said Asher. Especially for Daniel—even if all he does is take typewriters apart and sleep with Maria.

But aren't you glad for yourself?

Asher took a long drag on the cigarette. He was wearing a shirt with rolled-up sleeves. Elie looked at the blue numbers on his arm and said they nearly matched his eyes. He shook his head, remembering the morning when he'd been tattooed by a fellow prisoner—the needle embroidering numbers that became his only name at the camp. Elie noticed, and said:

Maybe those add up to a lucky number.

Are you into that occult garbage too?

It was just a funny idea, said Elie.

Asher added the numbers, and they came to nine, the number of sacrifice.

Maybe there's something to it, he said.

Maybe, said Elie. She began to sew the quilt she'd been mending and kept her eyes on it in such a deliberate way Asher was sure she knew he was looking at her.

Elie, he said. They say you saved me and Daniel.

Through a lot of bungling. That's how it is these days.

He took her hand: Thank you.

The mineshaft began to groan. Elie startled and got up.

So, still a secret, said Asher.

Nothing's secret here, said Elie. I'm not sure anything needs to be.

Geehrte Elisabeth,

Du würde nie denken welches ich hörte aber ich muß sitzen du persönlich. Begegnen mich am Baracken.

Liebe ,
Andreas

* * *

Dear Eliza,

You would never guess what I heard but I must tell you in person. Meet me at the barracks.

Love,
Andreas

Even though Daniel now slept with the Scribes, Asher Englehardt kept sleeping in the storage room, impervious to Sonia Markova and Sophie Nachtgarten, who made it clear they'd enjoy sleeping there too—although not at the same time.

Daniel still brought typewriters to Asher's room, and one day set a typewriter on the bed and took it apart, until it was a mere shell, and the floor was filled with mysterious pieces of dull metal. Then he explained every mechanism—how it worked, what could go wrong with it, how things fit together, where they belonged. It was the first time Daniel had explained anything to him and Asher was proud and astonished. He was even more astonished when Daniel showed him how the typewriter could be reassembled. This was far better than *infinitely reversible.* What was dismantled into unrecognizable pieces could be made whole again.

Now and then, Asher brought typewriters to his room, took them apart, and reassembled them. He memorized gears, springs, the order of keys—metal with a special power because it could produce any combination of words in the world. He loved going to sleep, surrounded by the smell of ink.

Once, he had brandy with Elie, Lodenstein, and the Solomons and made everyone laugh by telling Mikhail that once he'd owned a car, and Mikhail could have used it as an example in his letter to Heidegger about the mysterious Being of machines. The laughter, the presence of Elie—and the Solomons, who knew about everything—all of it still transported him to the time before the war and pushed him against everything he'd lost. The evening made him miss his wife. So he never wanted to have brandy with the four of them again. When he ran into Elie, they always nodded quickly and hurried on. Except for once, when they both said *good night* at the same time.

For a while, then, he was able to live in relative silence—a silence he craved, because even the smallest gesture or manner of speech could unnerve him. A loud voice reminded him of roll call. Scribes rummaging for coats reminded him of inmates scrambling for bowls of food. When he was by himself, he could read or invent words for *Dreamatoria*. When he was with other people, he felt a minefield inside him that could detonate at any moment.

But his pristine silence was disturbed when Dieter Stumpf broke his glasses. He'd put them on his chair while he was labeling a box of letters, sat on them, and heard a crunch. Stumpf was nearsighted. Without his glasses, he couldn't drive to his brother's farm near Dresden to bury unanswered mail. So he brought Asher his broken glasses.

What do you want me to do with these? said Asher.

I was hoping you could fix them, said Stumpf.

With both lenses broken?

What if I get equipment?

Stumpf, who still wore his SS jacket, reminded Asher of the most obnoxious of the Auschwitz guards, as well as Mengele who once barely gestured to the right when he'd decided Asher's fate and often had crates of bleached bones outside his door. Asher was tempted to say *no*. Nonetheless, he agreed. Making glasses could be a distraction.

Stumpf asked Elie to get optometry equipment from the outpost, and she said she would, even though she didn't care whether Stumpf got glasses or not. It would be a chance to look around, to discover if there were more rumors about fugitives, and find out why they hadn't received any letters.

She asked Lodenstein to tie the red ribbon around her wrist.

Cher Marianne,

Encore une fois je ne te vu. S'il te plaît viens aux versant de les barracks. TRANSLATION TK

Amore,
Patrice

* * *

Marianne,

You wouldn't think anything could grow in a place like this—but there's grass where the red snow used to be.

Love,
Patrice

It was the time of feverfew. Before Elie went to the outpost, she picked a large bouquet from the forest. The feverfew grew in clusters, far apart, and Elie took her time. Without the weight of snow, the pines seemed buoyant, free of every burden. The first winter after the winter of Stalingrad had passed, and it seemed as though the world had come a full cycle. Elie sat beneath a pine—hidden, protected, smelling the bare earth. She remembered playing house with her sister under trees. The wooden sticks were dolls. The boughs were their dresses. Her sister Gabriela named her dolls after friends she had at school, and Elie named hers after characters she loved in fairy tales. One spring, they found a wild rabbit. They fed it carrots, and it kept them company under the trees.

By the time Elie emerged, it was late afternoon. She brought the feverfew to her jeep and drove through the slanted light, still looking for people in the woods. Yet she felt buoyant, released, and for a moment didn't care that she hadn't heard from Goebbels in months.

The houses in this village in Northern Germany were still clean, orderly, not yet bombed. Elie drove to the outpost and walked across the field, milkweed brushing against her shoes. She knocked twice, no one answered, and she let herself in. The place was more of a jumble shop than ever. Chair on top of chair, a sofa filled with filing cabinets. The officer was shoving clothes into a suitcase.

What are you doing here? he said. You must know there isn't any mail.

Lodenstein sent me, said Elie, handing him half the flowers. People need to amuse themselves.

The officer threw the flowers on an ottoman.

What could be amusing here?

Elie pointed to more playing cards. Then she pointed to some rusty metal instruments, polishing stones, and an eye chart. She'd wanted to find a box of cast molten glass from the lens manufacturer Saegmuller and Zeiss. But she only found glass from a manufacturer she didn't recognize. One of the optometrist's chairs was still against the wall. She pointed to it.

How can optometry equipment be amusing? said the officer.

Stumpf broke his glasses.

That bumpkin, said the officer. He began to shake sheets from the bed he once tried to get Elie to sleep in. A revolver fell to the floor, and he crammed it in his suitcase.

Has Stumpf been bothering you? said Elie.

No, said the officer. And I wouldn't give a damn if he was. I don't care about Goebbels either.

Elie smiled. Then your neck is safe.

I don't care about my neck. The whole thing's going to hell. Look at Ardennes, and the damn Allies past the Rhine. No one's safe. I'm getting out of here. Take whatever the fuck you want.

Elie watched while he ran to his Kubelwagen and found herself alone in the outpost. The blackout curtains flapped. A few beams from the roof were on the ground. And the floor was littered with papers. Elie looked through all of them. Each detailed shipments of confiscated goods except for a note that read: *NO MORE FUCKING PIECES OF FURNITURE. SOMEONE IS BOUND TO FIND THEM.*

Elie pulled out everything from the wall: the polishing stones, the metal, the eye chart, the box of molten glass, and the playing cards. Then she took rations of flour, dried milk, sausage, Knäckebrot, cheese—whatever food she could find. The food was in heavy cumbersome boxes, and she had to carry them one at a time across the milkweed-covered field. Last was the optometry chair, which she lugged in fits and starts. She set it down and paused to look at the sky.

It was almost night—still too early to see anything but the evening star, one soft beacon in the sky. She shoved the chair into her jeep and drove off in the spring evening. A half moon lit green rhododendrons by the side of the road and Elie's fear of the dark disappeared—as though every mote of dark evaporated in the clear moonlight. She looked in the rearview mirror and saw that no one was following her.

Enough, she thought.

Dinka,

Usted ha preguntado cuándo puedo estar detrás y puedo decirle solamente por la letra circuitious que el cada día oigamos el extremo él el venir. Con todo retrocede, una frontera que se esté ampliando siempre. ¡Puede viene pronto!

Amor,
Piero

*   *   *

Dinka,

You have asked when I may be back and I can only tell you that every day we hear the end is coming. Yet it recedes, a frontier that's always breathing in and out. May it come soon.

Love,
Piero

Asher had wondered, with some irony, whether he'd be getting back his own optometry chair from Freiburg. But this chair was light brown, and there were three bullet holes in the back. To make sure the chart was illuminated, he made Stumpf create a tent from bolts of black merino cloth Elie brought from the outpost almost a year ago. It was a haphazard tent with a large opening and that made Stumpf even more of a public spectacle. Scribes watched while he held a patch over one eye and whined *Besser* and *Nicht Besser* for different lenses. Since Elie hadn't been able to find the best materials, Asher struggled to make them work. He polished the rusty instruments, ground the cheap glass until he got the lenses right, made the ear pieces twice because Stumpf's chins rose around his face like a ruff. But when he finally produced the glasses, Stumpf said he could see better with these glasses than any he'd ever had. Suddenly, the Scribes wanted glasses too, whether they needed them or not. Asher made glasses whenever he felt like it. No one could object, least of all Stumpf, who was abjectly grateful because it meant he could drive to his brother's farm— a visit he kept postponing since now he was drawn to a psychic named Hermione Rosebury, who said she'd known Madame Blavatsky. Hermione was the only Scribe in the Compound from England, although she spoke perfect German with no accent. Her sense of isolation made her willing to ignore the fact that Stump slunk around the Compound obsequiously, forsaken by Sonia Markova who had taken up with Parvis Nafissian. He had long since been deprived of any authority, including the right to make people imagine Goebbels. Also, with no more letters coming to the Compound, he'd given up insisting the Scribes answer them. He stored them in his office and answered them himself, or—more often—thought about answering them, since he still only understood the German.

In the midst of the craze about glasses, Lars Eisenscher paced the small round room of the shepherd's hut. He hadn't received a letter from his father for almost three months and had no idea whether his father was back in jail, had gone to another country, been shot, or didn't want to cause trouble by writing him. Twice Lars had gone to the post office in town and was told the postal system barely functioned. Germany was exhausted, and the war had taken all of her resources, even the simple ability to send a letter. Paper, ink, people one loved—all seemed to be forgotten.

Lars was lost in his worry over his father until he heard a motor rumble in the distance and saw a Kubelwagen turn into the clearing. It drove quickly, flattening flowers in its path, making deep cuts in the patches of new and green grass. Then a short dark officer got out and asked for Obërst Lodenstein. If Lodenstein hadn't spent time with Goebbels in his odious office, he might have thought the officer was Goebbels himself, finally paying his mythical visit. Lodenstein kept the officer at the door of the hut while Lars stood at a distance. The officer was weighted with medals— more than Mueller, almost as many as Goebbels. Lars looked at him anxiously. So many medals signaled power.

That guard of yours needs a haircut, said the officer.

He's on duty more than seventeen hours a day, said Lodenstein.

I can't quibble about hours, said the officer. I can only point out standards.

He reached into his pocket and handed him a memo from the Office of Enlightenment and Propaganda. The paper was thick, strong, unblemished. It read: *The Office requests a roll call of all Scribes.*

Lodenstein, who acted as though the letter weren't worthy of attention, felt his heart thumping. What do you make of this? he said.

There's nothing to make of it, said the officer. Just get everybody up here with their papers.

But they're imagining Goebbels.

The officer looked confused, and Lodenstein said:

Hasn't anyone ever told you about this important ritual?

The officer shook his head, and Lodenstein explained that every day the Scribes spent half an hour invoking an image of Joseph Goebbels—the mind behind this vital project.

If they didn't remember him, he said, nothing would get done. Interruption could mean catastrophe.

The officer agreed to spend time in Lodenstein's room—he referred to them as *quarters*—until the Scribes had finished their imagining. He even went back to his Kubelwagen and brought back a bottle of brandy. Then he walked down the incline slowly, examining the walls and taking note of everything in the room. He was a non-communicative man who stared with the pinched reticence of someone who has learned to observe carefully. He asked about the trunk on the floor in the corner of the room: Lodenstein said he was keeping mementoes to exhibit after Germany won the war. The officer looked pleased and asked about a camisole on the dresser: Lodenstein said one woman or another was always in his room. The officer asked about the clerestory windows. Lodenstein told him about the architect, Hans Ewigkeit, who disguised the mine as the shepherd's hut and created this tiny room above the earth. The officer asked about the playing cards. Lodenstein explained he liked to play solitaire. The officer picked up the camisole again and said he liked the smell of the tea-rose perfume. Lodenstein agreed and gave him more brandy. Soon, the officer was pleasantly drunk and leaned back on the bed and closed his eyes. The order slipped from his hands. Lodenstein wished it would float away like the letter on the train. But it stayed—so heavy and inert Lodenstein doubted it would even float in water.

The order was scribbled on the letterhead of the Ministry of Enlightenment and Propaganda, and the signature was unclear. Below was an old German saying appropriated by the Reich: *Ubersetzter sind Verrater.*

Translators are traitors.

Lodenstein put the orders on the bed and watched the light from the windows. It was hazy, the light of late afternoon, and fell in shafts on the quilt, the pillows, the officer's face, and a deck of playing cards lying on a bedside table. Because he'd stopped playing cards, the suits now looked like real-world images instead of symbols to be sorted, stacked, and swept. Lodenstein saw hearts as something lovers would carve, diamonds as stones. The court cards were mirror images, and Lodenstein remembered someone telling him this was a superstition: if an image appeared as a mirror image, then the royalty was safe and couldn't be beheaded. He set the cards down, walked to the windows, and wondered if the roll call were only a ruse. But when he read the orders again he saw Asher's name. And Daniel's. There was also a note that said: *nameless child.*

The memo on the side table seemed to speak out loud: translators are traitors.

Suddenly, without forethought, he grabbed the pillow on Elie's side of the bed and held it over the officer's face. He pressed the pillow against the officer's ears and held it around his mouth—not looking at the pillow, only at his hands, which bent the pillow with the force of someone bending steel. His hands didn't look like hands, but block-like objects with a will of their own, separate from his heart and mind. They pressed and pressed until the officer began to gasp and flail. His kicking made the night table inch towards the bed until playing cards crashed to the floor. It occurred to Lodenstein that these cards once belonged to someone who had been deported, probably dead by now, and while his hands pressed the pillow he had a vision of all the dead conferring with the officer and making such a fuss no letter in the world could stop them from gathering, gossiping, complaining, accusing him.

These thoughts only made him press harder, until the officer's body went limp. He left the pillow over his face and tried not to think *I killed someone*, and he tried to distance himself from the torn, ragged feeling in his heart. He looked at his hands and thought—as if he were talking to hands that belonged to someone else—*you killed someone.* They were in knots. He had a hard time unclenching them.

The pillow had burst and was leaking eiderdown. The quilt was covered with mud from the officer's thrashing boots. Lodenstein looked at the pillow long enough to imagine a scarecrow-like impression of his face. Then he looked away and began to think about burying the body: He couldn't bring it to the woods because the ground was still too hard from winter. He couldn't leave it unburied because it might be discovered, and there would be a smell. The only solution was a room only he knew about. This room was in the tunnel that led to town and wasn't on any existing map of the Compound.

The Tunnel

Lodenstein took a spade and three keys from the bottom of the trunk. One belonged to the door to his room, which he locked. Another belonged to the door that led to the tunnel, that led to the town three miles away. The third opened the room only he knew about. It was on the left side of the tunnel that dead-ended at the Compound. It had been placed there mysteriously. No one explained why when he'd been given the keys.

Lodenstein walked past the Solomons' to the same arched door Gitka had made Maria trace with her hands—the *trompe l'oeil* that looked just like the earth. He looked to see no one was watching then struggled with the key. Perhaps the door had never been opened. Or maybe the key didn't fit. But the door gave way, suddenly pushing Lodenstein into darkness and cold air and the smell of foul waste rushing from the downhill stream. He edged slowly, holding his gun in one hand, feeling the wall with the other. He unlocked the room in the dark.

It consisted of three walls that abutted the mine and a dirt wall built to accommodate the door. Except for the fourth wall, the three other walls and the floor were jagged earth and rocks, so the whole enclosure was a terrain of coal hills and dirt valleys.

The odor vanished as soon he closed the door. Lodenstein was in absolute quiet, surrounded by the smell of clean earth. This made the room seem like a sanctuary—small, and safe, carved of earth. Lodenstein sat against the wall, lit a cigarette, and tried to forget he was about to bury someone he'd just murdered. It could have been long ago when he and his friends played hide and seek, finding the most obscure places to wait and be found. It could have been an ordinary day in childhood.

He finished the cigarette and dug with the spade. The earth was hard, digging was laborious, and he had to rest. He lit another cigarette and watched idly while he shone his flashlight. The beam traveled across the floor, making a clear white line. As it traveled up the wall, the rocks looked like large pieces of obsidian—a wall of black jewels. It was strangely lovely and made him forget about the officer until the flashlight shone on another object. These jewels were white, angular. They shone with bleached radiance inside the beam.

He came closer with his flashlight and let his eyes adjust to the deep encompassing darkness of the room. The white jewels seemed sharp and defined, from another world and yet familiar. He traced the outlines with reticence. It was starting to dawn on him that the white jewels weren't jewels at all, but something far more human. He saw the outline of pubic bones. Their curves made a place to sit and were attached to four femurs—a perfect box—which appeared to be attached to four skeletal feet. There was also a vertical back to this object —a rib cage. Every single bone was a human bone. And Lodenstein realized he was seeing a chair. There was an identical chair next to it. There was also a side table.

For a moment he had the outrageous thought that these once belonged to a whole living room, and if reunited with this room, would turn into ordinary furniture again. He imagined transporting everything to the right place where it would transform to a time before a war, when no one thought about answering the dead or traveling on moonless nights to a place where people were kept and herded like cattle. He imagined that these bones were only an apparition of stones and darkness. But there was nowhere to take them. Nowhere at all. And they weren't an apparition, but furniture. Furniture that had once been alive.

He gagged, clawed at the walls, got dirt under his fingernails, and managed to close the door. He rushed to the cobblestone street and locked the *trompe l'oeil*.

He gagged again.

Xavier,

Ou es tu? Ou es tu? Je te cherche partout. Je te cherche partout. Si je ne te trouve pas, me trouve.

Marianne

*   *   *

Xavier,

Where are you? Where are you? I seek you everywhere. I seek you everywhere. If I can't find you, find me.

Marianne

In the main room of the Compound, no one had an inkling that an officer had arrived. Elie was at her desk, Stumpf was in the watchtower, and the Scribes were trying on new glasses, waiting to be fitted for them, or basking in the pleasure of just having received them. Gitka had glasses on the end of her nose and was holding her long cigarette holder. Niles Schopenhauer wore rimless glasses and a raccoon coat. Lodenstein watched it all at a distance. His hands were shaking. His breath came in bursts. He held his elbows and tried to breathe more slowly while he watched the Scribes admire their glasses as if nothing had changed. They had no idea death was so close—in the forest, in the room with the clerestory windows, in the space with the black jewels. They had no idea he'd just killed an officer and found a bizarre mausoleum at the end of the hall. *Nothing will ever be the same,* he thought—*this Compound is a coffin.*

People were too preoccupied to notice when he began to riffle through a bag against the wall. He tossed out boots, hats, and scarves until he found a pair of leather gloves. But when a shovel clattered against the telescope, people looked up.

Nafissian said he ought to get glasses too. They would give you a kind of dignity, he said.

Without question, said Niles Schopenhauer.

But La Toya stood up and said: We all know the glasses are just a distraction. This is still the place where we write to the dead.

Or the almost-dead, said Nafissian.

Or about-to-be-dead, said Gitka.

And we can only hope that someone reads these letters, said La Toya. If we call this room anything, we should call it the Optimistic Mailroom.

No, no, said Nafissian. It will always be the *Dreamatorium.*

People got absorbed in the joke, and no one noticed when Lodenstein went to the broom closet—always a tangle of packing tape, candles, torn sou'westers, cardboard boxes, and now crowded with more fur coats. Lodenstein rooted around until he found a screwdriver, a hammer, and a shovel. *No one knows they've come close to getting their asses hauled up for roll call,* he thought. *They think this place is a carnival.* He kicked the broom closet shut.

The officer was lying calmly, without rancor, and looked like someone napping, with a pillow to shield his eyes from sun. Lodenstein had to fold him in half—difficult because the officer was still limp. He stuffed him into the duffel bag, shoving him so hard he heard a crack—perhaps he had broken a bone. He slung the duffel bag over his shoulders, locked his door, and took the mineshaft. He was prepared to say he was bringing extra letters to the hall—an unbelievable claim, since everyone knew he had nothing to do with the letters. But when he passed the Solomons' and Lars saw him with the duffel bag, the incredulous look on his face told him he didn't need an excuse.

Do you need any help? said Lars stepping forward.

Just keep the street clear, said Lodenstein.

Lars nodded and walked towards La Toya, who had already seen him.

He thought he heard La Toya saying something and couldn't wait to get back to the *trompe l'oeil*. But when he reached it, he stood by the lock, beset by accelerating fear. The Gestapo often shot people in this tunnel, years ago, at the beginning of the war. Sometimes, the arms fire was so furious, so frequent, they sounded like typewriters. When Stumpf was in charge, the Scribes wrote as many letters as they could because they were afraid of being dragged to this very same tunnel and shot. Suppose the SS were waiting for him now? Suppose the officer was someone the Reich wanted to get rid of, and they knew he'd use the room to bury him? Suppose there was an ambush? He forced himself to open the door, and once more the foul odor of waste overpowered him. He dragged the duffel bag through the moist, endless dark.

The chairs and table had been fastened with bolts and brackets. Lodenstein unscrewed them, furious at the time it took, but grateful that nothing clattered too loudly because even though the passage was soundproof, he was afraid the Solomons could hear. When they were unscrewed, he pried them apart with the hammer. But the seat of the chair—the pelvis—had been glued, and he had to smash it again and again until it shattered. One bracket stuck to a foot, and he pulverized the foot until the ankle turned to gravel. When the bones were in pieces, he covered the duffel bag with dirt, spread the dirt with bones, and smashed the heap with his shovel.

Before guards had been sent to the front, they had lived in Mueller's room. Lodenstein remembered it as a place of cards, drinking, and high-spirited arguments. Now it was crowded with rosewood furniture and still held a trace of Mueller's malevolent secrecy, as well as the faded scent of Elie's tea-rose perfume. Lodenstein hated the room, but was covered with dirt and bone and had to wash by sneaking to the kitchen, filling a soup pot with water, and dragging it to the room. He ripped sheets and scrubbed his face and hands and hair. The water grew thick and murky with dirt. He snuck to the kitchen again, refilled the pot, and dragged it back to the room. Mueller had left a green trench coat and long underwear in his closet. Lodenstein put them on and ripped the SS insignia from the trench coat. Then he swallowed some schnapps and listened to the Scribes getting ready for the night.

Shoes clattered and fabric rustled as people changed from one pair of street clothes to another. An argument erupted about the lottery. Then there was a barrage of typing—the last diary entry for the day or a new phrase in *Dreamatoria.*

He heard La Toya propose a game, and someone else say:

Not tonight. And no typing in that damned journal.

There's plenty to write about, said La Toya.

People were laughing about a word in *Dreamatoria.* Then there was a lottery for cigarettes. Then more laughing about another word. Lodenstein was incensed that people could laugh. He was incensed that the ordinary world could go on.

He stormed into the hall, thinking he'd get angry at the Scribes then decided he wanted to keep everything to himself— it would be too much for people who already lived in such fear, and since the incident with the officer, he felt even more protective of the Scribes. He stood outside Mueller's room, heard voices at the end of the hall, and, through flickering gaslights, saw Elie and Asher at the far end of the street. They couldn't see him, so he had the detached, nearly disembodied sense that he was watching a play. They were on a wrought iron bench sharing a cigarette, and looked gracious, slightly mannered. When they'd finished the cigarette, Asher went to his room, and Elie came down the hall. Lodenstein turned away. He felt relieved to be distracted by a twinge of jealousy. Elie touched his arm.

For God's sake, what happened to you? said Elie.

I can't tell you. But we'll sleep in Mueller's old room tonight. What were you two talking about anyway?

Whether we're safe, said Elie. She stood back and looked at him. Your hands are freezing. And what are you doing with Mueller's long underwear and his trench coat?

She led him back into the room and closed the door.

Sit down, she said.

She began to unlace his boots and startled when she saw they were caked with earth and splinters of bone.

Gerhardt, she said. Tell me what happened.

But he couldn't say a word—as though his throat were clogged with dirt.

Gerhardt, tell me.

He turned and held her shoulders.

Are you sure you want to know? he said. Are you sure you'd want to know if something I did helped turn you into a murderer? Tell me—would you really want to know?

Elie began to cry, and he let go his grip and held her. Her collarbone moved effortlessly, like wings. But the curve of her bones beneath took him back to the dark, moist room and the sight of a chair in a beam of white light. He felt something else too—an ineffable place inside her that held all the unseen mechanisms that let her dream and walk and breathe and be Elie. Then he was crying too.

Gerhardt, please, said Elie. Whatever you did is in a good cause.

I don't know what's in a good cause anymore, he said. We'll never wake up to an ordinary morning.

You mustn't think like that, said Elie.

But he was convinced he would never have her the way he wanted, and his sobs spilled into the hall and reached the Scribes and the kitchen and echoed with the pots and pans. It was a mournful cry that carried through the keys of the typewriters and the loose sheets of paper and the meters of dead dirt above them. It stunned the Compound into silence. It was the sound of a man breaking apart.

Adelajda,

*Społecze stwo z nasz cellblock mie znikn ł rezygnowa
pewien toczy zawoła , pewien wieszanie, albo pewien przestroga.
aden ma nadmieniony im. Tam zostały nie publiczny wieszania.
My pomy le oni maj zostawia rezygnowa pewien trop.*

Miło ,
Kacper

* * *

Adelajda,

Two people from our cellblock have disappeared without a
roll call, a hanging, or a warning. No one has mentioned them.
There have been no public hangings. We don't know how they left
without a trace.

Love,
Kacper

Elie held Lodenstein until he drifted into a restless sleep. When he began to breathe calmly, she eased into the covers but was beset by an image of his boots: mud, dirt, and splinters of bone. She closed her eyes, and the boots became more vivid. She moved towards Lodenstein and smelled earth. *No sleep tonight,* she thought.

But when she opened the door, she wasn't sure she could stand the silence of the Compound so late at night. It was pristinely, uncharacteristically silent without typing, lovemaking, even night cries. She wanted to talk to Asher again. She sensed that something more terrible than she could imagine had happened in the Compound, and Asher, who'd lived through shootings and hangings, would probably sense it too. She remembered he had a way of listening with great calm. He had listened to her this way in Freiburg when she started to worry about the war. And even though his own wife had disappeared, he was able to listen with an indescribable sense of peace.

She walked to the crates on the wall that dead-ended into the tunnel. The shadows of the large boxes were almost solid on the floor—light from the stars mere pinpricks. She traced her hands over the arched *trompe l'oeil* and knew, beyond any rational knowledge, that a dead officer was in the tunnel beyond her. It was why Lodenstein had cried and why his boots were caked with mud and bone. She heard a door open. Asher came over and stood beside her.

How's Lodenstein? he asked.

You heard him, said Elie. He says I've turned him into a

murderer. She sat on the cold floor and moved a crate over to make room for Asher.

People don't say what they mean when they come apart. And they usually put themselves back together again, said Asher.

He sat next to her by the crates. No one's a murderer here, he said.

I don't know what I think anymore, said Elie.

Asher took out a cigarette.

I've never heard this place so quiet, he said. The Scribes have even stopped fucking.

They have a lot to think about.

At least they've stopped with their questions. And their typing. A few of them just went to sleep, and a few others talked about their families. I don't even know what happened to most of mine. I'm just grateful Daniel's here.

You must miss your wife, Elie said.

Yes, Asher said. My mother as well.

I have no idea what's happened to my parents, said Elie.

And your sister? You never mention her anymore.

Elie waited, listening to pulleys and gears creak so the moon could rise. Then she said:

You first saw Gabriela more than ten years ago.

Yes, he said. He looked at her directly and his blue eyes took her back to Freiburg. Do you remember the time we went to that coffee house? Asher said. Gabriela was imitating Hitler. She was a great mimic. We laughed so hard we couldn't breathe.

I don't want to remember, said Elie.

She would want you to, said Asher. You two were so close.

Elie lit a cigarette and leaned back against a crate. Do you know you're the only person I know who remembers her? Maybe that's why I think of her whenever I see you.

You'll find her again, he said. People will come together when this war is over.

Elie leaned back and began to cry. She cried without moving, as though she imagined Asher wouldn't notice. Asher had seen people cry this way at Auschwitz: the slightest movement attracted attention, so they cried as if they were not.

He didn't try to hold her. Talking about her sister, stuck in this place, the crates around them filled with letters to the dead—everything overwhelmed him. All he did was offer another cigarette.

Elie rested against one of the crates, the wooden and ghoulish links between the dead and the living. She finished her cigarette and went back to the rosewood bed. Lodenstein was still in a deep, deep sleep. She touched him again —his hair, the scar on his forehead— and tried not to think about what he had done. Instead she thought about what Asher said and then about Gabriela, long ago, before the war. She remembered their childhood in Krakow, skating, swimming, playing street games on summer evenings—wild games where boys chased them. She remembered their decision to study in Germany and the night they told their parents they wanted to leave their house. She remembered Gabriela's first piano recital and the way she looked after she'd finished—illuminated, joyful—holding white roses. Bunches of white roses. Gabriela had been married to a man near Berlin just after the war began.

She'd always believed the reason she'd never told Gerhardt about Gabriela was to keep her past secret so he wouldn't know too much if he were ever questioned. But now she realized it was because she was afraid he wouldn't understand her relentless sense of heartache, the way she missed her sister every day. Asher had a particular way of understanding—a way that absorbed pain so unflinchingly it made it bearable. This made her feel unfaithful to Lodenstein, and she held him more tightly. He still smelled of earth, and she remembered the officer. There had been a shovel against the door, and Elie shifted to see its outlines: rough wood leading down to smooth, dull metal. Her movements woke Lodenstein up. He began to shake.

Gerhardt, she said softly, almost a whisper. It will pass.

He sat up and kept shaking—a violent rocking Elie had never seen. She persuaded him to get up with her and make tea. She led him into the kitchen.

It was still quiet in the Compound—although the quiet seemed comforting now. And the tea was warm and familiar. Elie rubbed Lodenstein's neck and kept telling him to drink more, holding the mug for him. All at once they heard the mineshaft open and Lodenstein rushed into the hall holding his gun.

But it was only Lars, walking towards them. He looked at Elie, not certain what she knew.

Are you okay? he said to Lodenstein.

I'm okay, said Lodenstein.

Elie poured Lars a mug of tea, but he shook his head no. He took an apple and peeled it the way his father had taught him—a single, perfect spiral, as if he were removing skin. Then he said:

There isn't any point in pretending we'll win this war. We should all just walk into the forest.

From the mouth of babes, said Lodenstein.

It's safer here, said Elie. Because we're all together.

Lars shook his head and handed them soft slices of apple. Fruit was becoming rare.

Do you know what my father once told me? he said. If you go to the heart of a city at night, you should know the safest way out before you start.

I wish more people had thought of that, said Elie. She looked as though she were about to cry again.

I should comfort her, Lodenstein thought. *I shouldn't let her dwell on this.* Yet he was drained from what he'd been through and kept looking at the rose-colored street that had become his world. It looked comfortingly soft with its flickering lamps, as though it might be a real street from a time that was still safe. The Solomons' house was lit. Everything felt bundled up inside him: He had to talk about what he'd been through. The murder, the dreadful room, his need to protect Elie, who must never hear the things he needed to say. But Mikhail might listen. Mikhail might understand.

He kissed Elie, told her to get some sleep, and walked to the Solomons' alone. Mikhail stared at Lodenstein's rumpled trench coat and long underwear when he answered the door.

We've been worried about you, he said. We thought you fell asleep.

I'm not sleeping at all.

Then why don't you come in? said Mikhail.

Lodenstein sat down and looked through the thick window at the frozen sky. Mikhail watched him quietly. Lars had told them to stay inside: it was too dangerous to climb the watchtower to see the stars tonight. He and Talia had spent the entire evening sequestered in the house. When they'd heard him crying, Talia said again, *This place is as bad as Lodz.*

After a moment, Mikhail said:

Lars said it was best not to go out tonight.

He was right, said Lodenstein. You won't see the stars for a while. No one should go out except to the well.

I know that, said Mikhail.

I'm sure everyone knows something about what happened, said Lodenstein. But there are things I don't want to talk about. Terrible things. Then he told Mikhail about the room. His flashlight. The bones.

For a moment Mikhail closed his eyes. Then he got up and went to the tiny kitchen for brandy and two glasses.

It's unbelievable what happens, said Mikhail, when he came back. Unbelievable that anything could be worse than my son being shot in a town square.

There's more, said Lodenstein. The room was full of furniture.

I understand, said Mikhail. But it doesn't help if you think about it too much. I would go mad if I thought about Aaron bleeding to death in the town square, his head rising and sinking.

I didn't think about it. I broke it apart. I buried everything.

I mean don't think about it now. If I thought about Aaron every night, I'd go crazy.

He poured Lodenstein another glass of brandy and sat next to him.

You should never think you have blood on your hands, he said.

You've never killed someone, said Lodenstein.

I never had the chance to, said Mikhail. He glanced toward Aaron's picture, which had been taken a year before his death. Aaron was smiling and looking directly at the camera.

Sometimes Mikhail imagined him looking straight into the direction of his death.

Terrible things go on all the time, said Mikhail. They're atrocities. Most of them are unbearable. But what you did wasn't one of them. People will thank you. You should thank yourself. You're fighting for what's good.

Lodenstein put his face in his hands then touched the scar on his forehead.

Did I ever tell you I got this from running into a fucking sled? he said. Wouldn't it be better if I got it from dueling?

Mikhail smiled: I think you're getting a little drunk. Which might be the best thing to do.

Maybe I am, said Lodenstein. He looked in the direction of the window and asked Mikhail if he had ever heard anything coming from the tunnel: Any gunshots. Any clattering.

No. And we hear everything. Talia has ears like a fox. Were you thinking of that room for a hiding place?

Yes. Until I saw it.

It would work in a pinch, said Mikhail. No one else has to know what you found.

They talked about Daniel, Asher, and Dmitri, and how they could hide them in the earthbound room. But Mikhail kept coming back to what Lodenstein had done and how he should always remember that everything he did was to save people. His voice was comforting, almost melodious, as though he were telling a bedtime story to a child. Lodenstein fell asleep, his head against a velvet chair.

Stefan,

Ik ben nog hier maar ik kan aan de omheining meer komen niet. Pietra neemt u deze brief. Ik houd van u. Hebt u om het even welk voedsel? Ik mis u en ik zie overal u.

D.

* * *

Stefan,

I am still here but I can't come to the barracks anymore. Someone is bringing you this letter. I see you everywhere.

D.

At four in the morning, Lodenstein woke up on the Solomons' velvet chair and raced out of their house to look for Elie. He'd dreamt he was walking in a city with narrow, labyrinthine streets and couldn't find her. But he saw her right away, sleeping at a desk near the main room. Elie had brought this desk from the outpost so Dmitri could pretend he was at school. But it was for the fifth form, much too big for him; so she'd moved the desk near the main room, defying Ewigkeit's vision of a city park. Now, with her head on the desk, she looked like a child kept inside for breaking a rule while the other children are allowed to play outside. Lodenstein edged onto the seat and nudged her awake.

Why are you sleeping out here? he said.

I've been thinking about when I was a kid, said Elie. Annoying nuns. Playing under the pine trees. This reminds me of being at school.

Did you have a desk like this?

Yes.

Did you ever fall asleep at it?

No. I was too busy bothering the nuns.

Lodenstein said he'd had a desk like it too. And even though this particular desk was set so incongruously in the hall, and even though it came from a school where children had been deported, it seemed to him as though everything—even light from the gas lamps and the crescent moon—was part of a world they'd once lived in above the earth. He took out his knife and began to carve their initials on the inside of the desktop.

What are you doing? Elie said.

Remembering us, he answered.

Elie said they could remember themselves, but he said they wouldn't necessarily remember themselves this way—not in the Compound, not so late at night, not so alone. He carved *ES + GL* inside a heart, and the time—*4:35*. Then he carved: *I love you.*

Elie traced the heart quietly. Everything seemed tilted in the light, as though it were cast in sepia and framed by the sheer certainty of having happened. Lodenstein allowed this sense of certainty to extend into the future and imagined a time when the murdered officer and the room with the bones would become smaller than the white stars above the watchtower receding at high tide. He could even imagine a time when the war was over, and he and Elie woke to an ordinary morning in a house with many windows. He felt capable of grand gestures, reckless proclamations—about where they would live after the war and how many children they would have and how they would read books to these children and play games with them in the snow and go through season after season, every one of them filled with happiness.

But all he did was lift Elie in his arms and carry her to Mueller's old room. He set her down, opened the door, and picked her up again. She'd been smoking while they talked, and her cigarette became a point of light that moved close to him, then far away. She threw it to the floor. He put it out with his foot. Then he set her on the bed and pulled the covers over both of them.

Are we safe? she asked.

We're safe for now, he said.

Lizavita,

Lepsza pogoda ma wyrabiany pracuj l ejszy: Ni jest twardszy
(trudniejszy; intensywniej) ni podniesienie kamieni w chłodzie. I
ludzie (lud) znalazł drog (rodek) do urz dników ' kuchnia, i znajdowa
(odkrycie) i kła (poło ył; poło ony) listy (litera) i rzucaj oni nad
płotem. One wołaj dzwoni do oni lagnappes i Ja daj wam jed po raz
nast pny widzimy siebie. Wy obmy laliby cie co wszystek udawałby si
lepiej, ale był zniszczony i tam jest coraz bardziej rozmawia
(rozmowa; mówi) po miertnych pochodów (granica; marzec). musimy
mie plan, Lizavita. I wy musicie przybywa do płotu. Mo e wy uwa acie
to? Ja przybył (przybywa ; wchodzi ; wszedł) kocha ten (to) okropny
płot dlatego e to jest gdzie widz was: długie zagrodzenia i criss-cross
elazo przypominaj o uwagi. Ja ' pewnni one graj * piew. Co najmniej
nikt pami ta (pilnuje) płoty wi cej. I mog mówi wam kocham was.

    Krill

              *   *   *

Lizavita,

    The better weather has made work easier: Nothing is harder
than lifting stones in the cold. And people have found a way to sneak
into the officers' kitchen, and put letters in the bread dough and throw
them over to the next barrack. I'll give you one the next time we see
each other. You would think everything would be better, but the ovens
have been blown up and there is more and more talk of death marches.
Can you believe I've come to love this strange border because this is
where I hear your voice?

    Krill

After he murdered the officer, Lodenstein took turns with Lars keeping watch at night. Goebbels's office remained silent, and there were no investigations about the Compound or the missing officer. Perhaps Goebbels had ordered the officer to ask for roll call and got distracted by Germany's losses. Or maybe Goebbels would send someone to investigate when they least expected it. And there was always the chance that the officer had come on a whim of his own, and not under the orders of the Reich. The Scribes took a gun when they went to the well and surrounded Dmitri while he was outside. Asher hardly went out at all.

Late spring came, then summer. Feverfew and milkweed spilled to the path, and purple flowers bordered the edge of the forest. Long ago they'd planted a winter garden, but now, because there was hardly any food, they planted one in summer as well. Since no one must know that anyone lived in the hut, they planted the vegetables far apart—in the clearing, in the forest, among wild flowers and feverfew. Rations were fewer and fewer. Lodenstein wouldn't let Elie go to the nearest town, but sent Lars, who came back with a paltry array of boxes. Even ersatz coffee was scarce. La Toya planted chicory to make the brew stronger.

In early autumn, some nightwalkers arrived with news that the Russians were closer to Berlin. The Compound celebrated with a feast—except for Stumpf, who sat uneasily at the end of the table polishing the glasses Asher had made him. There was excitement about the Germans and Allies getting closer to Berlin. People lifted their glasses often—even Dimitri, who sat next to Elie with a glass of water—and whenever Stumpf heard the word *defeat,* he closed his eyes. All during the feast— a meal now comprised of a few cans of tinned ham, a few root vegetables, and watered down wine—he stayed close to Hermione Rosebury. But after the meal, when people still were toasting, Stumpf asked for her help with another séance, saying: the dead mustn't feel neglected.

Hermione got up with reluctance, and they walked up the spiral steps to the shoebox of a watchtower, now crowded with crates of letters. Stumpf didn't bother with the seven latches on the door; but Hermione moved slowly, lighting candles strewn about the crowded space. Hermione was expert at channeling letter writers from every century. She had channeled the button makers, coach makers, furriers, boat makers, wheelwrights, printers, illusionists, and artists. She had channeled letters from old warehouses, government offices, and dusty, forgotten shops.

And although he wanted to talk to someone whose letter came from the camps, Hermione told him to proceed slowly so the dead could assemble peacefully. It was best to start with someone long before the war, she said, perhaps the button merchant in Dresden who never answered three letters from Frau Weil, a dressmaker in Alsace, who wanted jet buttons for a faille dress. Or better yet, Herr Ditcher in Köln, who had ordered a barouche coach from Herr Rahm, the famous coach maker in Stuttgart.

I don't care who you channel, said Stumpf. He kissed a crystal ball for luck. The glass clouded from his breath.

I want to talk to the coach maker, said Hermione, lighting the last candle.

They sat on wooden crates. Hermione called for Herr Dichter and began to read Herr Rahm's letters. The first was deferential, hesitant... *if you please... would you be so kind.* Herr Rahm wanted to know whether the interior of the coach could be painted light fawn instead of the agreed-upon Prussian blue. The second asked about the possibility of glass siding on the coach. The third said was abrupt and to the point.... *three months and no answer...it is now well into the summer months.....*

Hermione read each letter and Herr Rahm began to talk in an English accent.

I meant to write to him. But no coach is made of glass. This man was living a fairy tale

You should have found a way to tell him that, said Hermione.

There was silence. Stumpf, as he often did, patted Hermione's ample bum. Hermione rapped his hand and told him to stop.

Convey my apologies, said Herr Rahm.

I don't think an apology is enough, said Hermione. It's beautiful where he is. But he can't enjoy himself because he's waiting to hear from you.

Hurry up, said Stumpf. I don't want to talk to him all night. Just tell him about the other letters he didn't answer.

Don't coach me like that, said Hermione. Even so she said:

There are other people like him there, with ears against the sky.

Stumpf tried to sit still. But news of the Russians advances tumbled around in his mind. It was terrible, devastating news; yet he was sure the cracks in the world leaked through to the other side and that the dead knew things the

291

living couldn't, even if the news about Germany losing the war was a rumor He stood up and spread his hands -addressing every member of the dead whose letter was in the crate.

Tell me what's really going on with this war, he said. The truth!

There was silence. Stumpf wrung his hands.

Aren't we working hard enough for you? he said. Don't you know we have crates of your letters? We answer letters every day! What do you want?

Stop, said Hermione.

I deserve to know, said Stumpf. He threw the crystal ball on the ground. It shattered, and every candle in the room went out. The room was filled with the smell of smoke and melted wax. Hermione jabbed him.

We've lost them, she sad. You should never have done that.

Stumpf put his arms around Hermione and said this time he would let her speak and he would help her light more candles. She wasn't as willowy as Sonia Markova, but there was more of her and he took comfort from her body in the dark.

But all at once, Hermione pulled away and bolted to the corner of the shoebox. Stumpf felt an electric presence in the room. He couldn't see Hermione, but heard her gasp. Then she said she had a message from the future—a disconcerting message because she wasn't clairvoyant. She buttoned her blouse, ran down the spiral steps of the watchtower to the main room of the Compound, and shouted for everyone to listen. Her voice was wild, unleashed, and echoed through the enormous room. Scribes froze and looked at her.

Germany is going to lose the war, she shouted.

How do you know? the Scribes asked—almost in unison.

I just saw, said Hermione. Cities were burning everywhere. The Allies broke into the camps. Yes, she said. I just *saw*.

Only one person in the Compound wasn't excited about Hermione's vision, and this was Elie Schacten. True—as Lodenstein argued—Germany was losing the war, and there was always the storage room for Asher, Daniel, and Dmitri if warrant troops arrived on the premises. Still, nobody felt safe, and once again the Compound turned silent. Rations were dwindling; the gardens had to be replanted constantly. Lars installed an extra lock on the door of the shepherd's hut, and they hid what extra food they could beneath coats along the far wall and in desks where the Scribes pounded away at *Dreamatoria*.

The more Elie thought of what the nightwalkers had said, the more the Compound became two worlds—By day a place of silent anticipation and the spinning out of a novel in *Dreamatoria*. By night a solitary hell, where she paced the cobblestone street and still tried to think of people who would help Asher, Daniel, and Dmitri go to Denmark.

Night was especially dangerous at this stage of the war. Deserters were everywhere, and so was the Gestapo, hunting them, shooting on sight and at will anything that moved. Elie and Lodenstein cleaned the bed where the officer had been murdered. They laundered sheets and left the quilt to air. Then they moved back to the room to be close to the door leading to the shepherd's hut. No one was supposed to go out at night, but the Scribes craved warm summer air, and Lodenstein left two guns in a bucket by the door.

Elie took her own revolver and placed it in the shallow pocket of her coat as she smoked cigarettes under cover of a scarf. Sometimes she thought she saw figures moving in the woods—the SS, fugitives, Gestapo, deer—she couldn't know. Lodenstein often came looking for her—chiding her, pushing her back to the hut. And Scribes still came out to smoke.

No one stayed for long. The Scribes measured time by one cigarette, Elie by three. Now and then someone rooted for vegetables. Before going to bed, she took the mineshaft to the Solomons' house and looked at Dmitri through the window. Dmitri had become her touchstone: if she saw him sleeping, she believed the Compound would be safe for another night.

In this frame of mind, she sometimes forgot she was Elie Schacten, bringer of food as well as disaster, and became Elie Kowaleski, renegade daughter of two Polish Catholics with a sister who was a pianist. Both Elies made lists and walked on the cobblestone street. Both Elies looked at the Scribes under the cover of her scarf. And it was from this vantage point that she watched Stumpf disappear, with twenty-two crates of mail packed in the back of his Kubelwagen.

One late September night, the air was unseasonably warm, reminding Elie of summer nights when she was a child. She took a deep breath and felt the world had forgotten the war. The pine trees were swaying and breathing with the wind—they reminded Elie of notes on a piano. They had no sense of fugitives, deserters, or SS who might be weaving through them. The warm air lulled Elie. She felt free of lists and schemes and worries.

All at once she saw something move on the edge of her vision. The door to the shepherd's hut opened slowly and a figure stepped over its threshold. It was Lars. He carried a large duffel bag and crossed the grass quickly in the direction of the woods. Elie was about to call out to him, but he was surrounded in an aura of secrecy, almost absolute silence. So she waited and watched him move toward the thicker part of the forest. When he came to a copse of trees, she saw an arm reach out, grab him, and shove him against a pine.

Where are you going? said a voice in the trees.

I'm going to find my father, said Lars. This war is shit.

Elie startled when she heard a shot. Lars fell to the ground, collapsing in a heap. He twitched; she heard another shot, and his body was still.

A figure in a long coat emerged from the woods. It came closer, and Elie put her hand on her revolver. It was Mueller.

Fraulein Schacten, he said. I'm so sorry you had to hear that commotion.

Believe me, I've heard everything, she said.

I admire your perspective.

Mueller smelled of gunpowder and pine needles—the combination made Elie's stomach lurch. Mueller asked for a cigarette, and Elie handed him hers. She kept a hand on her revolver.

Where did you come from? she asked.

From the trees, said Mueller.

Like a troll, said Elie.

Like the Reich, he said.

He put an arm around her and asked how she was managing. Elie said she was managing very well and Mueller said she probably wasn't managing as well as she thought.

Elie looked at Lars's body, as still as a fallen tree. She wanted to rush over to him—this desire was strong, like a heartbeat, but she forced herself to stand still.

I've been lucky in this war, she said.

And you may still be lucky, said Mueller. If you listen to me.

He took her arm and walked her toward a large pine tree. He walked with verve, as though they'd just left an opera and were promenading down a boulevard. The air had a stale, cloying sweetness.

It's lovely to see you, said Elie. But I have to go.

Maybe to my Kubelwagen, said Mueller. But not to stay here.

Elie edged away. Mueller came closer and held her chin.

I have news for you, he said. And not the kind you get on Radio Free Europe.

I have all the news I need, said Elie.

Not this news, said Mueller with reckless gaiety. Elfriede Heidegger has been poking around. She says her husband made a useless trip to Auschwitz and then was left all by himself in the snow at an empty train station. Neither of them are pleased.

A useless trip, he continued. And now Goebbels has your name.

What other lies are you making up? said Elie.

He slapped her hard across the face. She felt it in her teeth.

I don't have to make up lies, said Mueller, who was almost shouting. Goebbels knows you disobeyed an order, and he's going to kill you. But I can hide you. I'm getting out of this war. You'd be surprised at the places I could take you.

I don't want to be anywhere near you.

Come with me, he said. You've been with that joke of a Nazi much too long.

He edged Elie into the tree. She felt sharp branches and needles piercing her back. He ripped open her blouse and she felt warm air against her breasts. He shoved a hand against them. She held tight to the gun in her pocket.

There's always been something between us, he said. I've been patient for over a year.

There's never been anything between us.

Of course there has, he said. He jerked a sleeve of her blouse by the shoulders. Elie heard the hiss of ripping silk and in an instant felt the pines turn to glass needles, the air a sweet poison. She imagined how he would tear off her clothes and his ring would dig into her face and his moustache would froth against her mouth—all while he forced himself into her. She pulled her revolver from her pocket, pointing its barrel against his ribs. Mueller took a step back.

So you have a gun, he said. Like everyone else in this fucking war.

Except I'm not afraid to use it, said Elie.

She fired a shot, just into the woods. And then another.

If you ever touch me again, I will kill you, she said.

I don't think so. They'll be after you soon enough. And that little boy with the *Echte Jude*? They know about him, too. I made sure of that.

Elie fired another shot. Get out of here, she said.

Mueller pulled a bottle from his coat and took a long pull. Then he threw it on the ground and walked in the direction of the road. He hadn't come from the forest but from his Kubelwagen. When Elie heard it grumble into the night, she walked over to Lars's body. Without blood blooming on his chest, he might just be asleep. She pushed back his hair and stroked his forehead. She shut his eyes. She took a handkerchief and wiped blood from the corner of his mouth. She gathered pine boughs and covered his body. Then she picked up the bottle;

it was French cognac with a small note around the neck—the same words on the order Lodenstein had seen:

Translators are traitors.

Francois,

Peut-être tu ne me vu pas encore. Sais-tu qu t'aime.

Robin

* * *

François,

You may not see me again. Please know that I love you.

Robin

Elie raced downstairs and looked through the Solomons' window. Dmitri was sleeping near Talia and Mikhail, who were once again playing chess—so engrossed in the game they didn't notice her. She went upstairs where Lodenstein was putting a note into the trunk.

Do you ever stop finding things? she said.

They keep washing up, said Lodenstein.

Like stuff from the sea, said Elie.

Like stuff from the war, he said.

Elie took off her ripped clothes and got into bed. Lodenstein got into bed with her.

You can't go out so late, he said. You know they blew up the gas chambers.

Elie hesitated. Then she said:

Mueller was in the forest. He's a deserter now.

I'm not surprised, said Lodenstein. We should drink to never having to worry about him again. He reached for the last of their schnapps.

Gerhardt, she said. I have terrible news. Mueller shot Lars. He killed him.

Lodenstein's reaction was immediate: he began to cry; large gulping sobs. Elie stroked him, feeling the bruise of the pine needles against her back, wishing she never had to tell him such news.

Look at what I've brought to this place, she said.

Lodenstein forced himself to stop crying. You only bring good things, he said.

I don't, she said. Not at all.

Lodenstein lit a lantern and put his arms around her. Elie watched the soft circle of light on the ceiling.

We're still in this room, he said. And we're still together. Mueller's not going to come back. He just wanted to scare you.

But there *are* things to be scared of, said Elie. Mueller told the Reich about Dimitri. He says the Heideggers are bothering Goebbels again. They told him my name.

He's bluffing.

No, said Elie, he isn't. He'd left the Compound by the time Stumpf went to deliver the glasses to Heidegger. He doesn't know Stumpf told them my name.

Elie, listen: We've been through the worst of it. We'll make it through now.

They could still come after me.

There's always the room in the tunnel.

Suppose the Gestapo's there?

No one's going to be there. We've come to the end of this war.

A bedtime story, Elie thought, *something I'd tell Dimitri.* Still, she leaned closer to Lodenstein, trying to ignore the stinging in her back and an image of Lars' body alone in the forest. Lodenstein was real, durable, alive. And the room almost felt safe. He turned off the lantern, and they lay beneath the grey silk comforter. It was tattered. Elie touched one of the holes.

We ought to get another one, she said. This is careworn.

Careworn, said Lodenstein, just before he fell asleep.

Elie lay next to him, trying to retrieve the comforting sense of dark. But it dissolved into images of Lars's body and the sensation of Mueller's hands ripping open her blouse.

The night has been broken for me, she thought, not knowing if she were remembering something she'd heard or if it were something she'd just thought of.

But no matter where it came from, the thought *the night has been broken for me* acted on her strangely. She couldn't lie still or enjoy the quiet comfort of Lodenstein's body. Nor could she trust what he'd told her. She dressed in her ripped clothes, covered them with her coat, and went downstairs again. When the mineshaft opened, she saw Asher coming from the main room.

Stupid of me, he said when he saw her. What does it matter if I stand next to them?

Elie said she didn't know what he meant, and he told her he was so worried about Daniel getting Maria pregnant he sometimes stood next to their desks—as if his presence were a kind of birth control. He said it was strange and aberrant, listening to his own son making love.

As strange as anything I've ever done, he said.

Don't worry, said Elie. Maria has a lot of French letters.

That's good, said Asher. They're the only letters here worth answering.

Elie laughed and was surprised that she could. Asher sat next to her on the bench. She touched the blue numbers on his arm.

Those match your eyes, she said to him again.

That's good, he said, because I'm going to have these numbers for a long time.

The phrase *the night has been broken for me* came back to her. She began to fuss with her blouse so Asher couldn't see it was torn.

What is it? he said.

Nothing, said Elie. Just: How do you explain that the night has been broken?

No one has to, said Asher.

Elie nodded.

She suddenly remembered getting out early from a lecture and seeing Asher and Gabriela walking in a little park in the rain. They were bathed in mist, and Elie saw them the way one sees distant figures about to disappear: she loved and yet ached at the sight of it. She'd raced to catch up, and all three of them had walked into the mist together. She hadn't thought of this moment in years. An ocean of fear swelled and subsided inside her.

What did you really see in Auschwitz? she asked.

Asher took a deep breath.

Everything, he answered.

Elie had an odd sensation that she and Asher shared a private universe—different from the one she shared with Lodenstein. This world was from long before the war—a world of unveilings, revelations, disclosures. She and Lodenstein were partners in a mission. They shared fear for the Compound as well as hope for the future. She looked at the mineshaft and a sliver of the kitchen where Lars once peeled apples in perfect spirals.

Can I talk to you alone? she said.

Asher nodded and they walked down the hall.

Once more Elie was reminded of Asher's office in Freiburg. She saw papers with phrases in *Dreamatoria*, as well as books. There were also typewriters in every stage of reconstruction and disarray and a blue and white coffee mug on the floor. Inside the storage room, Asher lit the Tiffany lamp and handed Elie a glass of wine.

But Elie pushed the wine glass away. She was close to tears and her voice shook when she told Asher that things were in a shambles: Mueller had just killed Lars. The Heideggers gave Goebbels her name. And Goebbels knew about Dimitri.

This place isn't safe, she said. And you and Daniel and Dimitri aren't safe. You have to find a way to take them to Denmark. Maria, too.

You know we'd all be shot our first night in the forest.

Asher, you don't understand. You're in too much danger if you stay. Elie began to cry. She couldn't stop and put her head in a pillow.

Elie, said Asher.

What? said Elie.

This, he said. And he put his arms around her.

Elie felt an arc of warmth through her body. Asher held her and stroked her hair. It was as if he knew everything—the pine needles at her back, the sound of gunshots, the hiss of ripping silk. And how, in spite of hundreds of forays, she could never find the one person she was looking for.

When she had stopped crying, Elie stood up and looked around his room—the collection of books, notes for *Dreamatoria*, cartridges, keys, spools, and all manner of metallic shapes.

Thank you, she said.

Moments later, she was surprised that the cobblestone street looked the same. She walked to the main room, where Parvis Nafissian was working with some fabric. Years ago he'd apprenticed as a tailor with his father in Turkey, and sometimes it amused him to make clothes for people in the Compound. When Elie came in, he held up a lace bodice.

Perfect for Gitka, she said.

Our siren, said Nafissian.

No one took notice of their conversation. Nor did anyone notice when Elie sat at the school desk, writing once again in the dark red notebook. This time, she wrote quickly, filling one page, then another, as if she didn't write fast enough the words would fly off the paper into the air. When she'd finished, she went upstairs and put the notebook in Lodenstein's trunk. He reached for her in sleep, and she got into bed, treasuring the careworn quilt, the sliver of forest—pine boughs on each edge of the blackout curtains. She could feel Lodenstein's strength. She could feel every bone in his body. And when he woke up and they made love, everything that happened in the forest disappeared. She only recognized her own face by the way he touched it—brushing her eyelids, tracing her mouth, caressing the curve of her cheekbones. She only recognized the room by the feel of his body. No lovemaking could be deep enough. She could not find him enough, could not touch him enough, could not kiss him enough. They had always been part of something larger than the war—something timeless, secret, unrecorded.

He drifted to sleep holding her, and Elie waited until he was in a deep sleep, far away from her, to untangle herself. She stood in the door for a long time watching him.

Lodenstein woke a few hours later in an empty bed, threw on his trench coat, and went outside. It was just dawn, and sun fell in shafts through the pines. He looked for Elie in the vegetable garden then saw the fresh tracks on the grass. Her jeep was gone.

He went down the incline and rattled the diamond grating of the mineshaft, as if that would make it move faster. A few Scribes were making their way to the kitchen, rubbing their eyes. He heard someone mention the lottery, then the strike of the match for the first cigarette of the day.

He went to the kitchen: Elie wasn't there. Maria, in a moment of being only seventeen, put her head on his shoulder and said she'd had bad dreams. He patted her and went to the main room of the Compound. No sign of Elie. He opened the door to Mueller's old room. She wasn't there either.

He knocked on the storage room. Asher answered.

Have you seen Elie?

Asher shook his head.

Her jeep isn't here, said Lodenstein.

Just then Talia Solomon came rushing from the main room of the Compound.

Dimitri's gone, she said.

His eyes met Asher's. Both shrewd, both blue, both like Elie's. Did this random resemblance bring her into the room? For a moment Lodenstein thought it did.

He went back to the main room, opened the top drawer of Elie's desk and saw a note that said *To Gerhardt*. He put it in his pocket and went upstairs, hurrying past their room on the incline.

The late summer had begun to turn cold. Pine trees shook with the wind as if simple people lived in the shepherd's hut and an ordinary day without the war was starting. Once Lodenstein believed that the mind and the weather worked in tandem, but he'd come to realize that the weather was oblivious to everything. It shone and rained on atrocities and kindnesses, stinginess, violence, and generosity. It showed up for wars, weddings, peace treaties, and betrayals. For a moment he felt jealous of the weather because Elie would always feel its heat, its snow, its rain. Indeed, she must be somewhere now, feeling the violent wind.

He had never known this place without Elie. She'd driven him on the narrow road, shown him the forest, the shepherd's hut, taken him into the earth, and introduced him to the Scribes. She'd explained the mechanical workings of the sun and the architect's dream about the street and the city park. He'd never seen this place without sensing her presence—even when they were fighting or she was gone on a foray. Now he looked at the forest alone for the very first time. It was blank, without dimension—not a forest, but a collection of trees. The feverfew waved in random clusters. The clearing where Elie parked her jeep reverberated with absence. He looked at the tracks of her tires and realized he would never again wait for her to come back from a foray or rush out late at night to confirm she was safe.

A few months ago, Lodenstein had taken another photograph of Elie in the clearing, which he always kept with him. Her hair was drawn back in a red bow and she wore a white silk blouse with a white velvet rose pinned to the collar. He looked at it and felt her next to him: he could even see her blue eyes and the bright white of the velvet rose. Everything about her came back to him—her delicate bones, her tea-rose perfume, the way she brought the entire world to the Compound.

Elie, he said, as if her name would invoke her presence.

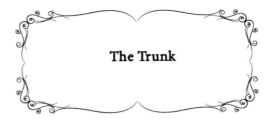

The Trunk

Dearest Gerhardt,

I know my actions have brought tremendous harm to the Compound. It's hard to believe this happened because of a simple pair of glasses. I thought I'd be able to handle everything. But I couldn't. I wasn't even sure I'd be able to leave. But Dmitri is in danger—and I need to save as many people as I can. I hope you will understand. You must make sure that Asher and Daniel don't go out anymore and that they have a clear passage to the room in the tunnel. There is extra flour hidden in the right-hand cupboard of the kitchen and five tins of ham in a crate underneath the sink. It's not very much, but I hope it will last.

I can't begin to tell you how much I love you. I can't begin to tell you how much I've thought about what you did for me, for all of us, and how you stood by me even when I brought unspeakable risk to this place. I know we both agreed to be nearly invisible for the sake of other people. I also know you did this much better than I did.

I wonder what people will think of the Compound after the war, and whether they'll remember us at all. I wonder if people will ever visit the cobblestone street piled with crates and the kitchen where La Toya made soup and the Solomons' house where Dmitri played with Mufti. Or maybe this place will be forgotten. How strange if no one ever knows about the room where so many people played word games and slept and cried out. How strange if no one ever sees the sun rise on pulleys or the fake stars that shone on Hitler's birthday. And how sad if no one remembers Dreamatoria.

Please keep everyone here safe for me. And please hold them close, as I will hold them close, as I will hold you close.

Love always,
Elie Kowaleski

311

Elie left eight months before the fall of Berlin. A week after Berlin fell, the Scribes smelled smoke and worried that fire would reach the forest. Only Asher and Daniel weren't worried. They'd both seen death up close.

But the forest around the Compound never caught fire. And a month after Berlin surrendered, Gerhardt Lodenstein guided the Scribes down the long tunnel, past the room with the bones, eleven kilometers in the dark next to the rushing stream, until they climbed into the sunlight of a northern town. Emaciated women cleaning the streets, not sure if their part of Germany had surrendered to the Russians, looked in amazement as almost sixty people in fur coats, many of them wearing glasses, emerged from a hole in the ground. They also saw an enormous trunk, followed by a wheelbarrow. Last to come up was a tall pale man in a trench coat.

Before they left the Compound, Lodenstein asked each Scribe to put a memento in the trunk. The ceremony was done with impatience and indulgence. The Scribes had spent nearly eight months with almost no food, but Lodenstein risked his life driving to town for the few rations they had, never wavering in his protection.

Into the trunk, Sonia Markova put a red glove. La Toya two cigarette holders. Gitka a fur coat. Mikhail and Talia Solomon their chess set. Nafissian a dictionary for *Dreamatoria*. Some tore a page from a coded diary. Asher put in his blue and white coffee mug. And Lodenstein added them all, right next to the pair of Heidegger's glasses.

Now the trunk stood before them like a living thing, as if it were waiting for a chance to speak. No one wanted it, and no one could say so out of respect for Lodenstein. All they wanted was to leave the Compound for good—to walk on real streets and travel to places far beyond this town. They wanted to see if they still had families. They wanted to see if they still had houses.

Lodenstein gave the trunk to Daniel because he was the youngest.

Keep it, he said. Keep it safe.

Daniel nodded, and Asher reluctantly took the trunk, which was still on the wheelbarrow. The Scribes hugged, kissed, and gave each other addresses of houses that might not exist. Then Maria and the Solomons had an altercation –the first one he'd ever heard –because Maria wanted to leave with Daniel.

Absolutely not, said Mikhail. You belong with us.

Lodenstein watched Daniel and Maria hug and kiss and cry. Asher and Mikhail exchanged a number of addresses so the two could write. He watched Gitka and La Toya disappear with their cigarette holders. And Sophie Nachtgarten walk away slowly, carrying Mufti. Indeed, he watched every since Scribe leave him, feeling more and more bereft. For so long his focus was on protecting them, feeding them, keeping them safe. Now he knew he would begin a long search for Elie. There were so many Kowaleskis in the world, and so many hadn't gone back to Poland because Poland had as many bad dreams as Germany.

Cari madre e padre,

Sto trasmettendo cinque copie di questa lettera alla gente differente che contribuisce a popolare il ritrovamento. Ora sono in un accampamento dove i soldati stanno alimentandolo e molto la gente.

Ero fortnato perché quando li hanno cominciati al mach via a, ho funzionato nei legno. E e per due settimane, ho vissuto su neve. Ma allora i Russi lo hanno trovato. Così sono giusto. Dove siete? Venga prego ottenerlo. Desaidero andare a casa.

Amore,
Nathalia Vernetti

*   *   *

Dear mother and father,

I am sending five copies of this letter to places that help people find each other. I am in a camp now where soldiers are feeding me and a lot of other people.

I was lucky because I ran into the woods when they began to march us away. For a week all I had to eat was snow. And then the Russians found me. Where are you? I want to go home.

Love,
Nathalia Vernetti

Elie never found a way to take Dmitri to Denmark. She went to a safe house in Berlin and stayed there until the city began to burn. For a few moments Elie and Dmitri saw preternatural brilliance from their window—an unholy illumination of roofs. Then flames leapt over chasms as if they'd lost each other and were reaching to reunite. A few days later when Berlin surrendered, Elie left the safe house and she and Dmitri saw Berlin in a haze – not the filmy haze of the Compound, but the smoky haze of dust and rubble. Elie found an apartment someone vacated long ago—a four-room apartment with bombed-out windows and dead plants. The building had seven other apartments with new residents in every one of them, all of them living among artifacts of lives they hadn't known, ranging from unfamiliar photographs to upright pianos. And since three of the residents spoke no German, they never asked Dimitri questions but only played him songs, taught him dances, gave him extra food from their own humble rations. Perhaps this was why Dimitri began to talk more and more – about his parents, about his favorite foods, about walks he liked to take.

In early autumn, Elie found a job as a translator in a hospital, an apartment with intact windows, another calico cat, and a school for Dmitri, who had developed a surprising gift for making friends. And all during this time she searched for Lodenstein. Berlin was an eerie switchyard where sometimes showing a photograph to a stranger led to a reunion.

Men and women whom Elie met—in restaurants, in banks, walking in the park— looked at Lodenstein's photograph and nodded. She'd been to beer halls, apartments, offices, and looked through hundreds of files—files with names of people in the 19th century, files of pardoned officers. She even knocked on doors of tenants with the last name *Lodenstein*. Nothing.

The hospital where Elie worked was near the center of Berlin, and a few times on her lunch hour she walked through the Brandenburg Gate. Dust rose through its columns which were pocketed with holes from grenades. She walked on to Wilhemstrasse and the burned, bombed hulk of the Reichstag: Here was the jail where Lodenstein had been thrown. And Goebbels's office where Lodenstein had bargained. Elie watched birds fly around beheaded statues on the roof and sometimes went close to the boarded-up buildings, as if she must pay homage to Lodenstein and even find him. Then she walked back through the befuddled city, lush with arching linden trees, smelling of lilacs and dust. Every cobblestone street had been blown to bits. She tripped over rose-colored shards.

Elie kept looking for Lodenstein—dragging Dmitri to the border of West Berlin on weekends or to different neighborhoods after school. No matter what their route, they saw houses bombed beyond recognition—windows that opened to the sky, empty doorways that led to rooms without floors or smoky halls and shattered furniture. A few houses had only one wall half standing, as though they'd been amputated.

Elie looked at every house, as well as every man on the street. One was as tall as Gerhardt. Another had his blue eyes. Another his shambling walk.

Tonight a man with brown hair waved, and Elie waved back. She knew him because they'd been in the same safe house. But strangers waved, too, because they assumed they'd met in a dark basement during a bombing: there were long hours in the shelter, and the combination of anonymity and fear encouraged complete strangers to exchange confidences. It was not that different from the Compound at night.

Elie stopped a neighborhood policeman to give him an illegal order for a *Brotbaum*—bread tree—the only way Berliners could get enough food. Tonight she'd written: *chocolate, fresh bread, potatoes in exchange for translation of Polish, French, Dutch, German, English, Russian, Czech, as well as expert advice about finding missing relatives.* As always, Elie walked slowly, hoping that when they came home, Lodenstein would be waiting on the steps. She imagined him in his rumpled green sweater—tall, tense, looking in her direction. But the steps were empty. They were always empty.

She began to search for her keys and heard excited voices inside the foyer. They were male voices and spoke with urgency.

Elie rummaged through her purse, found her keys, dropped them, and waited while Dmitri found them in the dark. She worked the lock and clamored to the landing as though she'd been trapped in ice, racing—as she always did—with anticipation. She was sure one of the voices had Lodenstein's pace and timbre—the way he emphasized words when he was making a point, or talked quickly when he sensed danger.

But all she found were her landlord and another man, a man who was not Gerhardt Lodenstein, talking about the price of potatoes.

Two months later, Elie took Dmitri to the least bombed-out place she could find—a neglected city park where grass was

319

starting to grow in patches. It was a damp spring evening, the air was filled with the smell of lilacs and moist earth, and she and Dmitri passed through a rusted wrought iron gate to an enclosure. Dmitri carried two fresh roses, and Elle carried—with some difficulty—a rough piece of granite. She put the granite in the earth and placed a white rose on top of it. Around the stem of the rose she had tied her frayed and worn red ribbon. Engraved on the stone were the words:

Gabriela. You are always with me. Your loving sister, Elie.
Is she really dead? Dmitri asked.
Yes, said Elie. Why?
I don't know. I just wondered.

Elie knew why Dmitri wondered. He lived in tenuous hope, because he didn't know if his parents were alive. It was the hope of imagined reunions, and Elie still lived with this hope every day, knocking on doors, going to beer halls, looking through the sort of files and letters that would have delighted Stumpf. The dead and the missing still haunted her: except now they were above the ground. Sometimes she wondered what had happened to the crates. Sometimes she thought about the Scribes: if they were still writing; what had happened to *Dreamatoria*; if Gitka and La Toya were still together. She remembered the twilit room, the pounding typewriters, the kerosene lamps, the cold. But she always returned to Lodenstein.

Now she lit incense by the grave. It smelled cold and sweet, reminding Elie of childhood cathedrals in Poland, where Gabriela poked her during mass when she fell asleep. It was unthinkable that she had been killed—something she couldn't tell Lodenstein or even Asher. For this was the truth about her sister, told by a friend who had seen it ten years before the war.

Gabriela had been marched to a small town square near Berlin and shot almost seven years before the Reich came into office. Her head rose up again and again in a pool of her own blood and her body had been carted off in a wagon and dumped somewhere in a field.

She had been in the earliest part of the Resistance—intercepting messages and sending them to England, starting to forge passports. *And you should help, too,* she'd told Ellie more than once. As soon as she heard the news, Elie had gone to the town to look for Gabriela's body, not believing her friend who said it was dragged off in a cart. But all she saw was a faint pool of blood in a town square surrounded by linden trees. A few months later she left Freiburg, with only a note to Asher and the university. She began to go to Party meetings. She used her charm to meet inner members of the Party until she found Goebbels, who needed a linguist. She was driven to find a way to rescue as many people as she could—an impossible, insatiable penance for Gabriela's death.

Are we done? said Dmitri.

Not quite, said Elie. She handed him the fresh red rose.

But she's not my sister!

It's for all the people you love.

What if I don't love anybody?

I love you enough for both of us, said Elie.

She leaned down and hugged Dmitri. He hugged her back. Now give this to my sister, she said.

Dmitri put the rose on the grave.

Do you remember how you found me? he asked.

I'll always remember, said Elie.

And how you brought me to that place?

I'll always remember that too.

And how all those people wrote letters?

I remember.

Dmitri stepped back and looked at the grave. That guy with the chins made me write them, he said. To kids. Did you write letters too?

Only one, said Elie. But I kept it in a notebook.

As for the trunk, it began a Diaspora: First to a Russian refugee camp with Daniel, Asher, and Maria, who stayed with them because she had no living relatives. Then across the Atlantic to New Jersey, where Asher's sister taught piano lessons on a tree-lined street in Hackensack. Then to an apartment in Greenwich Village, then to one in Brooklyn, then to a typewriter shop on the Upper West Side. The trunk stayed in attics, in basements, in houses with yards, in cramped one-room walk-ups. No one bothered to open it. The contents began to grow rife with mold. Forgotten.

Asher remarried. He refused a teaching job, saying philosophy was only an endless series of invented arguments, and set up a typewriter repair shop on Broadway in the Upper West Side. Daniel got a doctorate in chemistry. And Maria, who came to New York as soon as she turned twenty, became an art historian. Daniel and Maria were married in a small ceremony in a Brooklyn temple. They kept the trunk but argued about throwing it away.

Why not the East River? said Maria.

Or a lake in the Berkshires? said Daniel.

But throwing the trunk in the water seemed unthinkable, and one hot summer day, when they couldn't stand the sight of it, Maria and Daniel gave the trunk to Asher, who kept it in the back of his shop. It sat among the spools and ribbons, the keys, and dull metals.

322

It was Daniel and Maria's oldest child who was responsible for opening the trunk. Her name was Zoë-Eleanor Englehardt—everyone called her Zoë. Zoë was thin, blond, and liked mathematical puzzles. At least once a month, after school, she walked into her grandfather's typewriter repair shop with the commanding presence of someone distracted by something important.

That trunk, she'd say to her grandfather. I need to see it.

Asher never encouraged Zoë to open the trunk. But even as he tried to dissuade her, she would pry it open, breathing the smell of moldy paper, the faint aroma of tea-rose perfume. The top was covered with Ferdinand La Toya's handkerchief; folded and refolded so many times it looked like the bare palm of someone thousands of years old. Zoë-Eleanor saw stamps of every color and nationality, and pictures of statesmen whose names had umlauts, cedillas, tildes, and graves. She saw letters in every imaginable language. Most were on thin, brittle paper, a few typed on thick ivory stock, with deep seals and official letterhead. Some were on vellum in old-fashioned, calligraphic handwriting. Beneath the letters were green notebooks that reminded Zoë of her own diary. There was also a manuscript her grandfather said close to sixty people had written, in a language only they knew, and he'd never bother to translate it because— he said with an ironic smile—translators are traitors.

There were also numerous objects: velvet roses shredded from age, empty perfume bottles, a blue and white coffee mug, two fur coats, five fingerless gloves, a lace blouse, an ermine scarf, a black lace corset, a silver hand-mirror, a broken wool carder, black cigarette holders, two maps, a gun, photographs, and a pair of glasses marked *für Martin Heidegger*.

When Zoë tried on the glasses she saw the world in a blur, a place with no distinct edges, and her grandfather told her to take them off. Everything in the trunk had come from an unbelievable place, ten meters under the earth, he said. It was a place that had saved his life and the lives of her mother and father, even though none of them wanted to talk about it. And it contained an infinite number of objects. Every time he closed the shop in the evening, Asher had to pull Zoë away from it.

It's a magic trunk, he said to her. There will always be one more thing left to find. And one more thing after that.

Zoë turned into a wispy teenager and majored in philosophy of science to the mixed reviews of her grandfather, who said to her, more than once: *Philosophers only engage in endless arguments. They have principles but never live by them.*

Like Martin Heidegger? said Zoë, whose glasses she remembered.

Like everybody, said Asher.

Zoë was no longer interested in the trunk, and Asher never mentioned it. But when he was closing his shop for good, he summoned Zoë. She floated in with the same distracted authority she'd had as a child, except now she had a diamond in her nose and purple streaks in her hair. Asher took her to the back of the shop and pulled out the trunk.

I want you to have this, he said.

I haven't thought about it in years, said Zoë.

But you used to love it as a child, said Asher. Maybe you'd even like to archive this world someday.

Why didn't you?

You know why I didn't, Asher said. I never wanted to be another found object from the Holocaust. Neither did your mother and father.

Zoë, who'd heard all this before, didn't say anything. She opened the trunk, was overcome by the smell of mold, closed it and took it by taxi to her Lower East Side apartment. When she opened the trunk again, she couldn't remember why she once found it so compelling. Its contents, once mysterious and totemic, now bristled with darkness, captivity, and reproach. She picked up a letter in German—a language she could read now—and saw that it extolled conditions in the camps. She picked up a letter in Polish, which she couldn't read, and sensed terror in the short, hurried script. She knew she was reading lies.

Besides letters there were diaries, concealing old photographs. Zoë saw the illuminated face of a red-haired man named Benyami Nachtgarten. The slightly bewildered face of a baby named Shalhevet Nafissian. The studious face of a teenager named Alexei Markova. The whimsically elongated face of a woman named Miriam La Toya, who looked like she was laughing at a party. It was clear these people had died because there were two dates on the back of the photographs. Zoë assembled them and imagined these people in a country of their own. They looked alive, curious, happy together.

She also looked at the old letters—to a 19th-century dressmaker in Alsace, a button dealer in Dresden, a lawyer in Stuttgart. Letters from the time *before* the time that mattered; a time when no one ever thought about writing to make false records; a time when the dead didn't need letters to stop the world from falling apart; a time when people didn't depend on knowing languages to save their lives; a time when letters were helpful to the living, not used to sentence them to live below the earth. And a time when letters brought the living together and weren't used as weapons or to rewrite history.

Because most of the letters were just that—weapons, devices. And, like things that one didn't want to see but saw anyway, they reminded her of the numbers on the arms of her father and grandfather. Even worse, the letters conveyed terrible news because of what they left out. They reminded Zoë of silences she'd felt as a child when grown-ups pretended there wasn't tension while she knew—sitting at the dinner table, at her desk at school—that something unspeakable was being avoided. They even reminded her of silences now, when people hardly mentioned anything difficult—in their own lives, in the lives of other people. The last time she'd heard of anything painful was when a neighbor said that he'd told his son to see the world— meaning he should visit relatives in Italy, not join the Marines and take a piss by the banks of the Euphrates. But that, in fact, was just what he was going to do. *Holy places*, he'd said. *Bombed to ruins.*

What's the use of talking about what's difficult, if people aren't going to listen? Zoë asked her grandfather when she visited his book-strewn apartment. And what good would it do to archive a trunk?

Maybe no good at all, said Asher. But don't ever get rid of it.

When Asher died at ninety-five, Zoë was living on the Upper West Side in an apartment that had been chopped into three smaller apartments. She lived in the part that had a maid's room, and she gave the trunk to it so she'd never have to look at it. After his memorial service, where she'd shaken hands with innumerable people, she spent some time looking at the trunk, but she did not open it. It was the most vibrant link to her grandfather. She knew that at the very least she should look through it carefully. Instead, she shut the door.

A few mornings later, she got a call from a man with a German accent who said his name was Gerhardt Lodenstein. His English was precise, and he apologized for intruding. He said he'd just read her grandfather's obituary—they'd corresponded for a while. And he wasn't calling from below the earth but from Germany.

It took Zoë a moment to believe she was hearing from someone who had lived in that place. And before she was able to say she was glad to hear from him, Lodenstein said he understood her grandfather had given her the trunk and there were a few more photographs he'd like to send. He also asked if she'd consider exhibiting the contents.

Zoë knew her grandfather wanted this. He'd telegraphed his desire when he gave her the trunk. And he'd always made what happened to him clear by the way he kept his shirtsleeves rolled up, even in winter—exposing the numbers on his arm. But Zoë had come to loathe the trunk. So she told Lodenstein she would have to think about it—sure her final answer would be no—and surprised herself by bringing a few letters to the public library the same evening. People with stacks of five-by-eight cards looked curiously at the wispy woman with purple streaks in her hair. The letters emanated the dank mineral smell of the mine, as if determined to broadcast their history to the library.

That night Zoë went back into the maid's room and opened the trunk slowly. Here was an empty bottle. She could almost smell the tea-rose. And here was a red woolen glove. She could see the ragged edges where someone had cut off the fingers. And here were Heidegger's glasses—an object of such fascination when she was a child. She remembered putting them on, seeing the world in soft edges, her grandfather's consternation. And here was a blue and white coffee mug.

She took each letter to the laundry room of her apartment building and hung them on a clothesline. But they still smelled of dank minerals and mold—and emanated so much reproach Zoë started to believe that the dead really did expect answers.

As if they could see her dismay, people in the library began to give her things. A man studying bonding behavior in primates bought her an eraser that glowed in the dark. A woman doing a thesis on number sequence gave her pens with red and silver ink. Zoë got arrows for marking pages, paper clips, translucent folders. She took everything, whether she needed it or not.

Lodenstein kept sending things too—more than a few photographs: He sent typewriter spools, braided candles, diaries decoded by relatives of Scribes, more velvet roses, black merino wool, another red globe. German detective stories from the 1930s, a recipe for soup, a spade. There was no more room in the trunk. Zoë put them on her couch, where they formed a chaotic pile.

He also sent letters from raided houses—obviously interrupted while they were being written. They talked about lengthening hems on children's clothes, vacations to the Alps. Each letter pointed to a life far back in time, a life Zoë could never reach. Sometimes she stared at the fabric on her sweater, and thought she could see people from the Compound in the tufts. Sometimes she toyed with the idea of answering the letters—as if this would bring people back to life or at least help her to stop imagining their voices. And once, when she was visiting her parents, she started to talk about the number of unanswered letters in the world.

Are you doing something with that trunk? Maria said.

Yes.

I knew we should have thrown it away, said Maria. It belongs at the bottom of the Hudson.

They were in the kitchen, and Maria was making dinner. Zoë watched her pour spices into leek-and-potato soup and make dressing with three different kinds of vinegar. She said that Maria shouldn't go to all that trouble for a salad.

You might if you'd been in that place, said Maria. People worked very hard to make good food. And they were always kind. I was a lucky to be there during the war.

So you don't want that trunk at the bottom of the Hudson? said Zoë.

No, I suppose I don't, said Maria. And neither does your father. So do what you want with it.

One morning in May, over sixty years after Berlin surrendered, Zoë ran her hands along the trunk. She felt the same splintered wood on the top that she'd felt as a child— and on the bottom that her grandfather said didn't exist. The trunk was finally empty.

The man who studied primates had found a small museum in Manhattan—called The Museum of Tolerance— that wanted to exhibit the contents of the trunk. The head of the museum helped Zoe catalog and even found translators for the letters and diaries. Two of the translators, with numbers on their arms, said they would have given anything to have been in that place.

Zoë had annotated everything. She had even traced the origins of the grandfather clock, and—on the promise that she'd never tell—she'd gotten Lodenstein to confess that he'd broken the wool carder when he was angry. And now the objects and letters were ready for the exhibit. A brochure said that the Compound was one of the few places in the war that had sheltered survivors from Auschwitz. It also said the Scribes were, in a sense, bred for their languages. Maria and Daniel thought this was an exaggeration—as did Zoë, who had written the Scribes were chosen at deportations because they knew languages besides German. But the head of the museum liked it and put it in the brochure. It was the first time Zoë noticed how someone turned her words around to make a different sentence. She remembered how deeply her grandfather distrusted newspapers and history.

Lodenstein, who knew about the exhibit, hadn't sent anything for a month. That morning Zoë sent him the brochure and enclosed a note, asking whether he'd like the trunk back.

His answer—that he would not—came two weeks later with a package that included her grandfather's original prescription for Heidegger's glasses, a dark red notebook, and a photograph of a woman near a stand of trees. The woman had delicate features, penetrating eyes, and wore a white blouse with a rose pinned to the collar. Her blond hair was drawn back with a red bow and a tangle of curls spilled around her shoulders. Her face was lit by sun.

Zoë looked at the photograph for a long time. Then she looked at Heidegger's prescription in her grandfather's handwriting. How long ago had it been that the two of them were in that office, Heidegger looking at an eye chart, saying *Besser* and *Nicht Besser*, her grandfather pretending he wasn't terrified of his shop being raided or of his family being deported? She looked again at the woman lit by sun. Her face was so compelling she wondered if there were more photographs and realized if she didn't stop asking Lodenstein to send things, the exhibit would never be ready. It felt like a journey with no end.

But when she called him, Lodenstein sounded surprised that she didn't want anything more. He was sure Asher would want to include everything he had—and he kept running across memorabilia.

Zoë told him that Asher once said the trunk was a magic trunk, and she'd never see the end of it. The prospect of getting more and more objects from him was overwhelming.

My head is starting to spin, she said. And every time you send something, I only get more interested. Like that woman with the rose. Was she a Scribe?

Lodenstein paused. When he spoke his voice began to crack.

She was the heart of the Compound, he said. Without her, no one would have kept going. We would not have survived.

She looks lovely, Zoë said.

More than lovely, said Lodenstein.

There was grief in his voice—grief imbued with hope. Zoë imagined him after the war, looking for Elie wherever people gathered—in lines, under awnings, in bookstores, taking shelter in the rain. She imagined Elie looking too.

Suddenly Lodenstein said:

The red notebook was hers.

Zoë looked at the tattered notebook. The dark red cover had faded. The pages were brittle. Many were blank or had only a few phrases. Only two pages were filled.

Did you ever have it translated?

For a moment Lodenstein was quiet. Then he said: I never had the heart to.

My dearest Gabriela,

I had to write you before leaving this place. If you knew what this place was, the things we have done here, you'd understand why—because if there's a chance that you can ever read this letter, it would be from this place.

I helped save a lot of people in this war, but I never brought you back. And I keep thinking about what I would have done if I'd paid more attention. Whenever I go to a new city I imagine I'm going to see you. I see your face every night before I fall asleep.

Twice I drove to the town where you were shot because I thought I could find you. Instead there were brown shirts, and I left before I got to the town square.

I remember everything about being with you, Gabriela— making angels in the snow, swimming in the river, listening to ice crack in the spring. I remember the play where I forgot my lines, and you said them for me. I remember how you poked me when I fell asleep in Mass. And how we snuck eye shadow into the house and made each other into movie stars.

Heidi told me how you died. She said you kept raising your head again and again after they shot you.

Forgive me for not paying attention sooner. I should have known you were in danger. I should have helped. Instead, while you were forging passports, I was at Freiburg, acting as though nothing bad could ever happen to us. Never to dissenters. Never to Polish Catholics. And never, ever, to you.

I'll never stop talking to you, Gabriela. I'll never stop asking your forgiveness. None of the people I've helped rescue ever made up for losing you.

I love you forever,
Elie

The translator shut the dark red notebook and handed the translation to Zoë.

I shouldn't have done this for you, he said. Some things should stay between two people, whether they're alive or dead.

Zoë nodded. I won't let anyone see this.

Good, said the translator, pointing to the fragments on a page. Because she was trying to write this for a long time. He pointed to the blank pages, the false starts, the spaces in between. And then something—who knows what?—made her snap. Does anyone know what happened to her?

No, said Zoë. She disappeared before the war ended.

Like so many people, said the translator.

Zoë nodded. She was glad she didn't know. She could almost hear ice cracking in the spring; see Elie and her sister making angels in the snow. She felt a fierce sense of protection for both of them.

The translator was wiry, well into his eighties. He lit a cigarette, Zoë coughed, he opened a window and the Lower East Side wafted up. Zoë heard children's voices, the sounds of traffic. She smelled the sharp fumes of exhaust.

You look upset, said the translator. Do you want a drink?

No, said Zoë, who was trying not to cry. I just need to walk.

333

It was late afternoon when Zoë left the small cramped office. She crossed Canal Street, where bins overflowed with paraphernalia. She saw cheap watches, fake designer bags, mysterious pieces of metal, and every kind of tool.

A jumble shop, she thought, walking past another clot of fake designer bags, neon T-shirts, beaded rings. She noticed a bin of small wooden boxes: one had dark polished wood, with a clasp like a trunk. She stopped.

It's old, said the man behind the bin.

How old? said Zoë.

That I can't tell you.

Zoë smiled, walked away, then came back and bought the box. Maybe for the translation of Elie's letter, maybe for whatever Lodenstein kept sending. Or maybe just for herself—for whatever in her own life she wanted to keep.

She passed through Chinatown, Little Italy, and walked farther and farther north until it was dark and she was in Times Square among the tall looming buildings, the brisk stale air, its carnival of red and white lights.

Zoë wandered among throngs and hawkers and knew, as she'd never known before, that letters to the dead were for the living: They were justifications, records, appeasements, excuses, deceits, apologies, atonements, laments, confessions. They categorized. They beseeched. They invoked. Some told of unspeakable grief. Some tried to rewrite an entire history. And sometimes—more often than anyone could admit—even the most sophisticated letter writer imagined the dead could hear. Zoë was holding the translation of Elie's letter and felt it brush against a stranger's sleeve. For a moment she thought of letting it drift into the acrid air. Then she simply placed it in the wooden box.

The conversation with the dead goes on forever, she thought, and so does everything in the trunk: The spools and the candles. The letters and the lamps. The gloves and the roses. She wished the trunk were the Compound, and that everything in it could bring those people back. But nothing will ever do that. And there will always be one more thing left to add. And one more thing after that.

LaVergne, TN USA
11 March 2010
175637LV00001B/1/P